# POSTAL

## DELIVERANCE

### CREATED BY MATT HAWKINS

# POSTAL

## DELIVERANCE

CREATED BY MATT HAWKINS

Writer
BRYAN HILL

Artist
RAFFAELE IENCO

Letterer
TROY PETERI

Editors
ELENA SALCEDO & MATT HAWKINS

Production
VINCENT VALENTINE

Cover Art
LINDA SEJIC


*For Top Cow Productions, Inc.*
For Top Cow Productions, Inc.
**Marc Silvestri** - CEO
**Matt Hawkins** - President & COO
**Elena Salcedo** - Vice President of Operations
**Vincent Valentine** - Lead Production Artist
**Henry Barajas** - Director of Operations
**Dylan Gray** - Marketing Director

EDENVERSE

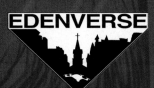

To find the comic shop nearest you, call:
*1-888-COMICBOOK*

Want more info? Check out:
**www.topcow.com**
for news & exclusive Top Cow merchandise!

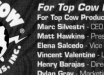

**IMAGE COMICS, INC.**
Robert Kirkman—Chief Operating Officer
Erik Larsen—Chief Financial Officer
Todd McFarlane—President
Marc Silvestri—Chief Executive Officer
Jim Valentino—Vice President
Eric Stephenson—Publisher/Chief Creative Officer
Jeff Boison—Director of Publishing Planning & Book Trade Sales
Chris Ross—Director of Digital Sales
Jeff Stang—Director of Direct Market Sales
Kat Salazar—Director of PR & Marketing
Drew Gill—Cover Editor
Heather Doornink—Production Director
Nicole Lapalme—Controller
**IMAGECOMICS.COM**

POSTAL: DELIVERANCE, VOL. 1. First printing. November 2019. Published by Image Comics, Inc. Office of publication: 2701 NW Vaughn St., Suite 780, Portland, OR 97210.



Printed in the USA. ISBN: 978-1-5343-1516-7.

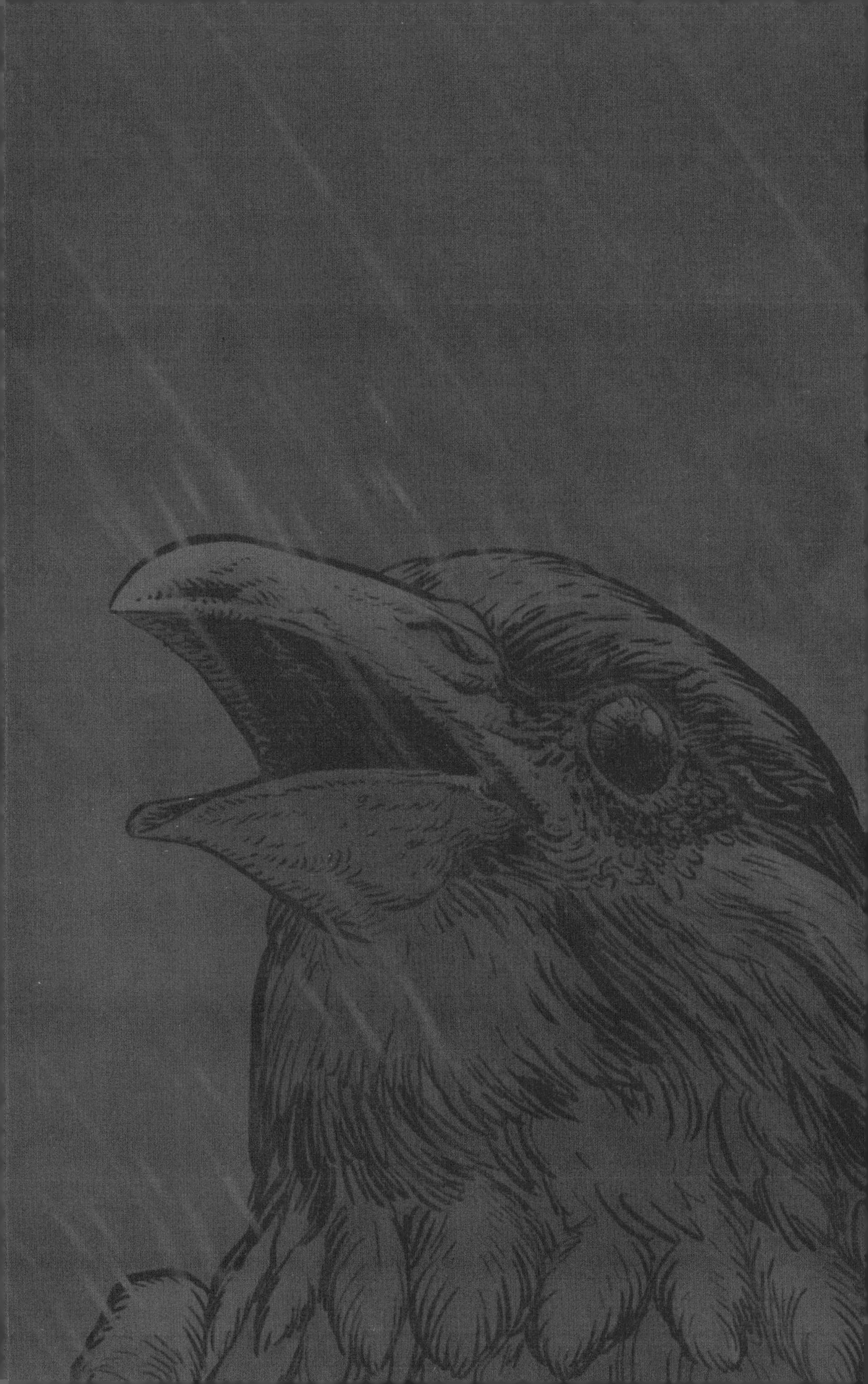

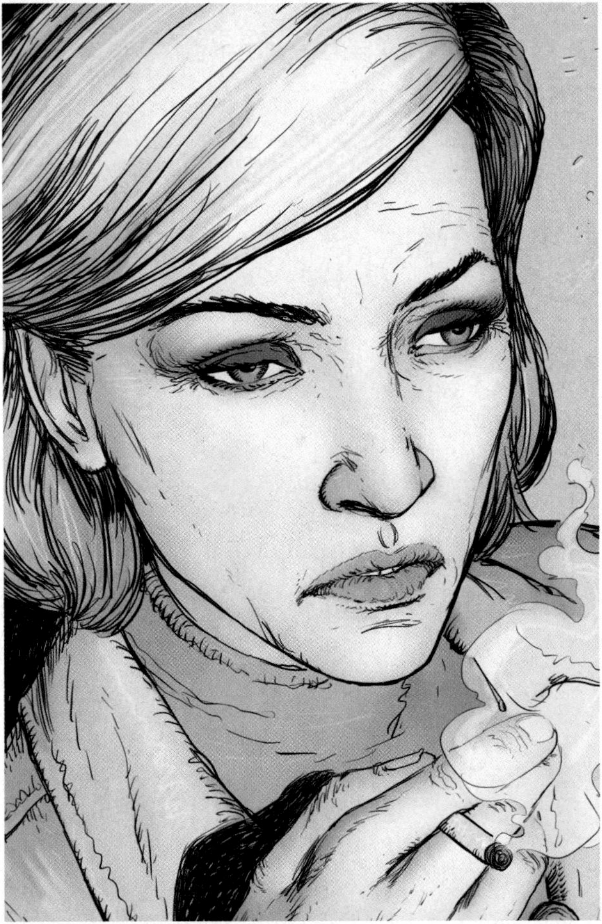

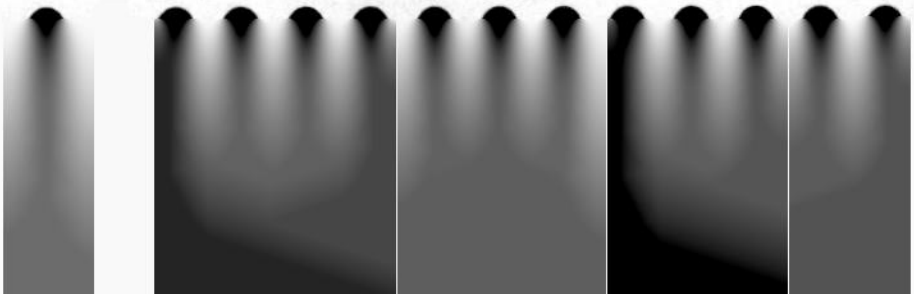

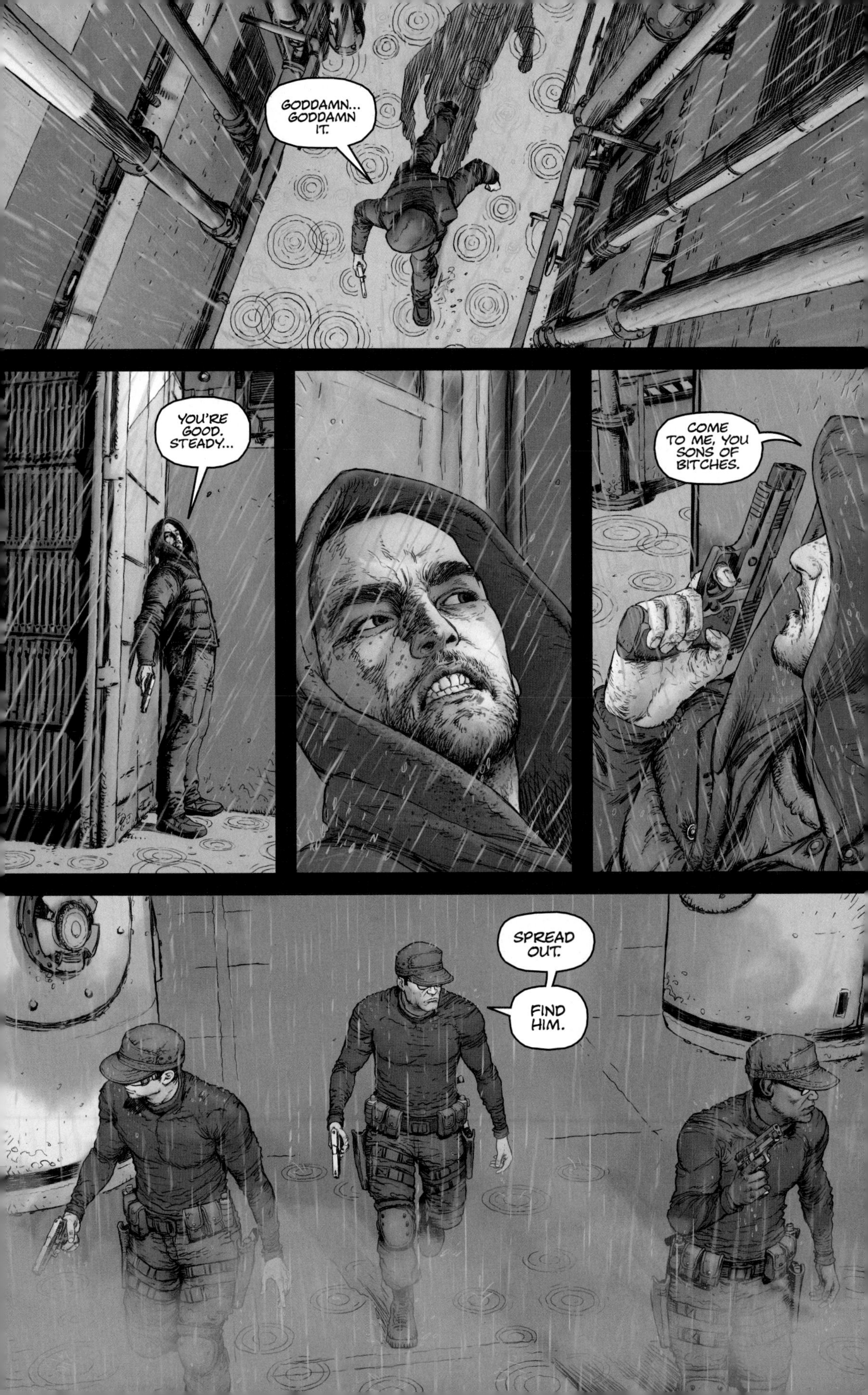
GODDAMN... GODDAMN IT.
YOU'RE GOOD. STEADY...
COME TO ME, YOU SONS OF BITCHES.
SPREAD OUT.
FIND HIM.

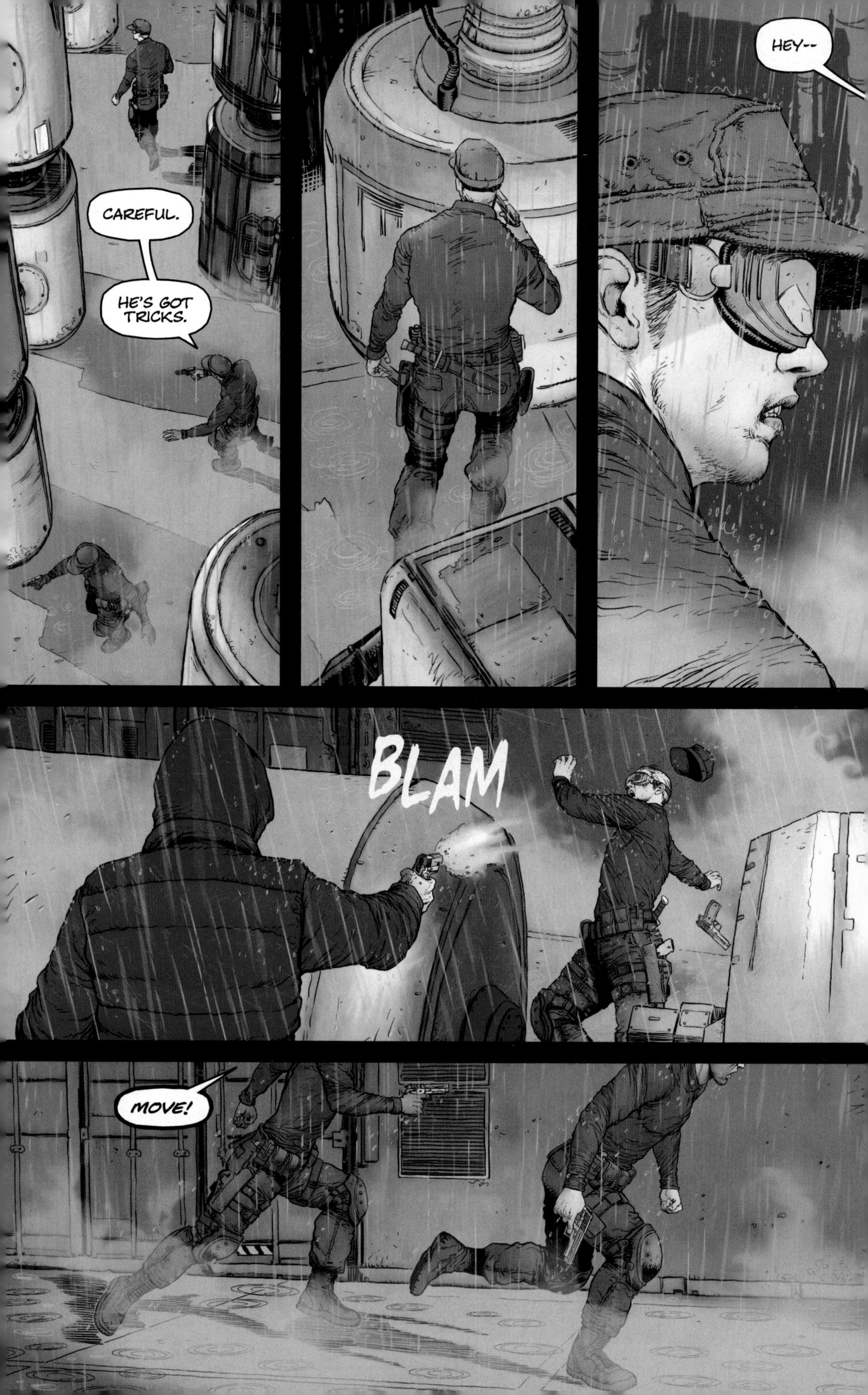
CAREFUL.
HE'S GOT TRICKS.
HEY--
BLAM
MOVE!

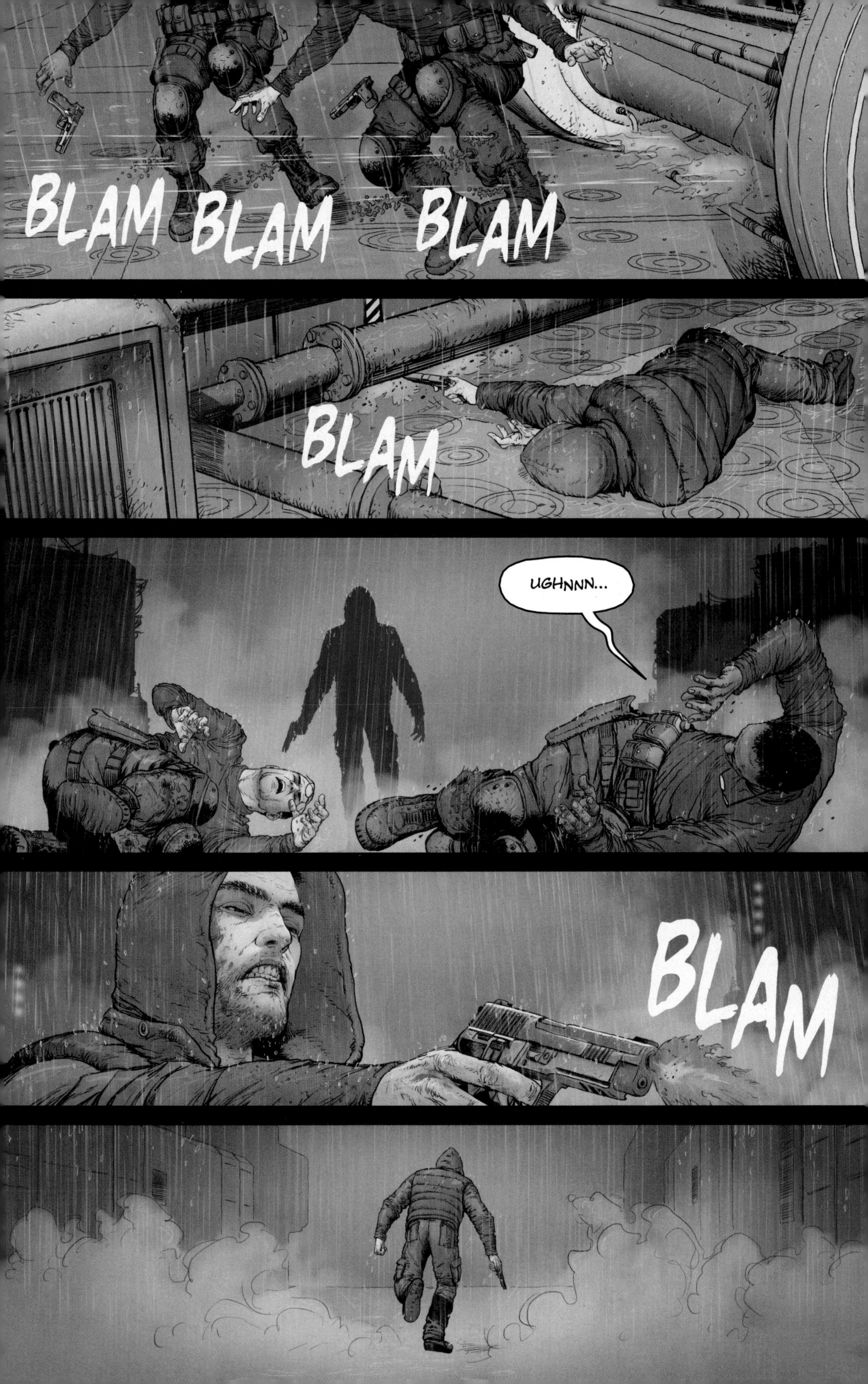
BLAM BLAM BLAM
BLAM
UGHNNN...
BLAM

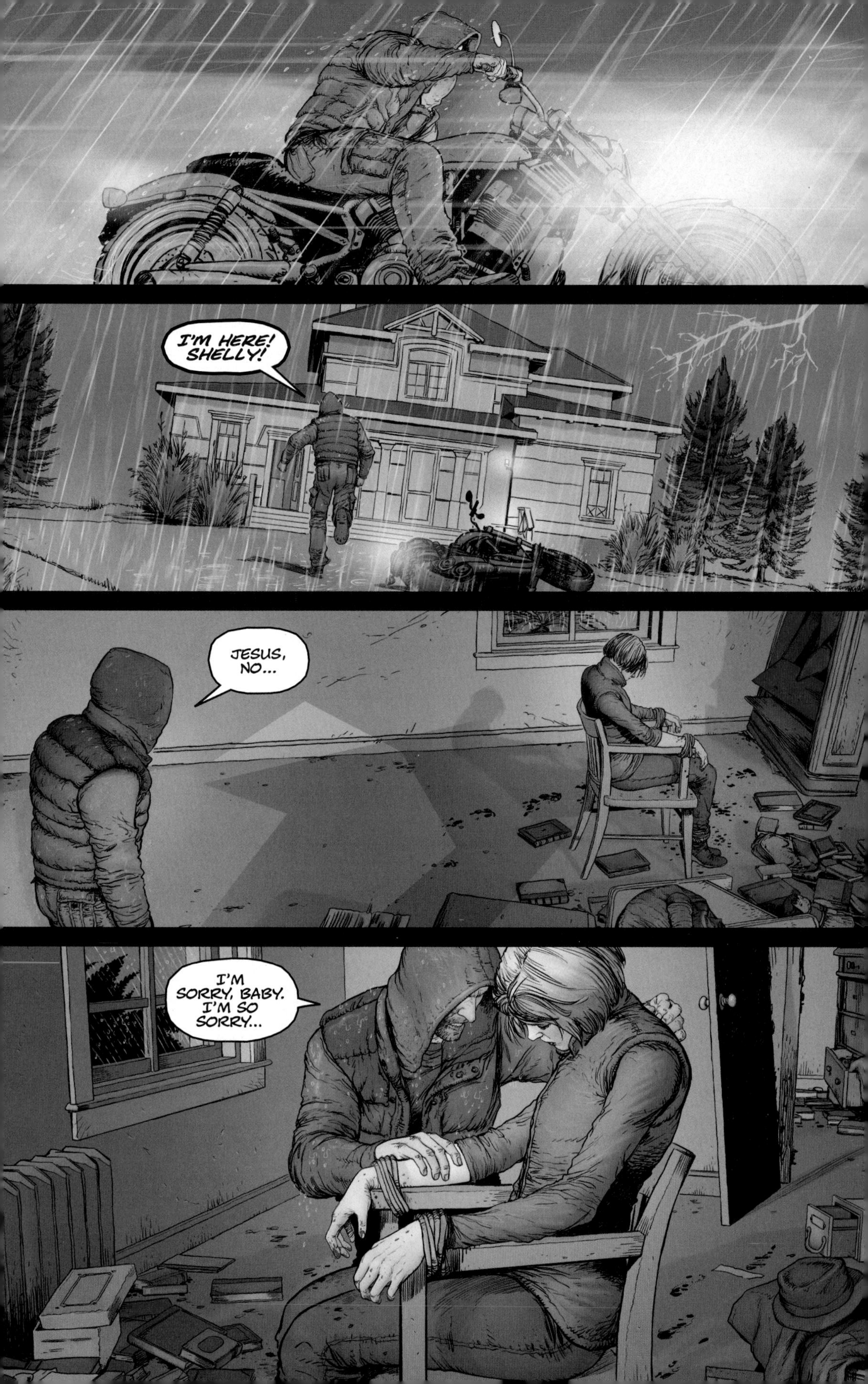
I'M HERE! SHELLY!
JESUS, NO...
I'M SORRY, BABY. I'M SO SORRY...

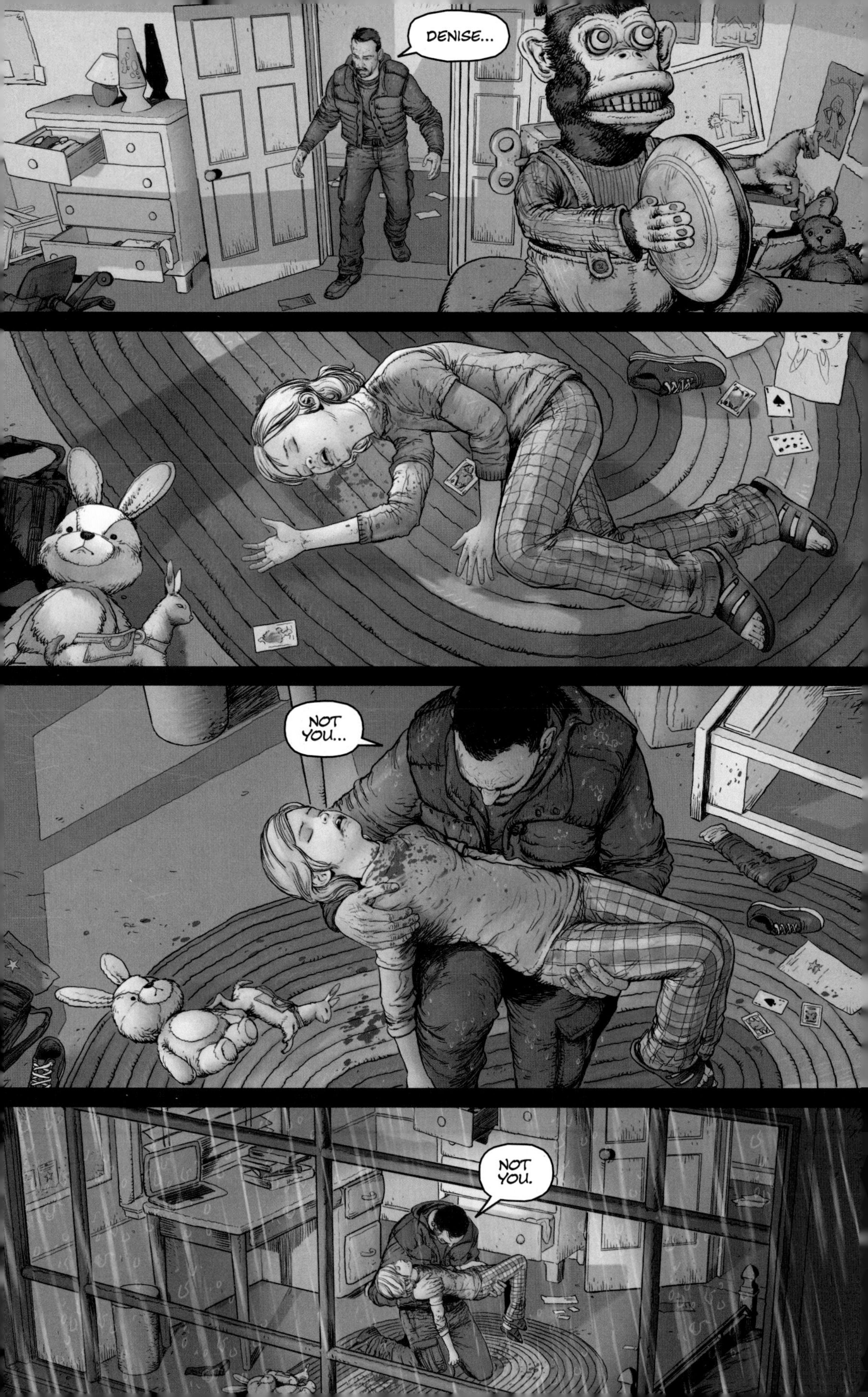
DENISE...
NOT YOU...
NOT YOU.

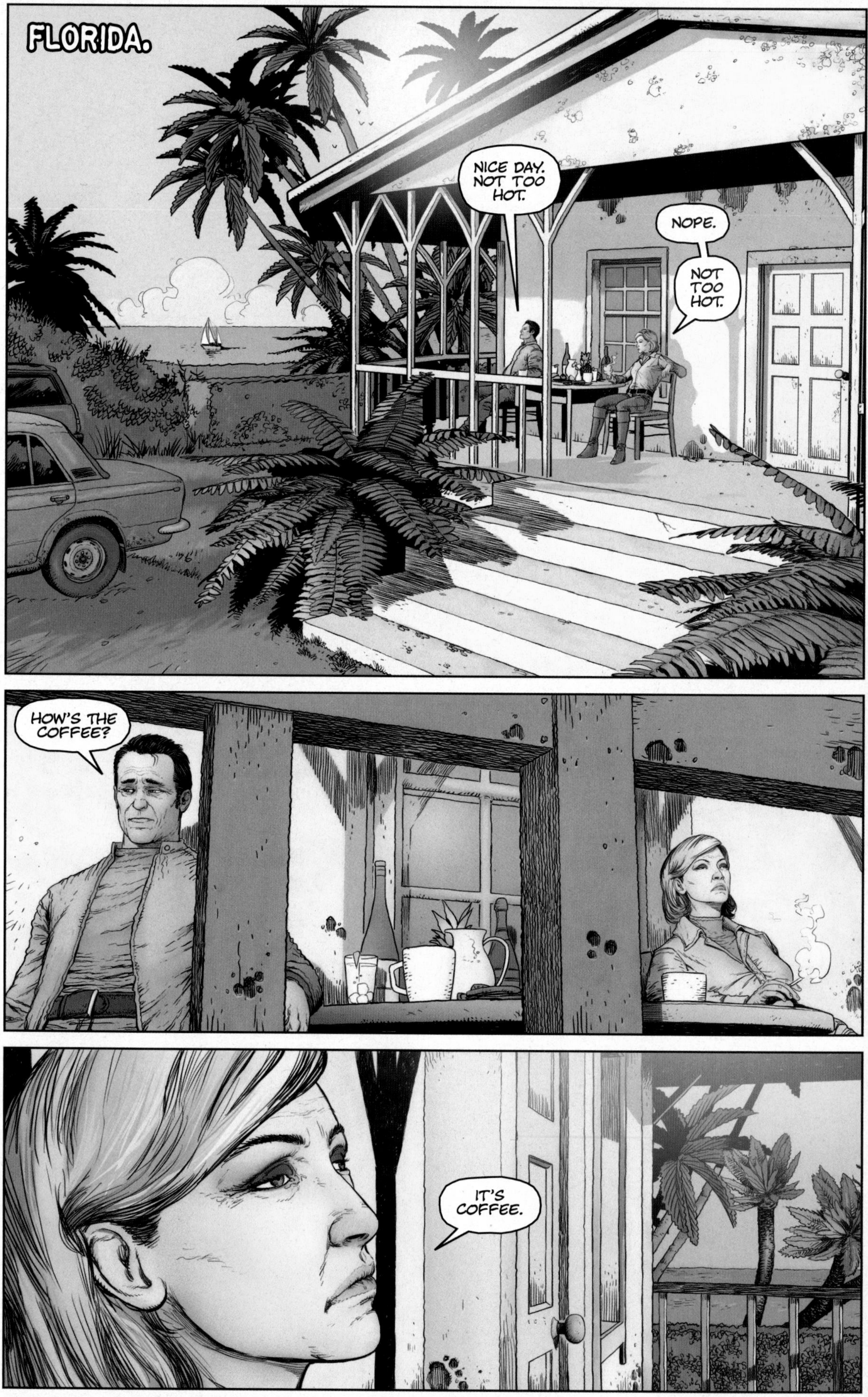
FLORIDA.
NICE DAY. NOT TOO HOT.
NOPE.
NOT TOO HOT.
HOW'S THE COFFEE?
IT'S COFFEE.

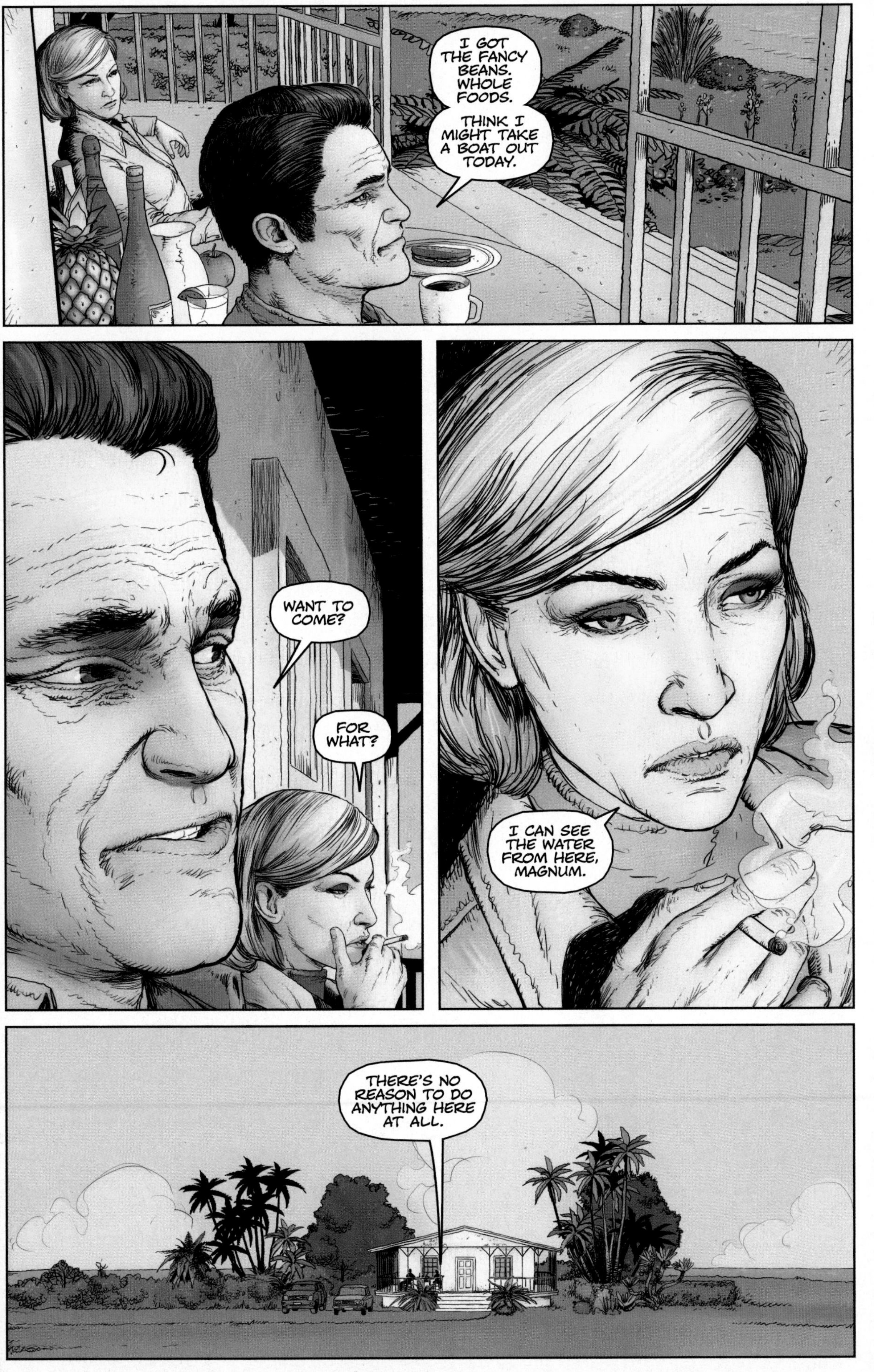
I GOT THE FANCY BEANS. WHOLE FOODS.
THINK I MIGHT TAKE A BOAT OUT TODAY.
WANT TO COME?
FOR WHAT?
I CAN SEE THE WATER FROM HERE, MAGNUM.
THERE'S NO REASON TO DO ANYTHING HERE AT ALL.

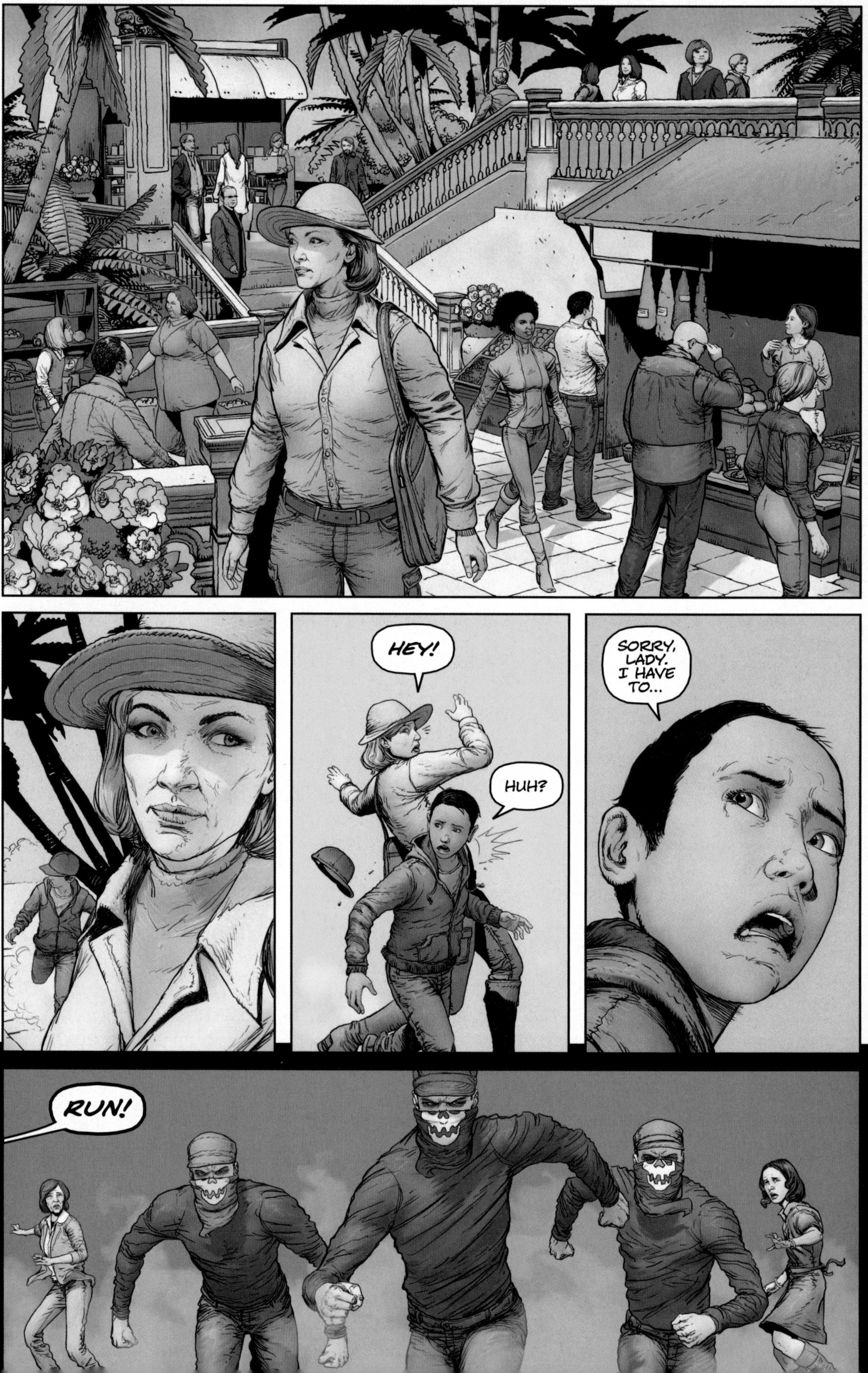
HEY!
HUH?
SORRY, LADY. I HAVE TO...
RUN!

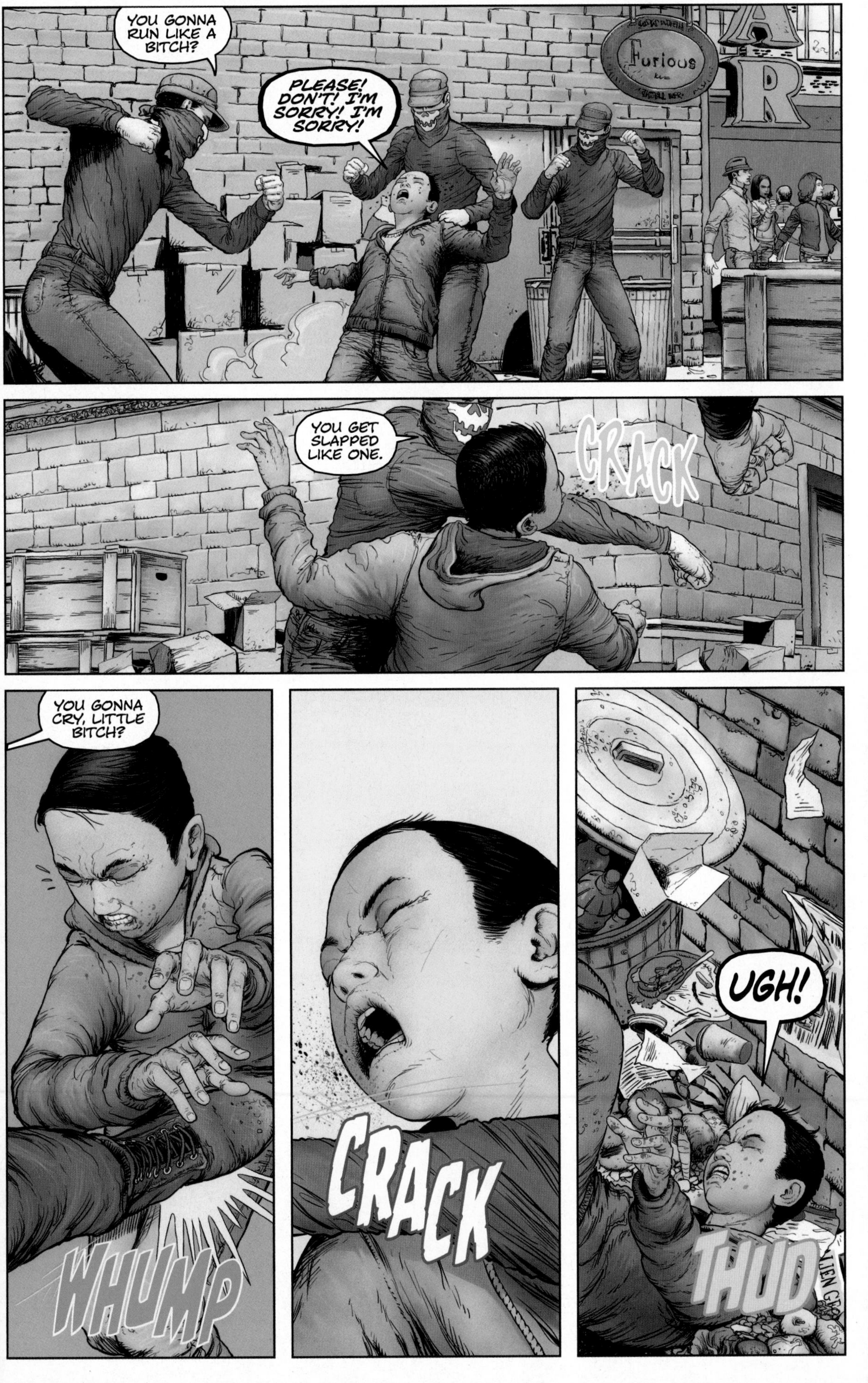
YOU GONNA RUN LIKE A BITCH?
PLEASE! DON'T! I'M SORRY! I'M SORRY!
Furious
YOU GET SLAPPED LIKE ONE.
CRACK
YOU GONNA CRY, LITTLE BITCH?
WHUMP
CRACK
UGH!
THUD

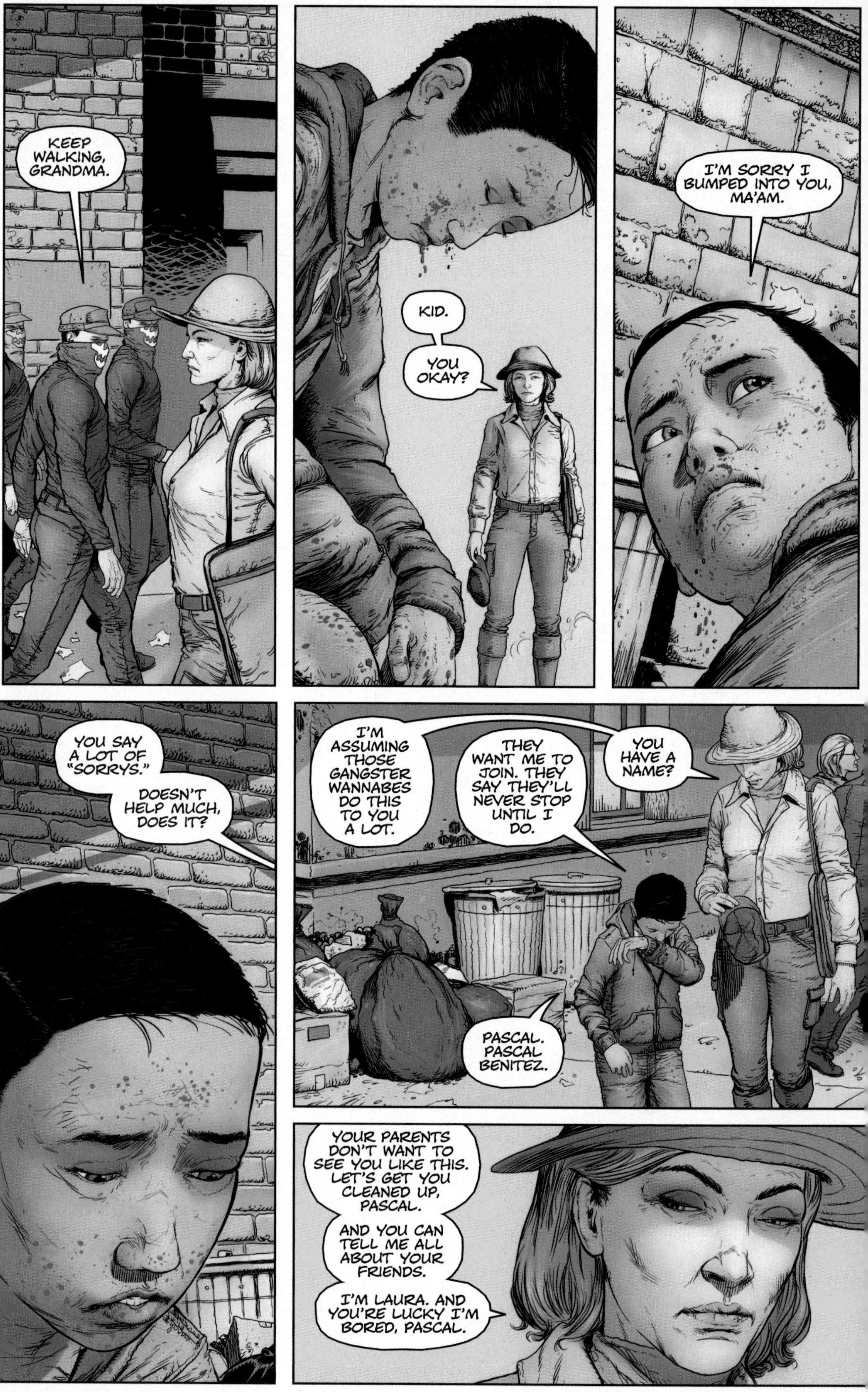
KEEP WALKING, GRANDMA.
KID.
YOU OKAY?
I'M SORRY I BUMPED INTO YOU, MA'AM.
YOU SAY A LOT OF "SORRYS."
DOESN'T HELP MUCH, DOES IT?
I'M ASSUMING THOSE GANGSTER WANNABES DO THIS TO YOU A LOT.
THEY WANT ME TO JOIN. THEY SAY THEY'LL NEVER STOP UNTIL I DO.
YOU HAVE A NAME?
PASCAL. PASCAL BENITEZ.
YOUR PARENTS DON'T WANT TO SEE YOU LIKE THIS. LET'S GET YOU CLEANED UP, PASCAL.
AND YOU CAN TELL ME ALL ABOUT YOUR FRIENDS.
I'M LAURA. AND YOU'RE LUCKY I'M BORED, PASCAL.

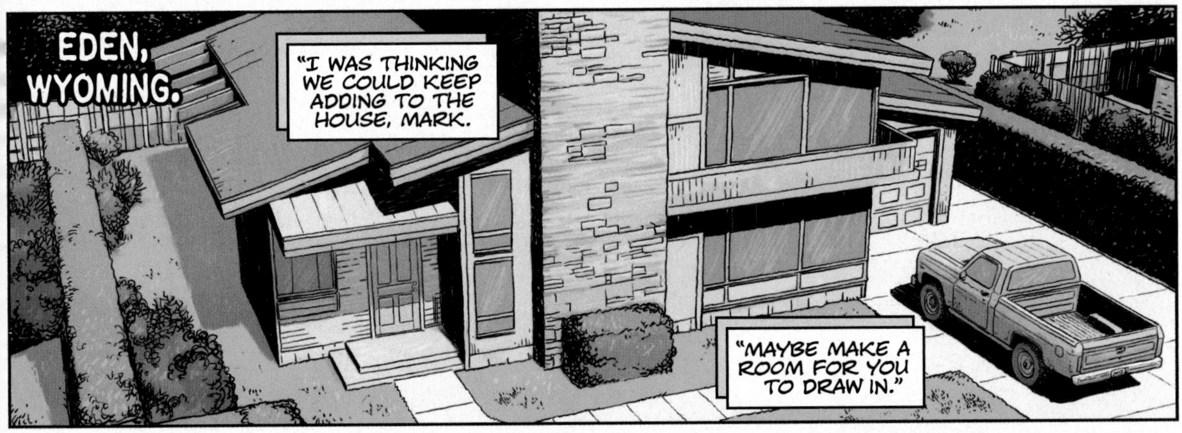
EDEN, WYOMING.
"I WAS THINKING WE COULD KEEP ADDING TO THE HOUSE, MARK.
"MAYBE MAKE A ROOM FOR YOU TO DRAW IN."

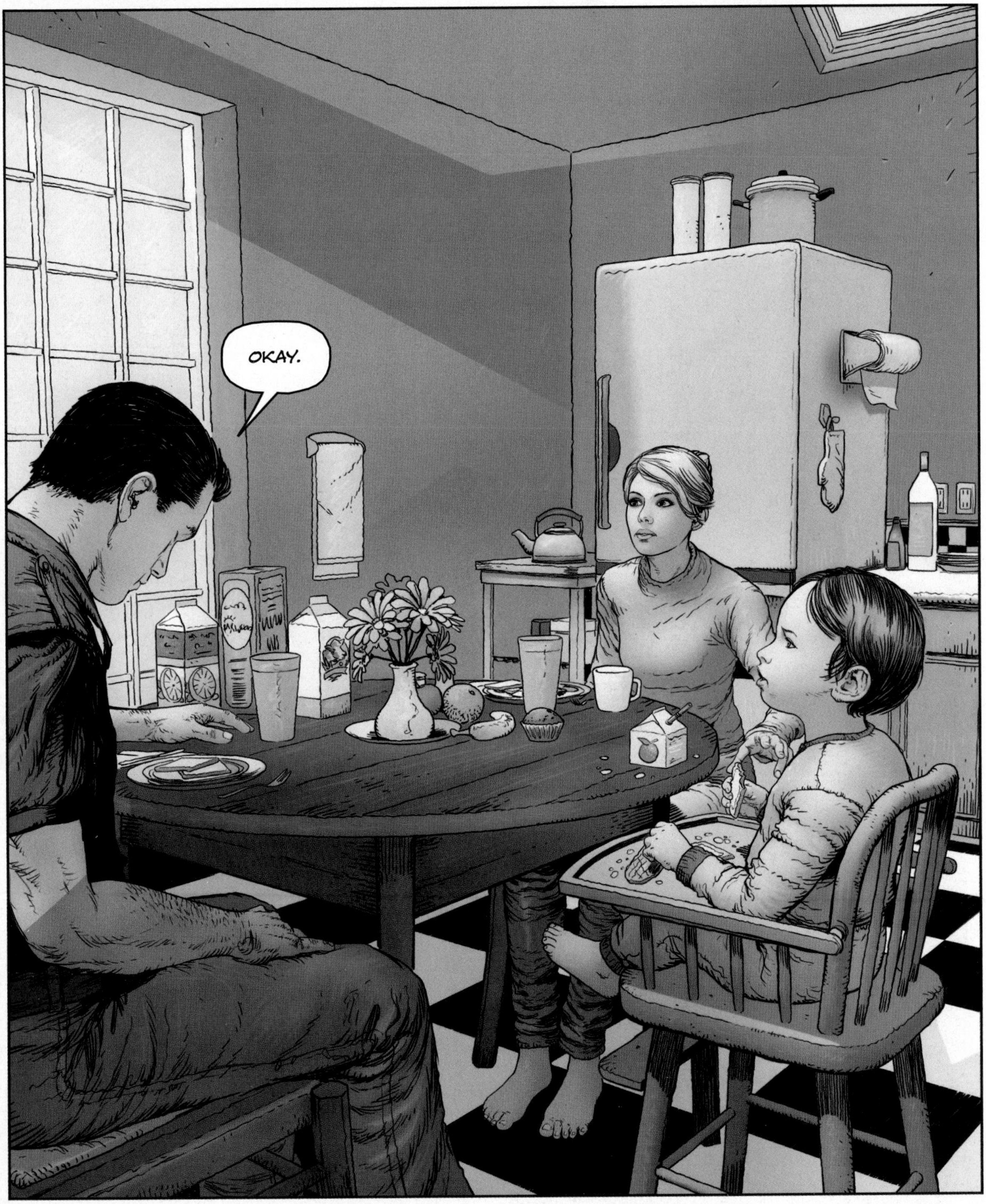
OKAY.

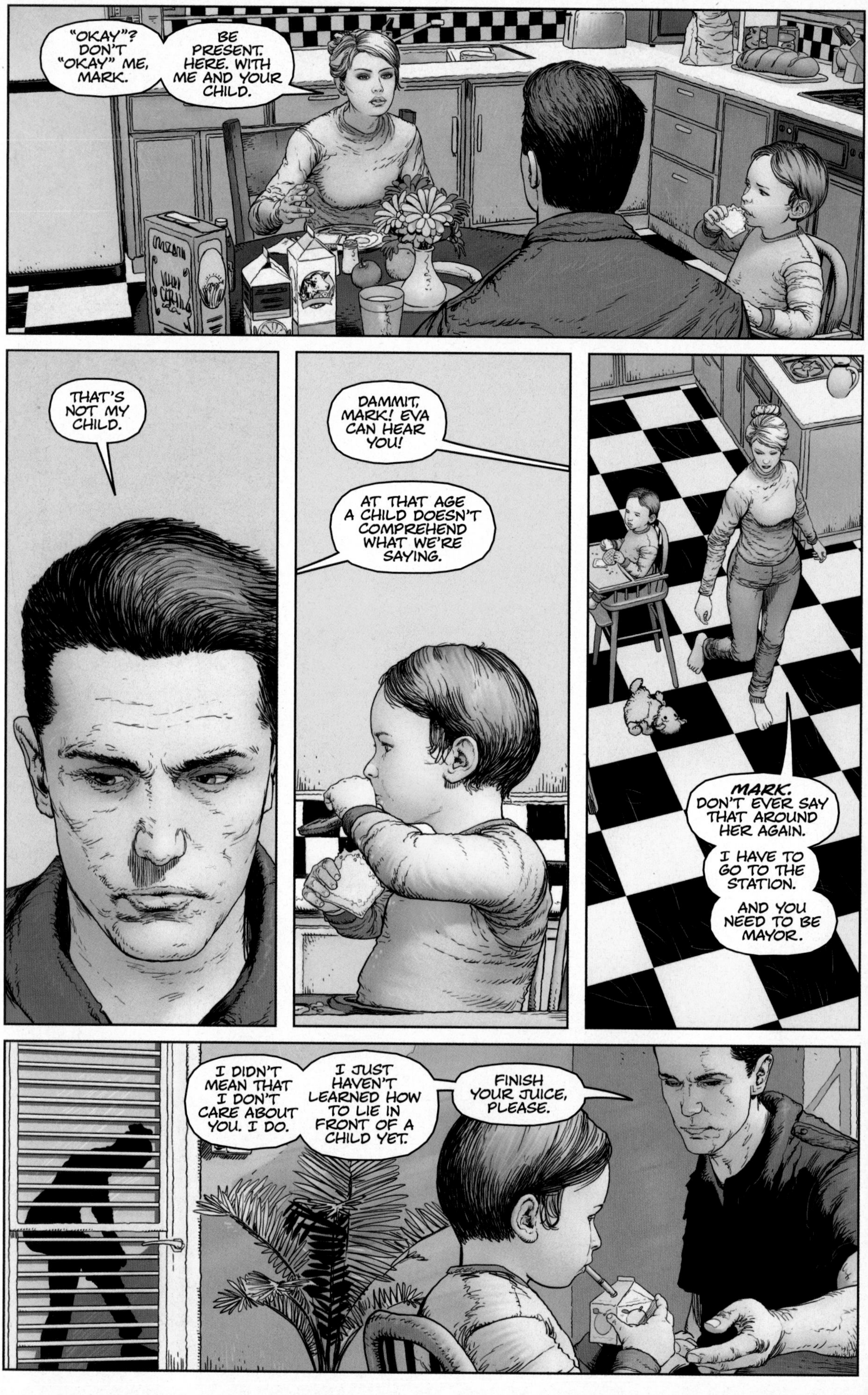
"OKAY"? DON'T "OKAY" ME, MARK.
BE PRESENT. HERE. WITH ME AND YOUR CHILD.
THAT'S NOT MY CHILD.
DAMMIT, MARK! EVA CAN HEAR YOU!
AT THAT AGE A CHILD DOESN'T COMPREHEND WHAT WE'RE SAYING.
MARK. DON'T EVER SAY THAT AROUND HER AGAIN.
I HAVE TO GO TO THE STATION.
AND YOU NEED TO BE MAYOR.
I DIDN'T MEAN THAT I DON'T CARE ABOUT YOU. I DO.
I JUST HAVEN'T LEARNED HOW TO LIE IN FRONT OF A CHILD YET.
FINISH YOUR JUICE, PLEASE.

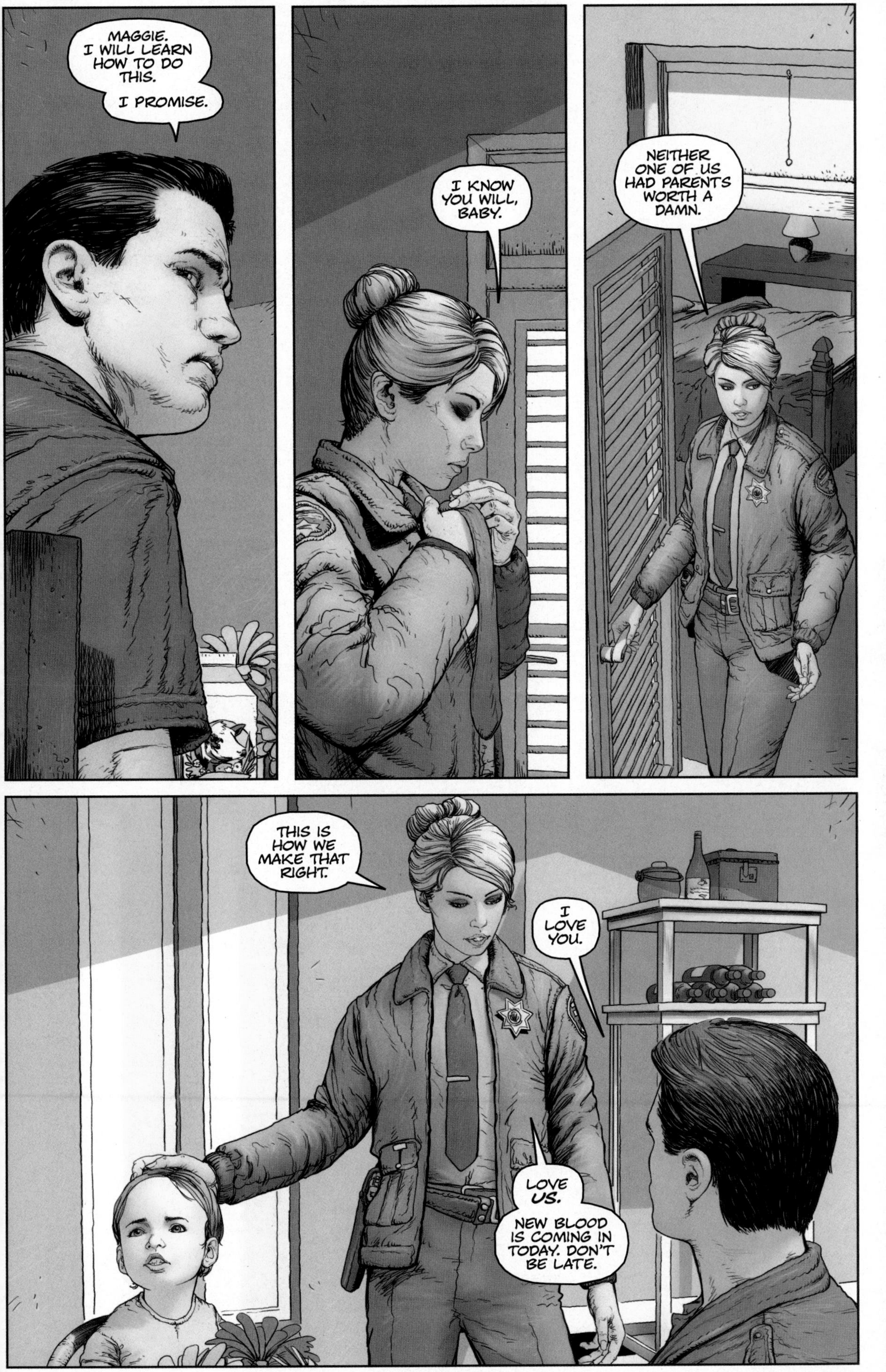
MAGGIE. I WILL LEARN HOW TO DO THIS.
I PROMISE.
I KNOW YOU WILL, BABY.
NEITHER ONE OF US HAD PARENTS WORTH A DAMN.
THIS IS HOW WE MAKE THAT RIGHT.
I LOVE YOU.
LOVE US.
NEW BLOOD IS COMING IN TODAY. DON'T BE LATE.

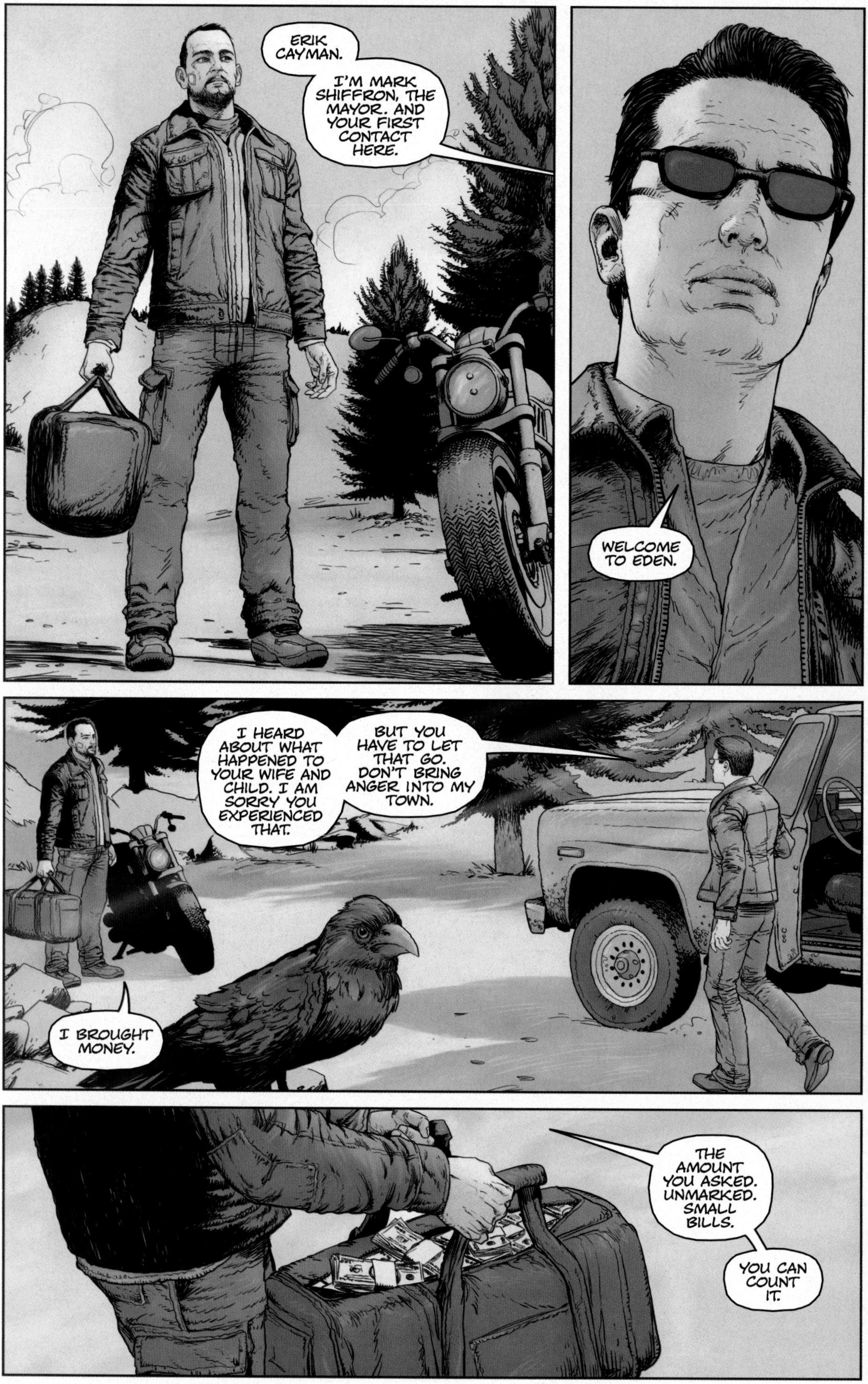
ERIK CAYMAN.
I'M MARK SHIFFRON, THE MAYOR. AND YOUR FIRST CONTACT HERE.
WELCOME TO EDEN.
I HEARD ABOUT WHAT HAPPENED TO YOUR WIFE AND CHILD. I AM SORRY YOU EXPERIENCED THAT.
BUT YOU HAVE TO LET THAT GO. DON'T BRING ANGER INTO MY TOWN.
I BROUGHT MONEY.
THE AMOUNT YOU ASKED. UNMARKED. SMALL BILLS.
YOU CAN COUNT IT.

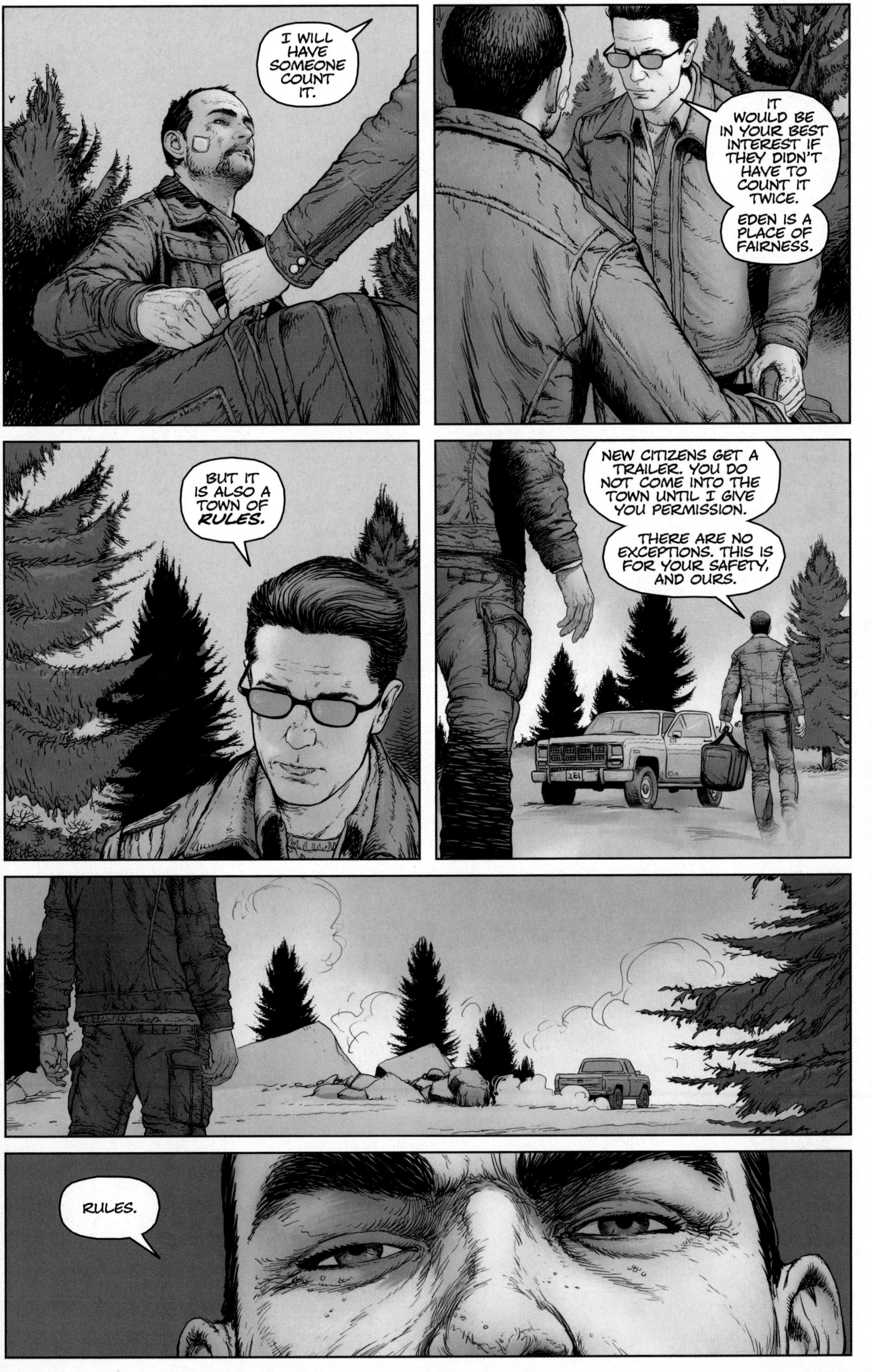

I WILL HAVE SOMEONE COUNT IT.
IT WOULD BE IN YOUR BEST INTEREST IF THEY DIDN'T HAVE TO COUNT IT TWICE.
EDEN IS A PLACE OF FAIRNESS.
BUT IT IS ALSO A TOWN OF *RULES.*
NEW CITIZENS GET A TRAILER. YOU DO NOT COME INTO THE TOWN UNTIL I GIVE YOU PERMISSION.
THERE ARE NO EXCEPTIONS. THIS IS FOR YOUR SAFETY, AND OURS.
RULES.

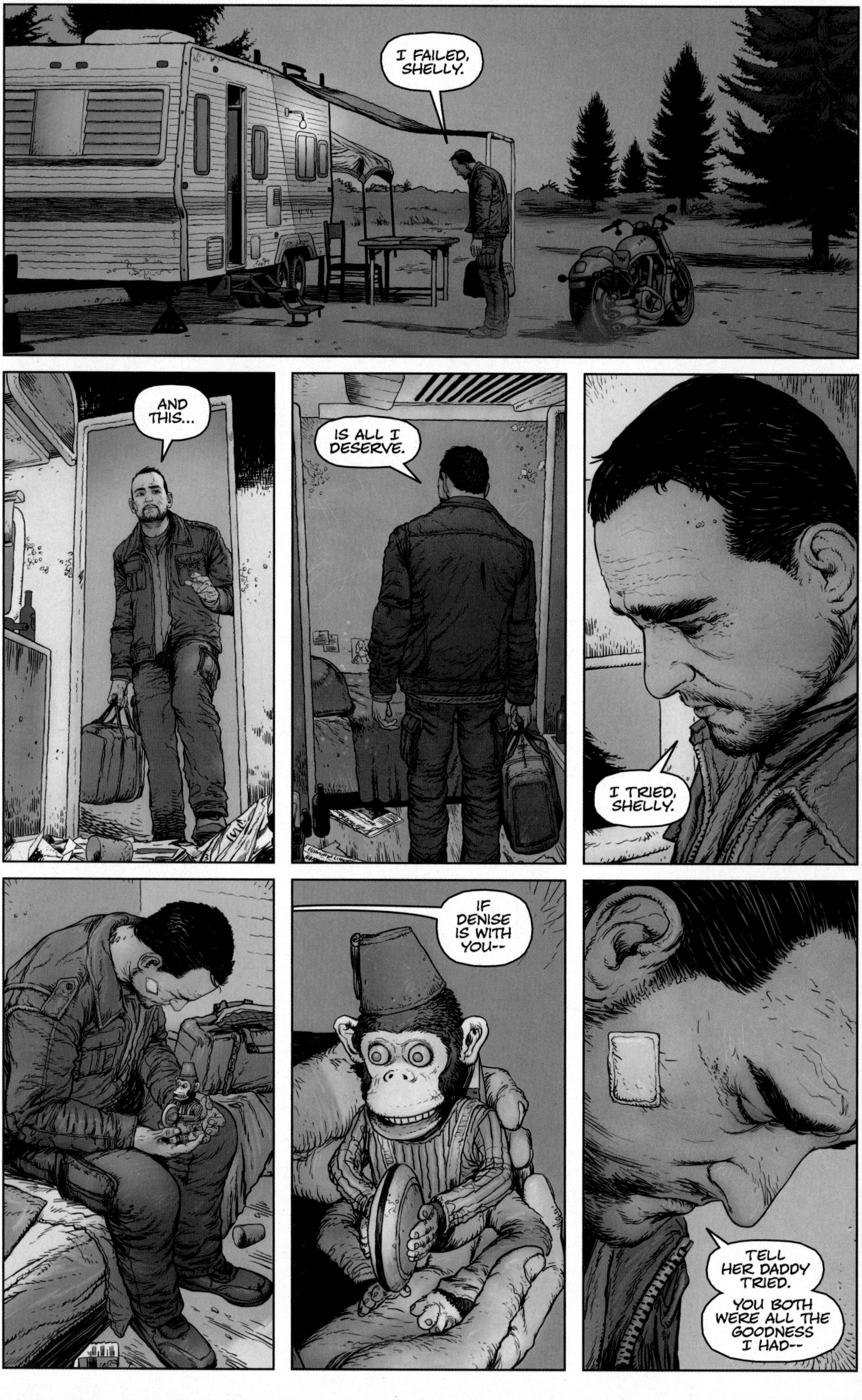
I FAILED, SHELLY.
AND THIS...
IS ALL I DESERVE.
I TRIED, SHELLY.
IF DENISE IS WITH YOU--
TELL HER DADDY TRIED.
YOU BOTH WERE ALL THE GOODNESS I HAD--

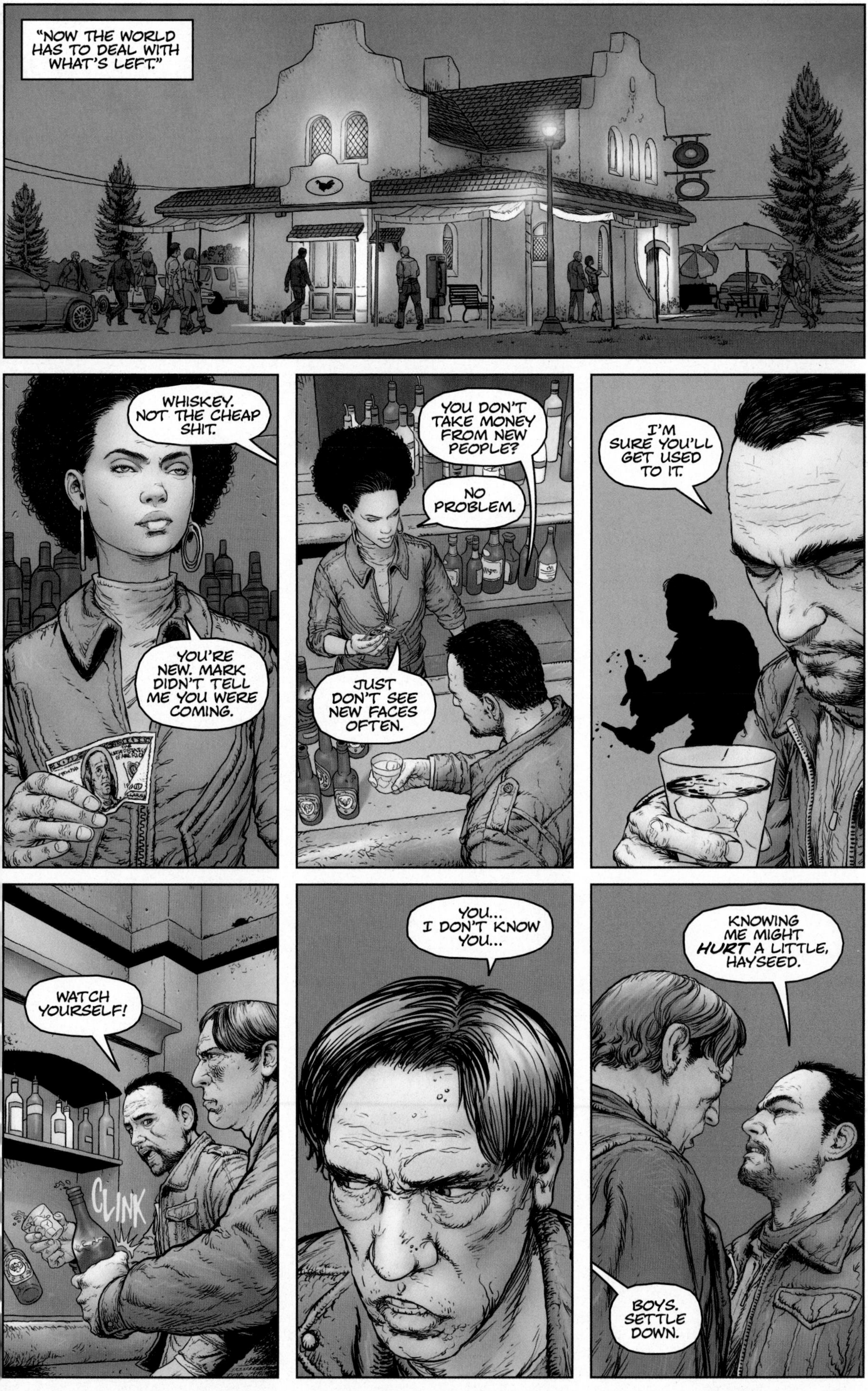
"NOW THE WORLD HAS TO DEAL WITH WHAT'S LEFT."
WHISKEY. NOT THE CHEAP SHIT.
YOU'RE NEW. MARK DIDN'T TELL ME YOU WERE COMING.
YOU DON'T TAKE MONEY FROM NEW PEOPLE?
NO PROBLEM.
JUST DON'T SEE NEW FACES OFTEN.
I'M SURE YOU'LL GET USED TO IT.
WATCH YOURSELF!
CLINK
YOU... I DON'T KNOW YOU...
KNOWING ME MIGHT HURT A LITTLE, HAYSEED.
BOYS. SETTLE DOWN.

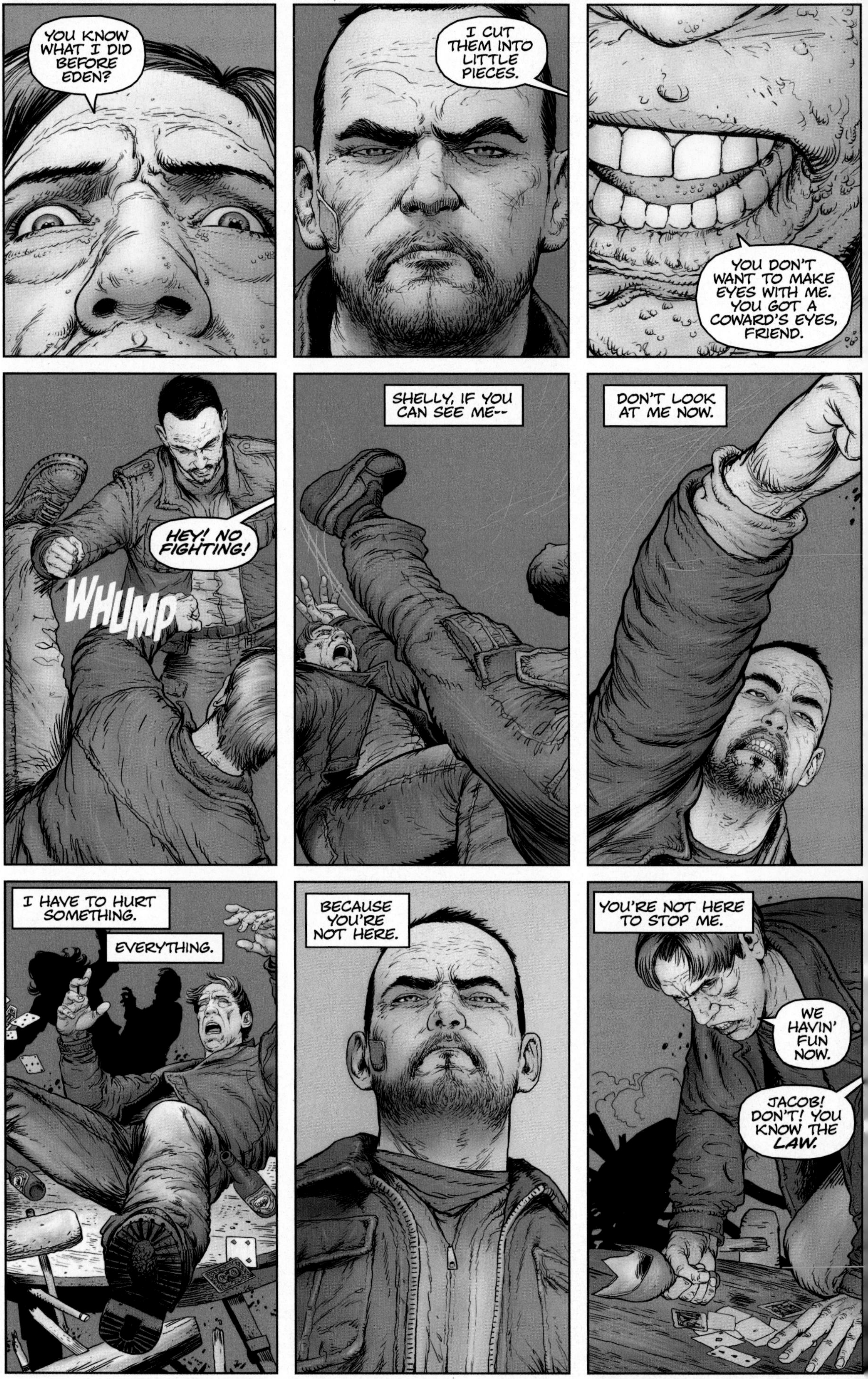
YOU KNOW WHAT I DID BEFORE EDEN?
I CUT THEM INTO LITTLE PIECES.
YOU DON'T WANT TO MAKE EYES WITH ME. YOU GOT A COWARD'S EYES, FRIEND.
HEY! NO FIGHTING!
WHUMP
SHELLY, IF YOU CAN SEE ME--
DON'T LOOK AT ME NOW.
I HAVE TO HURT SOMETHING.
EVERYTHING.
BECAUSE YOU'RE NOT HERE.
YOU'RE NOT HERE TO STOP ME.
WE HAVIN' FUN NOW.
JACOB! DON'T! YOU KNOW THE LAW.

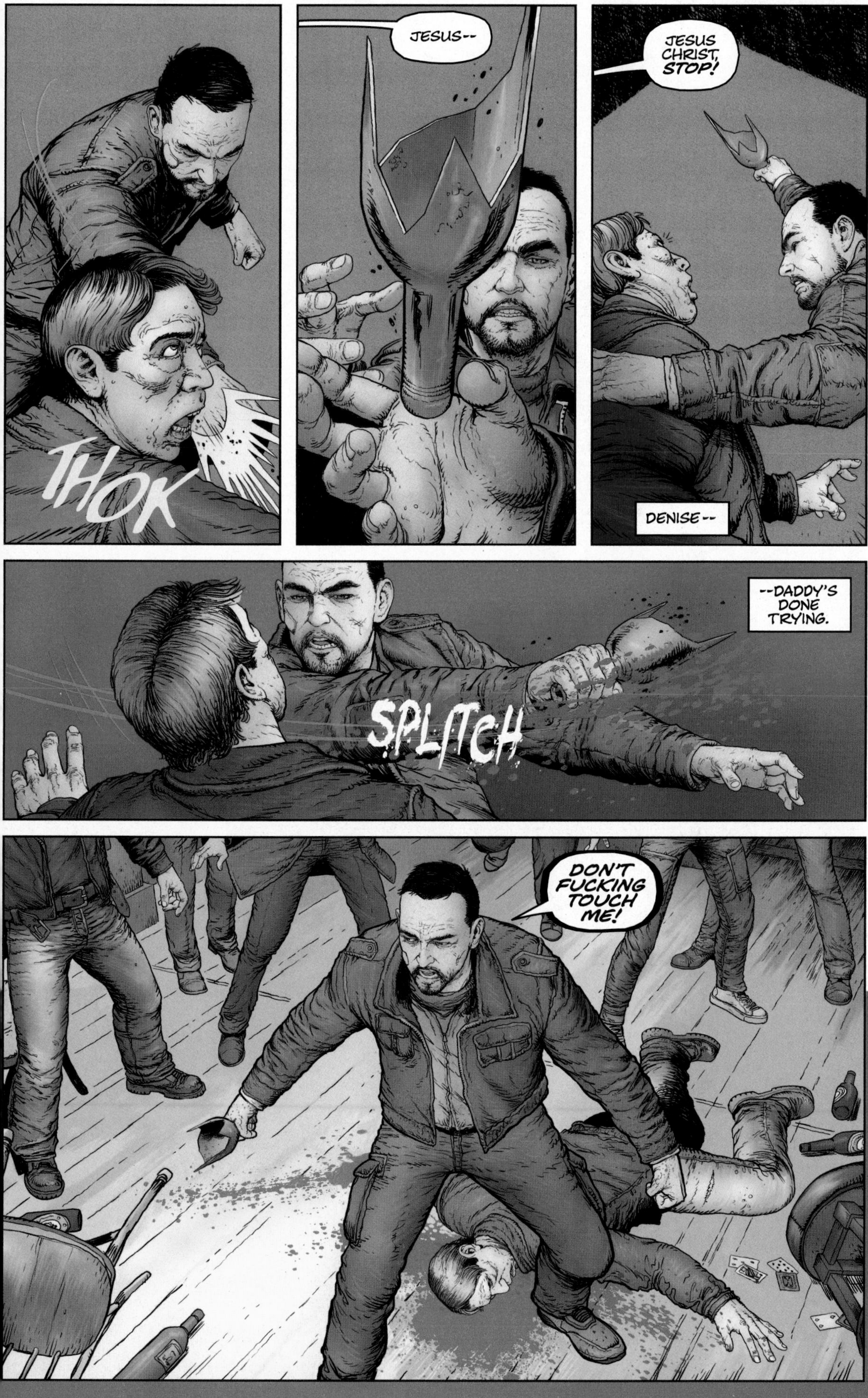
THOK
JESUS--
JESUS CHRIST, STOP!
DENISE--
--DADDY'S DONE TRYING.
SPLITCH
DON'T FUCKING TOUCH ME!

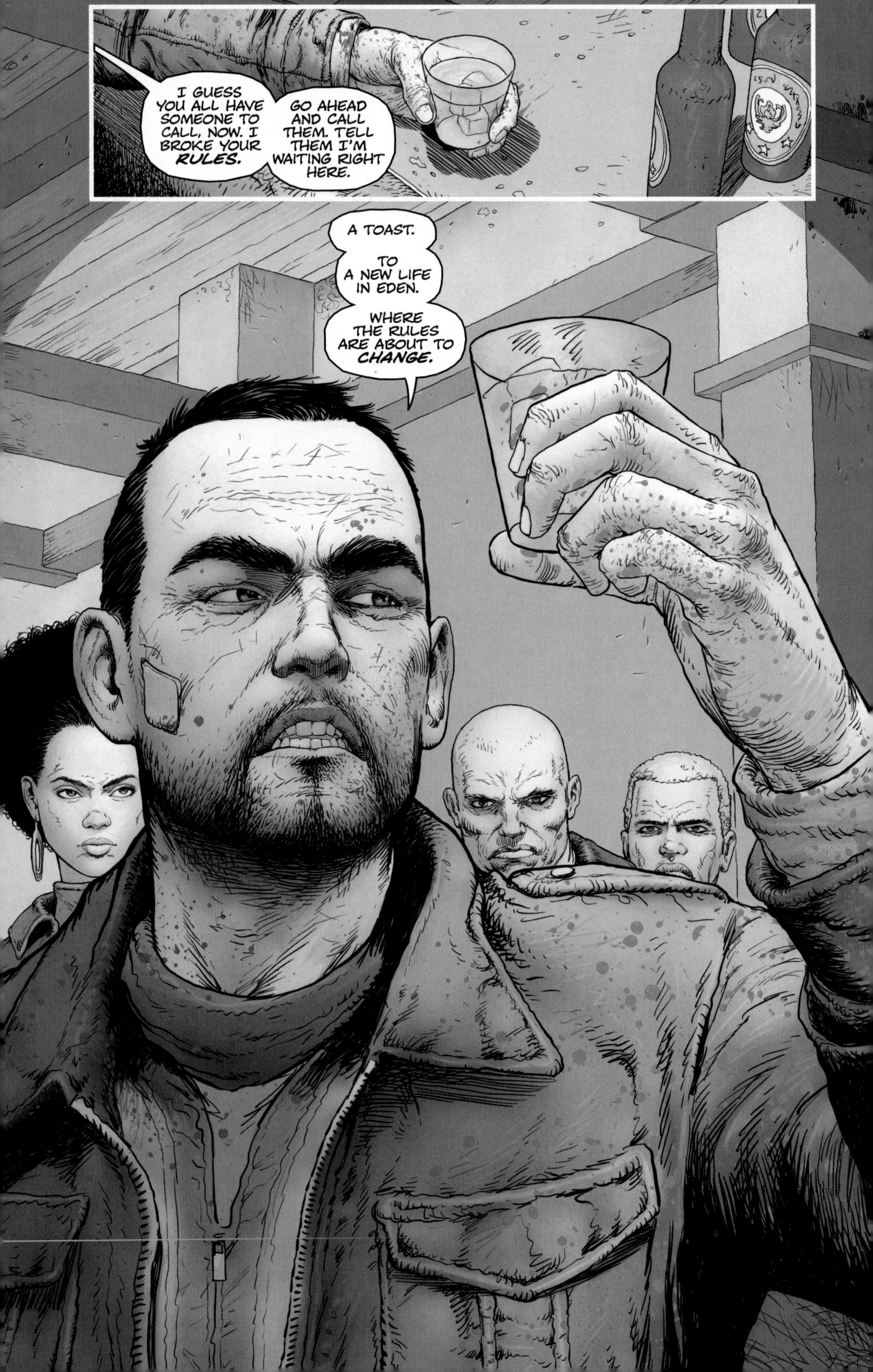
I GUESS YOU ALL HAVE SOMEONE TO CALL, NOW. I BROKE YOUR **RULES.**
GO AHEAD AND CALL THEM. TELL THEM I'M WAITING RIGHT HERE.
A TOAST.
TO A NEW LIFE IN EDEN.
WHERE THE RULES ARE ABOUT TO **CHANGE.**

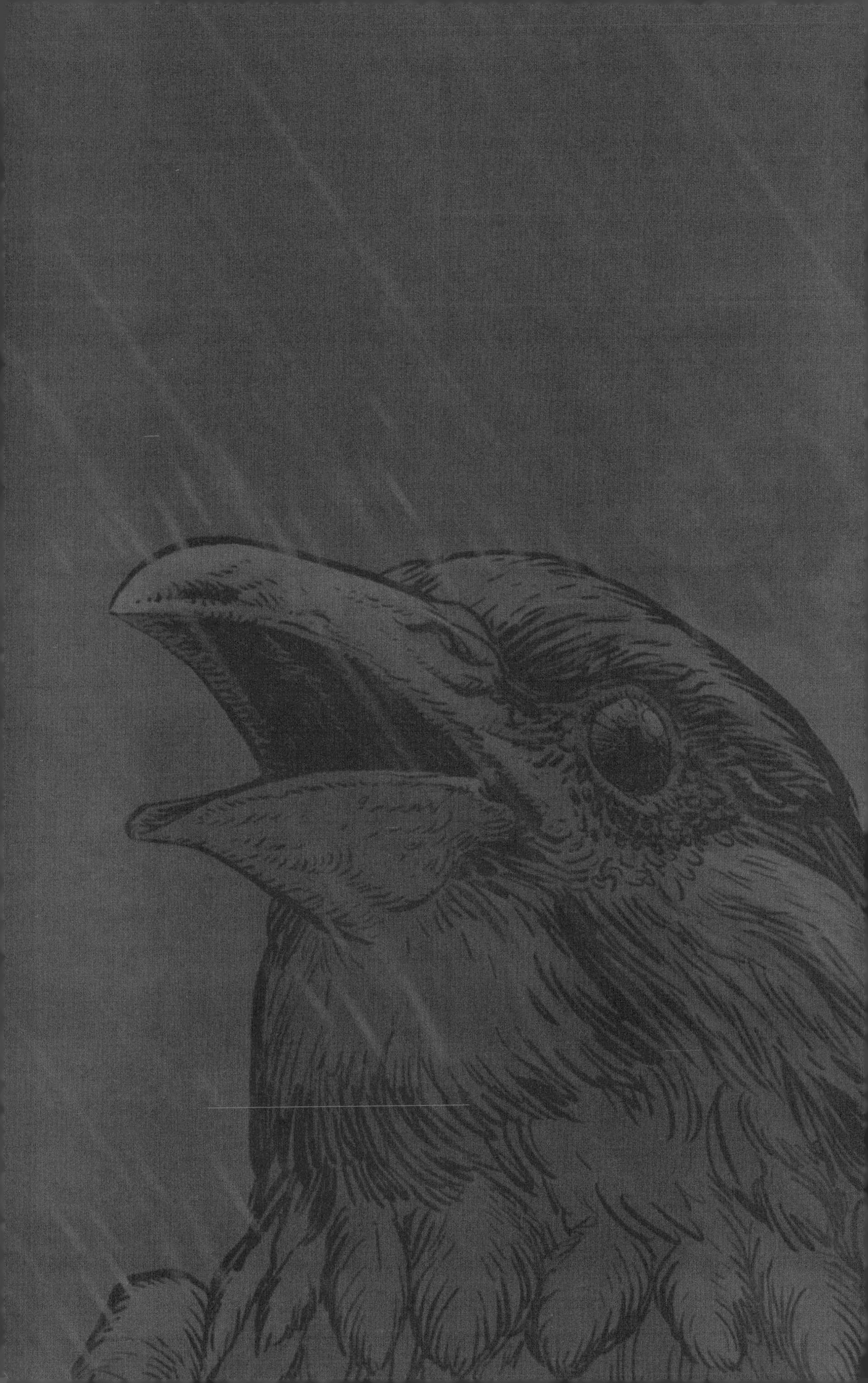

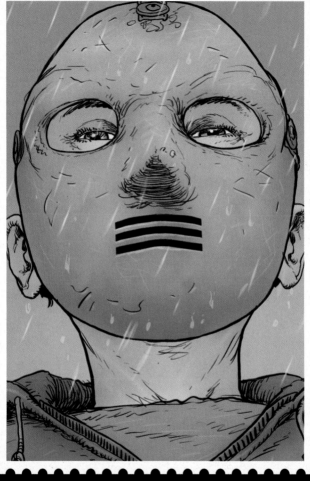

# CHAPTER 2

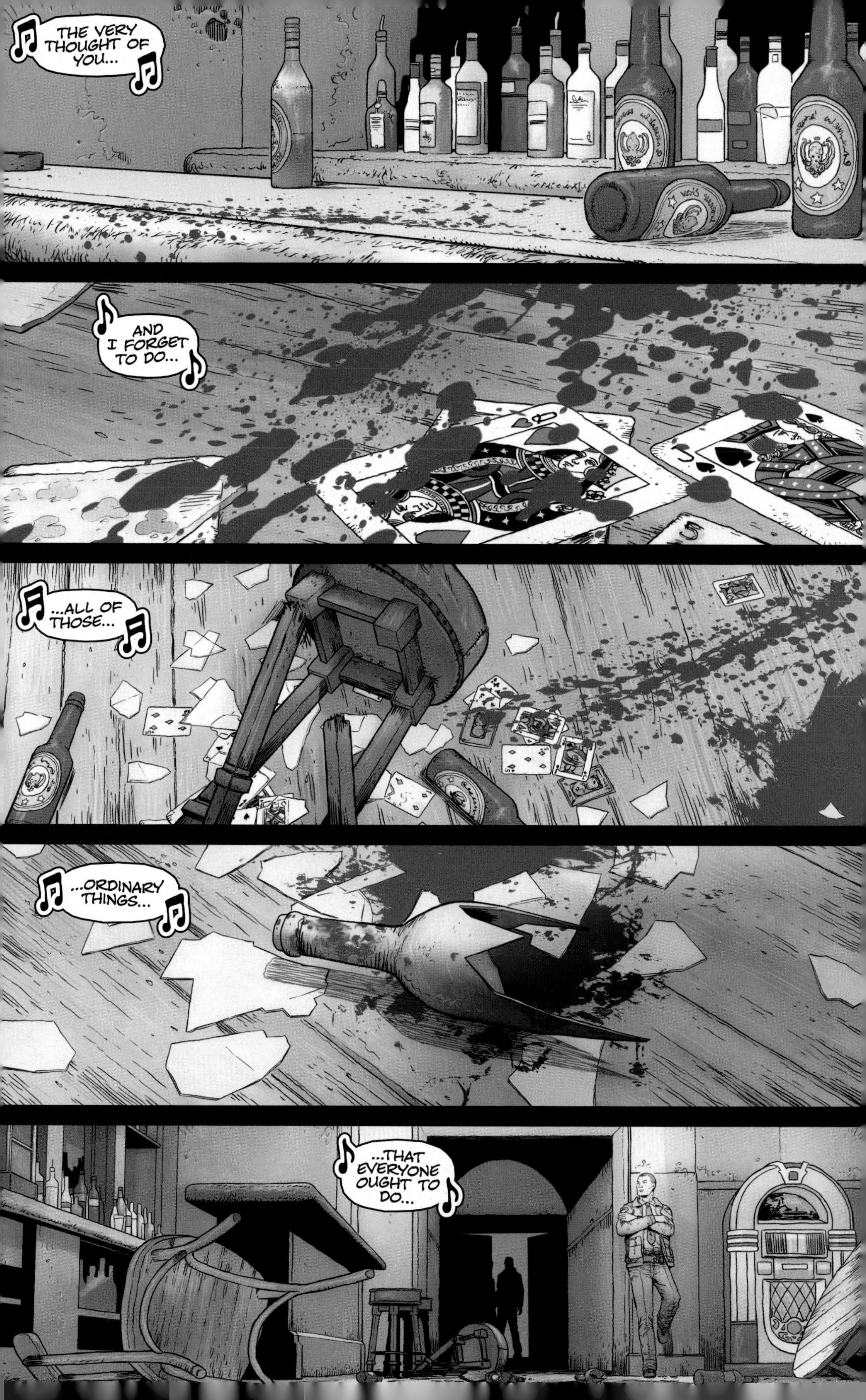
THE VERY THOUGHT OF YOU...
AND I FORGET TO DO...
...ALL OF THOSE...
...ORDINARY THINGS...
...THAT EVERYONE OUGHT TO DO...

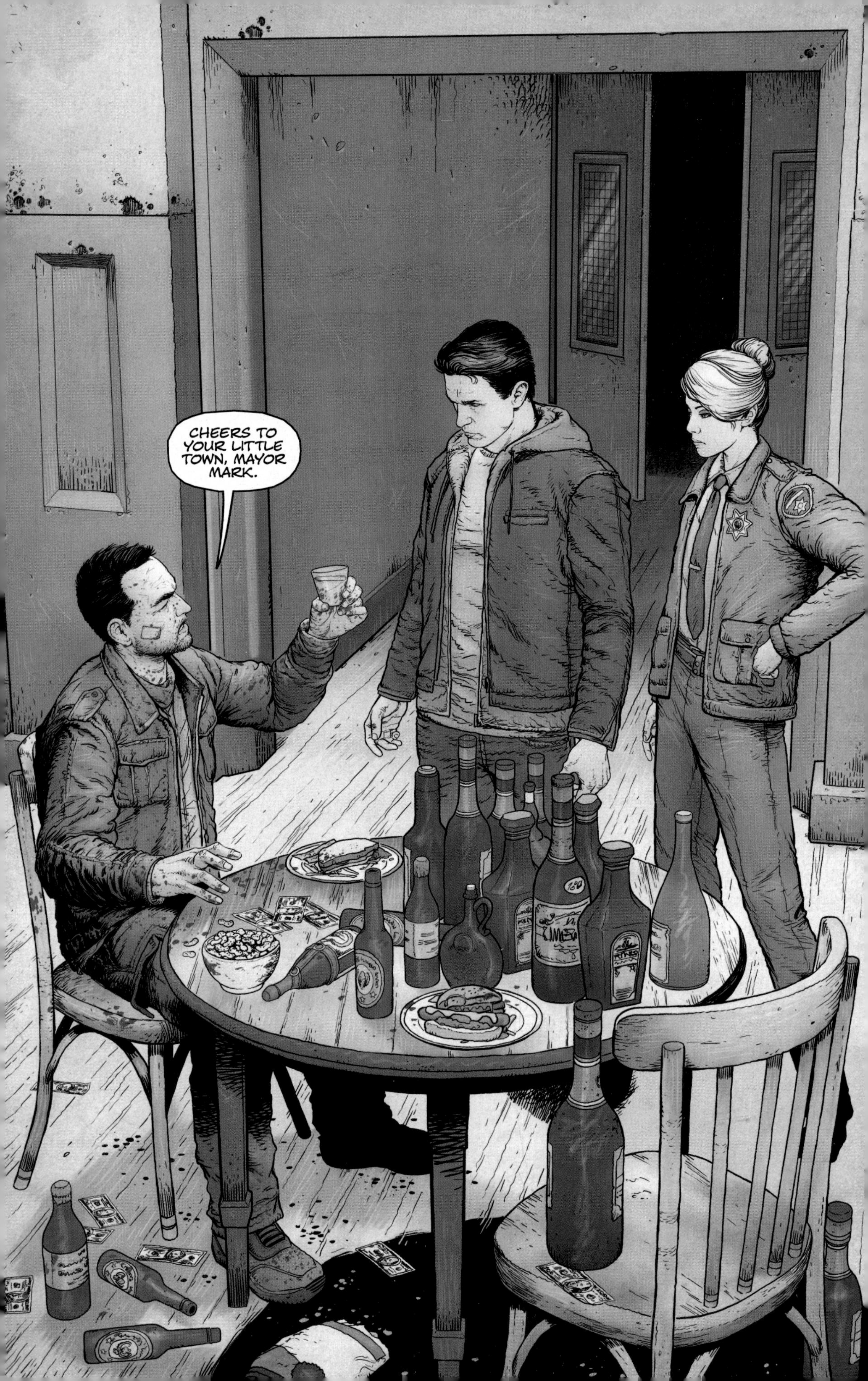
CHEERS TO YOUR LITTLE TOWN, MAYOR MARK.

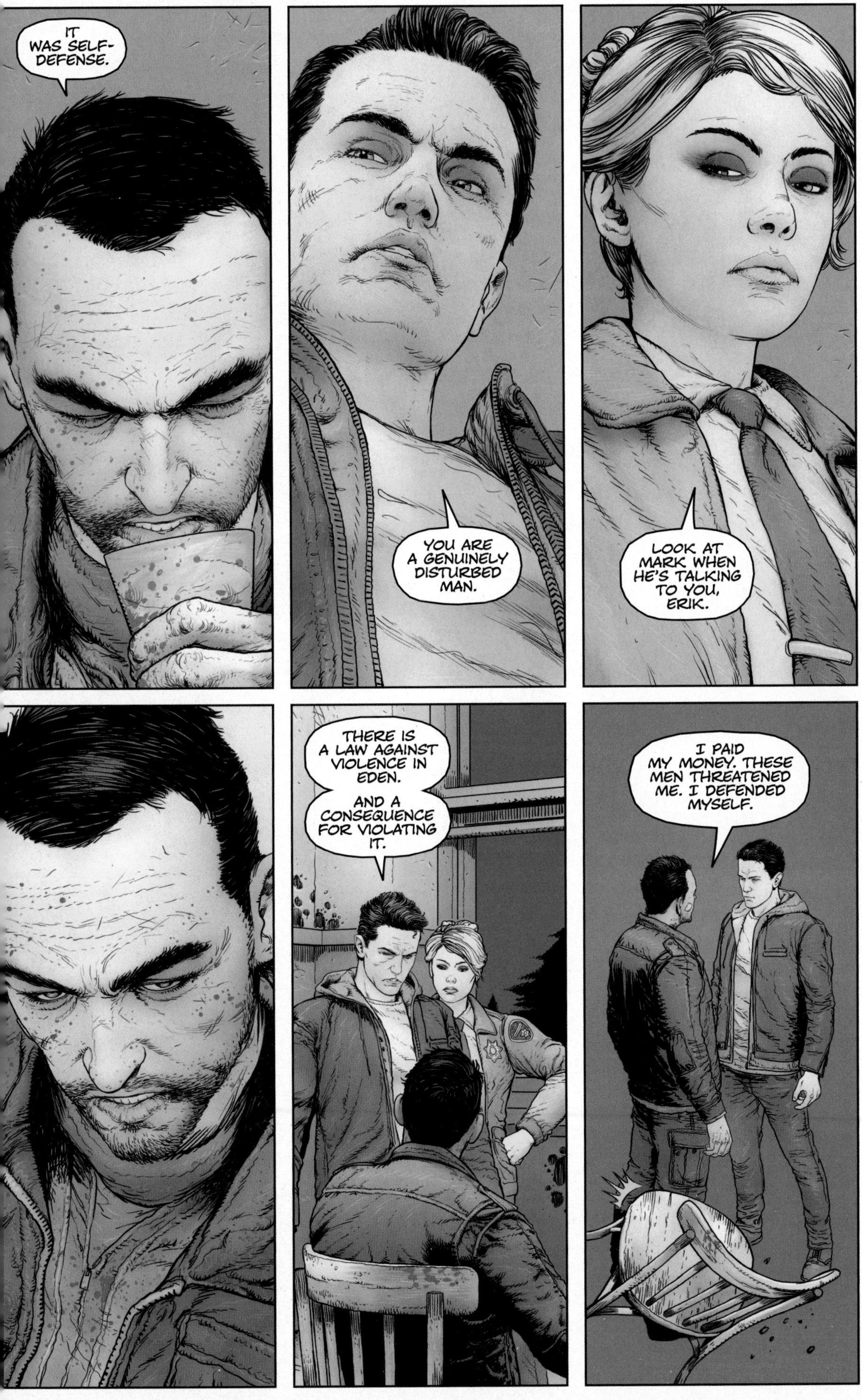
IT WAS SELF-DEFENSE.
YOU ARE A GENUINELY DISTURBED MAN.
LOOK AT MARK WHEN HE'S TALKING TO YOU, ERIK.
THERE IS A LAW AGAINST VIOLENCE IN EDEN.
AND A CONSEQUENCE FOR VIOLATING IT.
I PAID MY MONEY. THESE MEN THREATENED ME. I DEFENDED MYSELF.

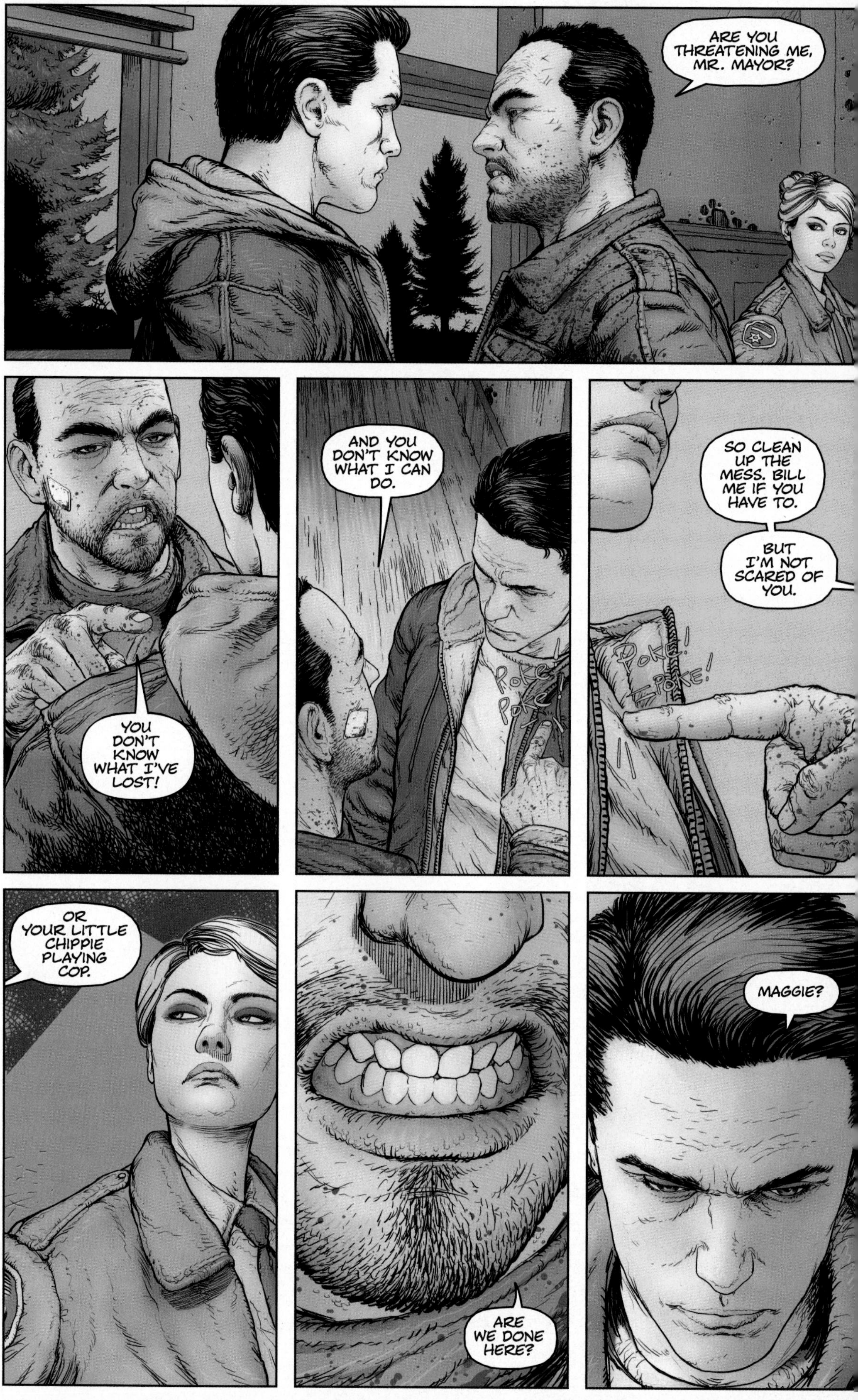
ARE YOU THREATENING ME, MR. MAYOR?
YOU DON'T KNOW WHAT I'VE LOST!
AND YOU DON'T KNOW WHAT I CAN DO.
POKE! POKE!
SO CLEAN UP THE MESS. BILL ME IF YOU HAVE TO.
BUT I'M NOT SCARED OF YOU.
POKE! POKE!
OR YOUR LITTLE CHIPPIE PLAYING COP.
ARE WE DONE HERE?
MAGGIE?

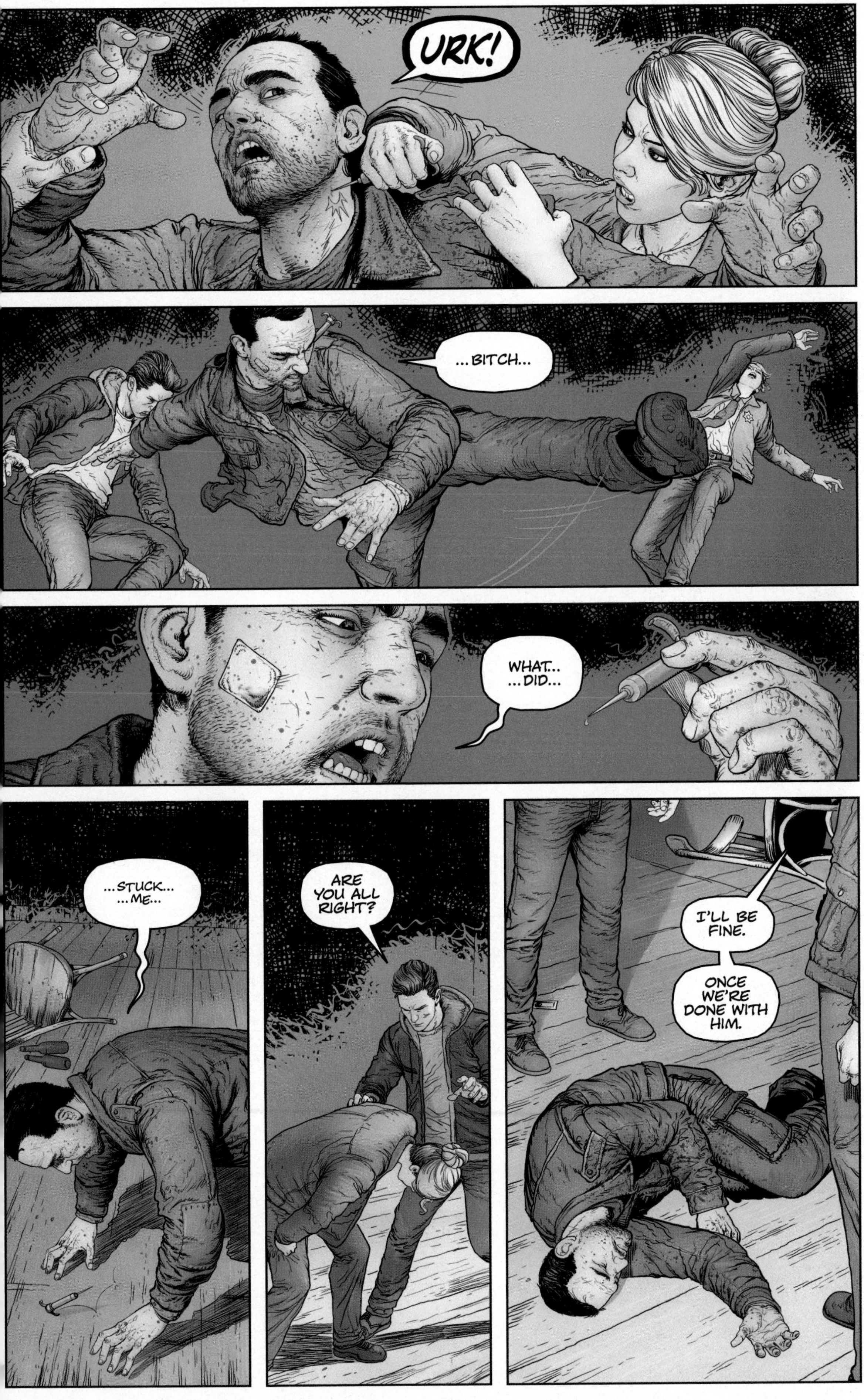
URK!
...BITCH...
WHAT... ...DID...
...STUCK... ...ME...
ARE YOU ALL RIGHT?
I'LL BE FINE.
ONCE WE'RE DONE WITH HIM.

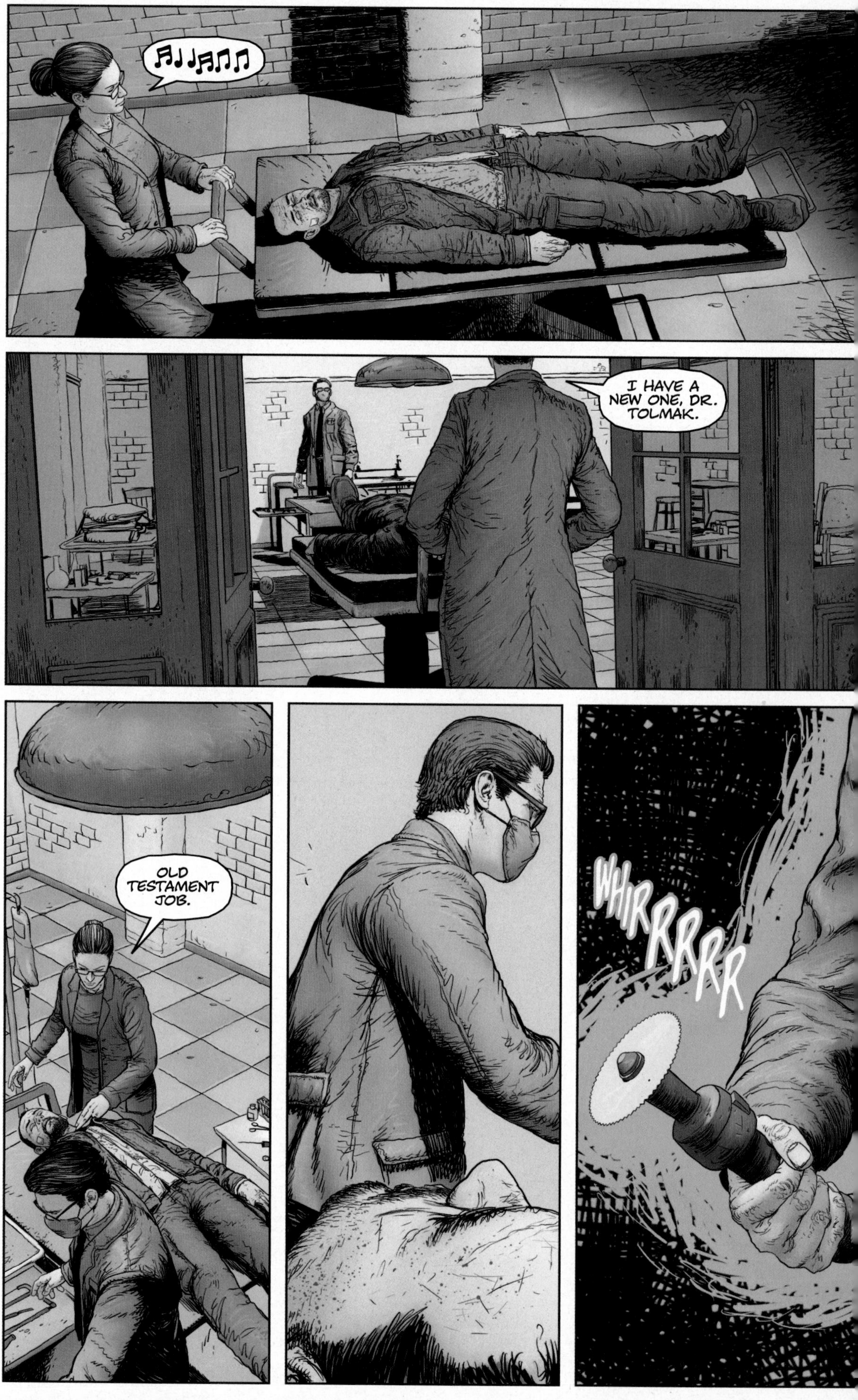
♫♩♩♫♫♪
I HAVE A NEW ONE, DR. TOLMAK.
OLD TESTAMENT JOB.
WHIRRRRR

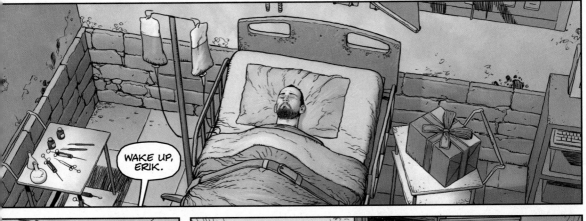

WAKE UP, ERIK.

YOU?

WHY AM I STRAPPED IN? GET ME OFF OF THIS BED!

YOU NEED TO RECOVER.

I BROUGHT YOU SOMETHING THAT YOU'LL WANT TO KEEP.

WAIT... WHERE IS...

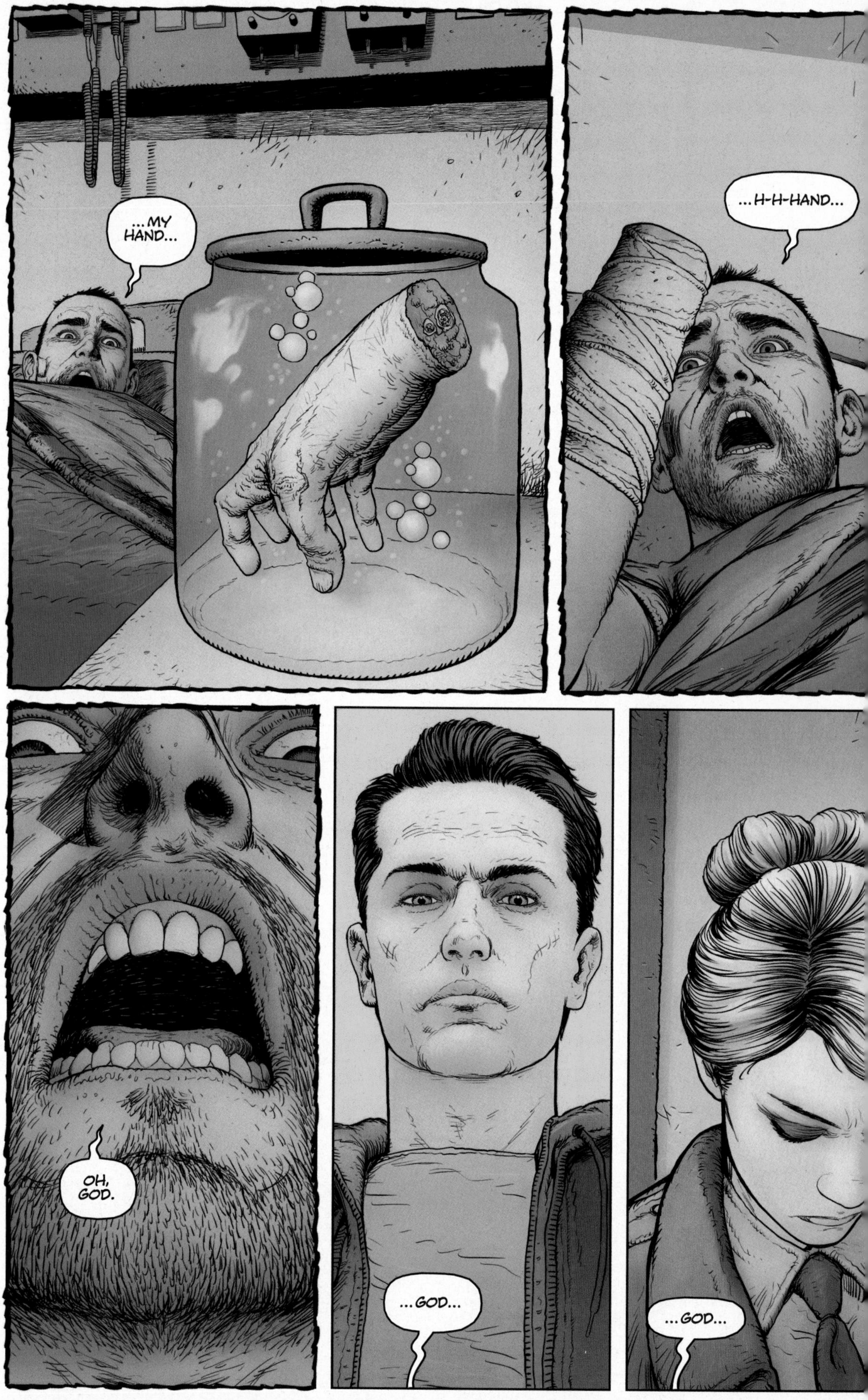
...MY HAND...
...H-H-HAND...
OH, GOD.
...GOD...
...GOD...

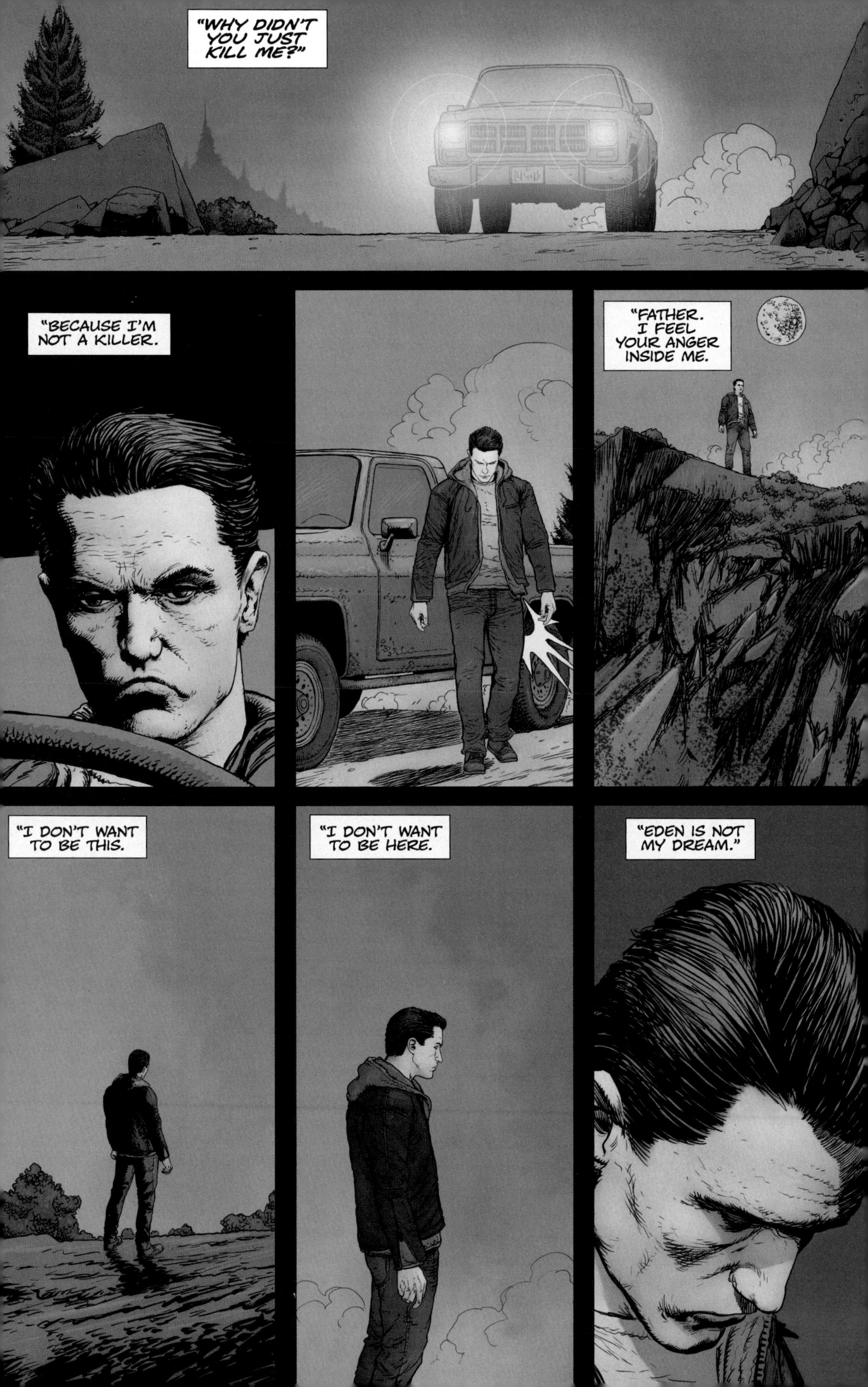
"WHY DIDN'T YOU JUST KILL ME?"
"BECAUSE I'M NOT A KILLER.
"FATHER. I FEEL YOUR ANGER INSIDE ME.
"I DON'T WANT TO BE THIS.
"I DON'T WANT TO BE HERE.
"EDEN IS NOT MY DREAM."

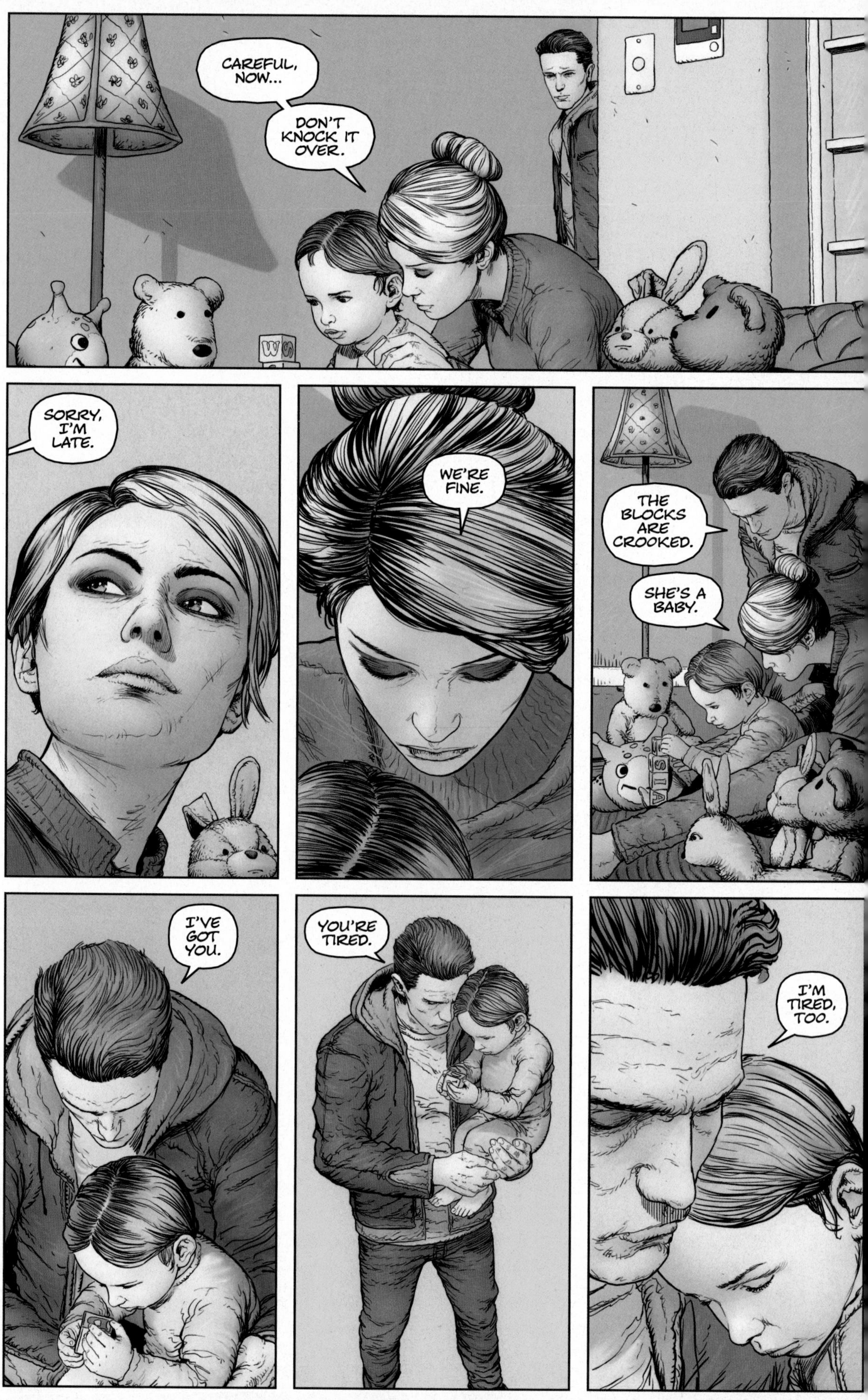
CAREFUL, NOW...
DON'T KNOCK IT OVER.
SORRY, I'M LATE.
WE'RE FINE.
THE BLOCKS ARE CROOKED.
SHE'S A BABY.
I'VE GOT YOU.
YOU'RE TIRED.
I'M TIRED, TOO.

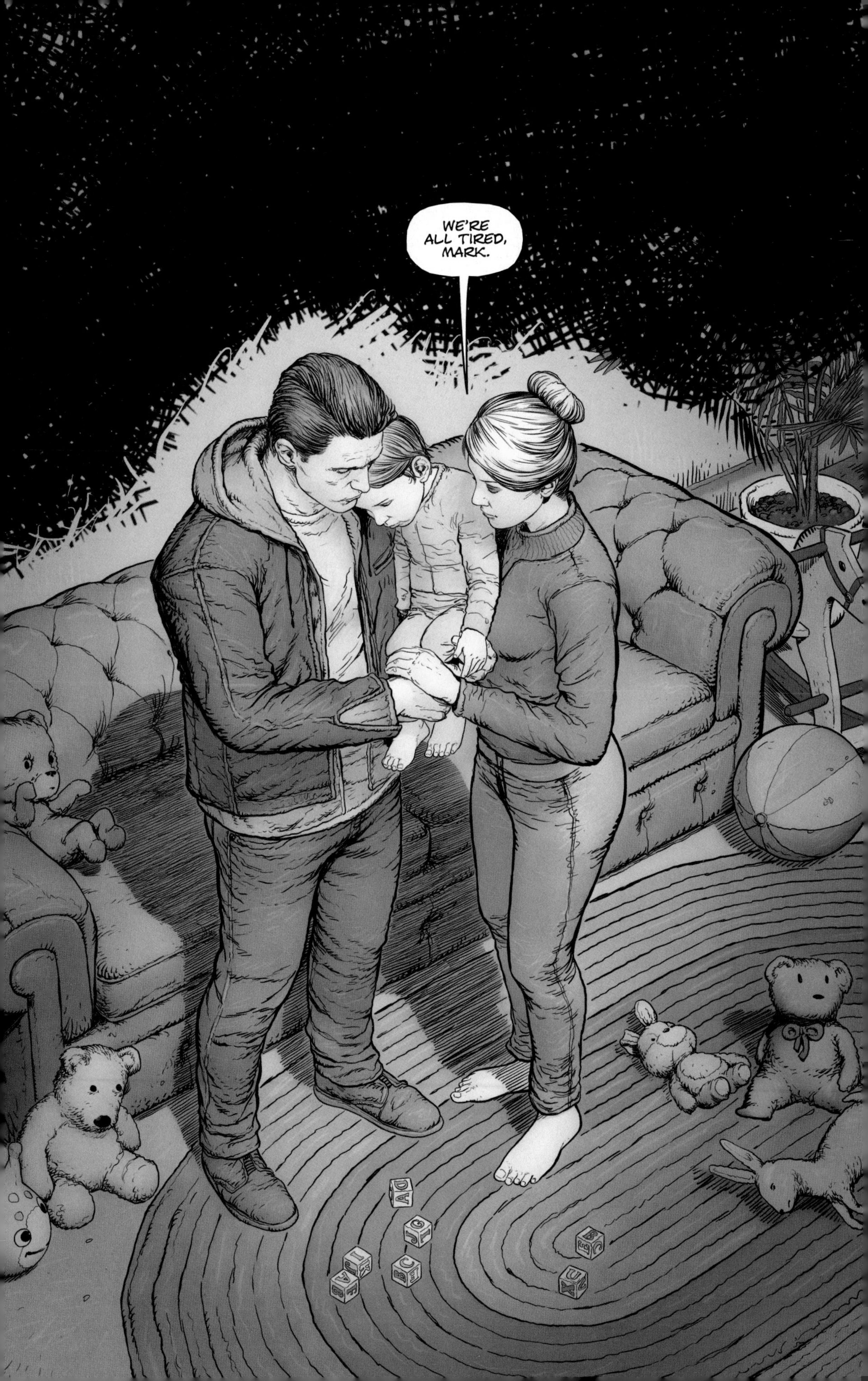
WE'RE ALL TIRED, MARK.

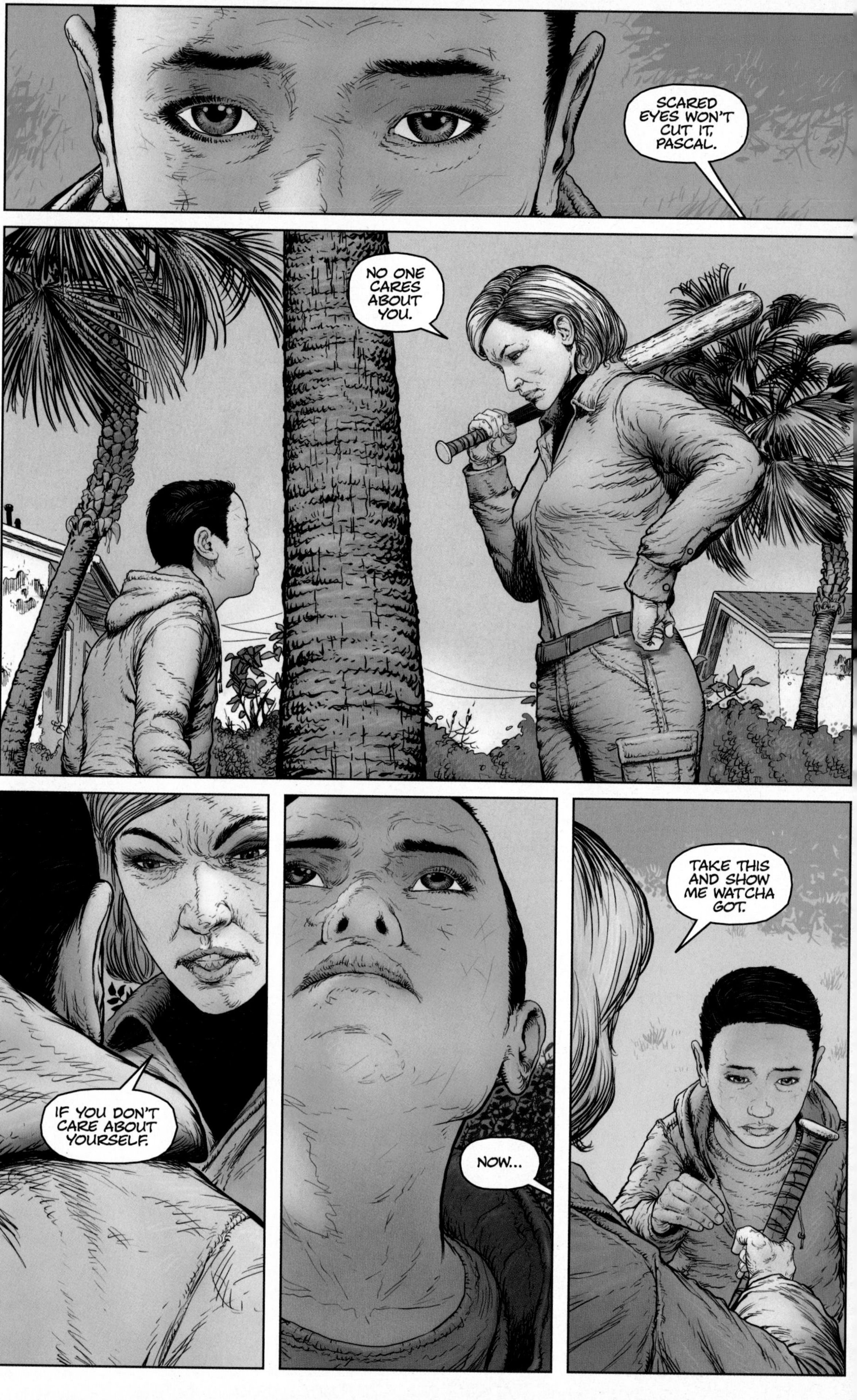
SCARED EYES WON'T CUT IT, PASCAL.
NO ONE CARES ABOUT YOU.
IF YOU DON'T CARE ABOUT YOURSELF.
NOW...
TAKE THIS AND SHOW ME WATCHA GOT.

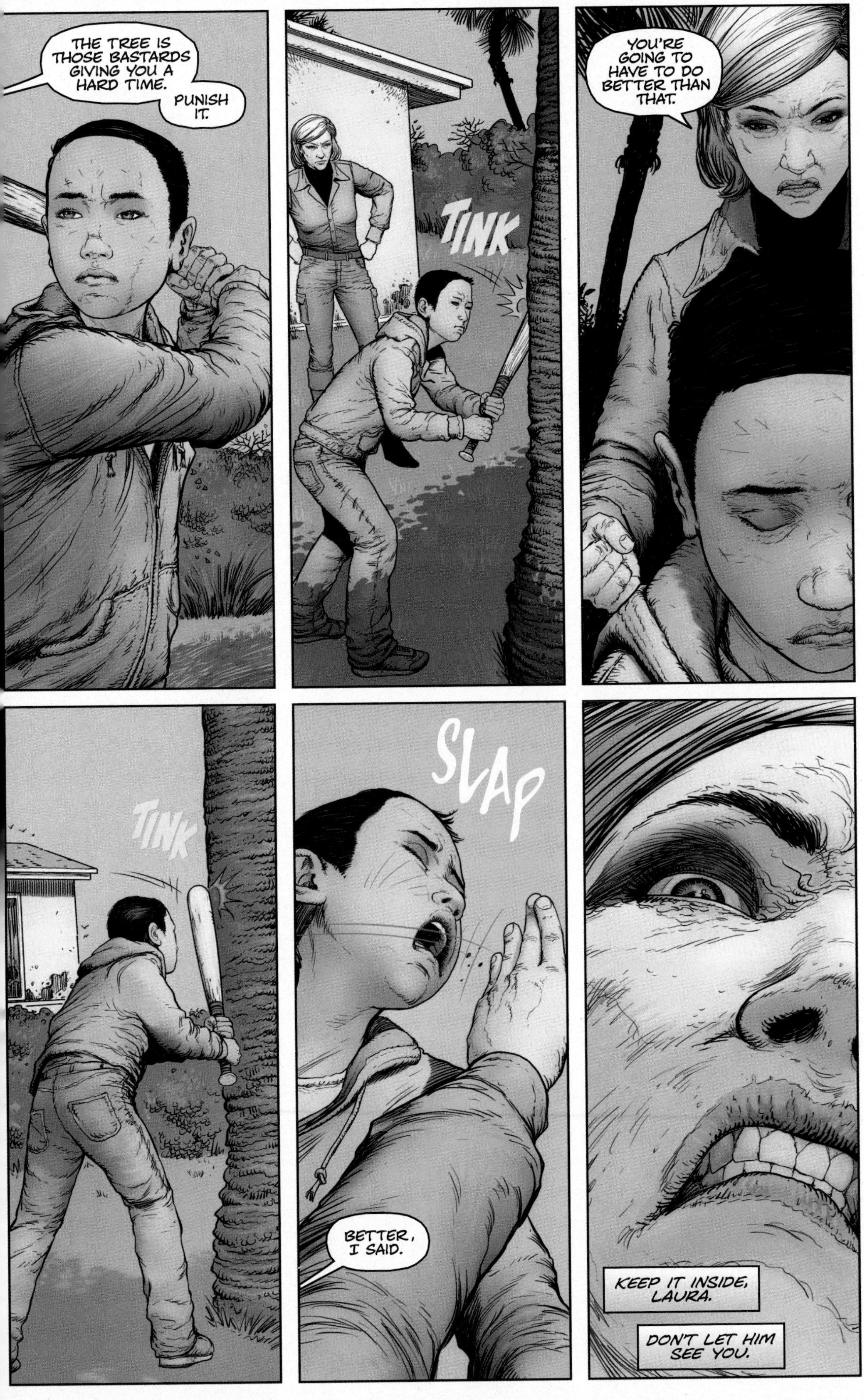
THE TREE IS THOSE BASTARDS GIVING YOU A HARD TIME.
PUNISH IT.
TINK
YOU'RE GOING TO HAVE TO DO BETTER THAN THAT.
TINK
SLAP
BETTER, I SAID.
KEEP IT INSIDE, LAURA.
DON'T LET HIM SEE YOU.

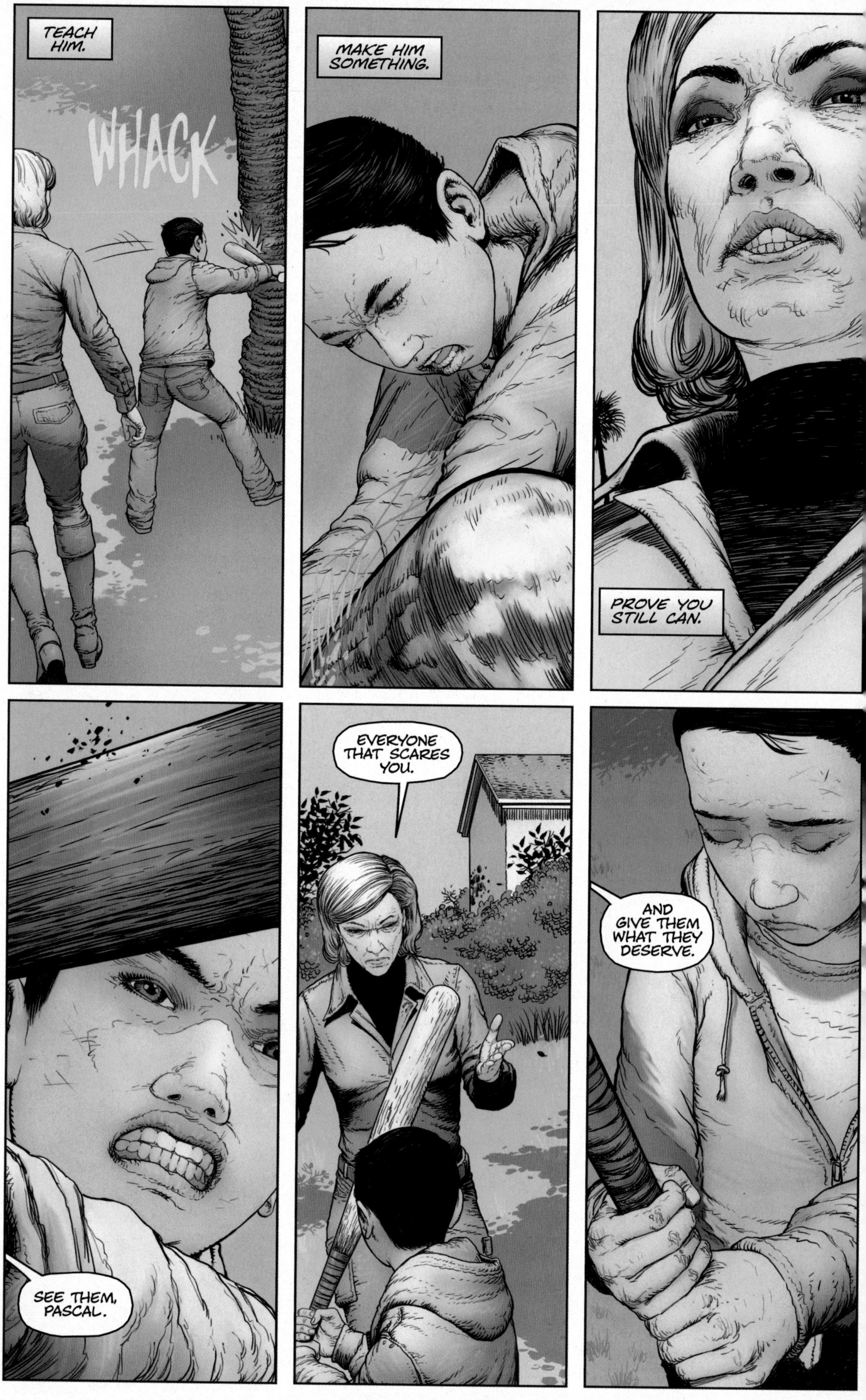
TEACH HIM.
WHACK
MAKE HIM SOMETHING.
PROVE YOU STILL CAN.
SEE THEM, PASCAL.
EVERYONE THAT SCARES YOU.
AND GIVE THEM WHAT THEY DESERVE.

THAT'S RIGHT.

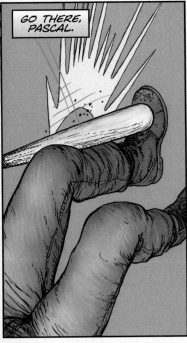

GO THERE, PASCAL.

SET IT ALL FREE.

THERE ARE NO VICTIMS.

THERE ARE NO VICTIMS, PASCAL.

JUST WINNERS AND LOSERS.

AND YOU BEAT THE TREE.

BUT THERE ARE MORE TREES AROUND HERE.

AREN'T THERE?

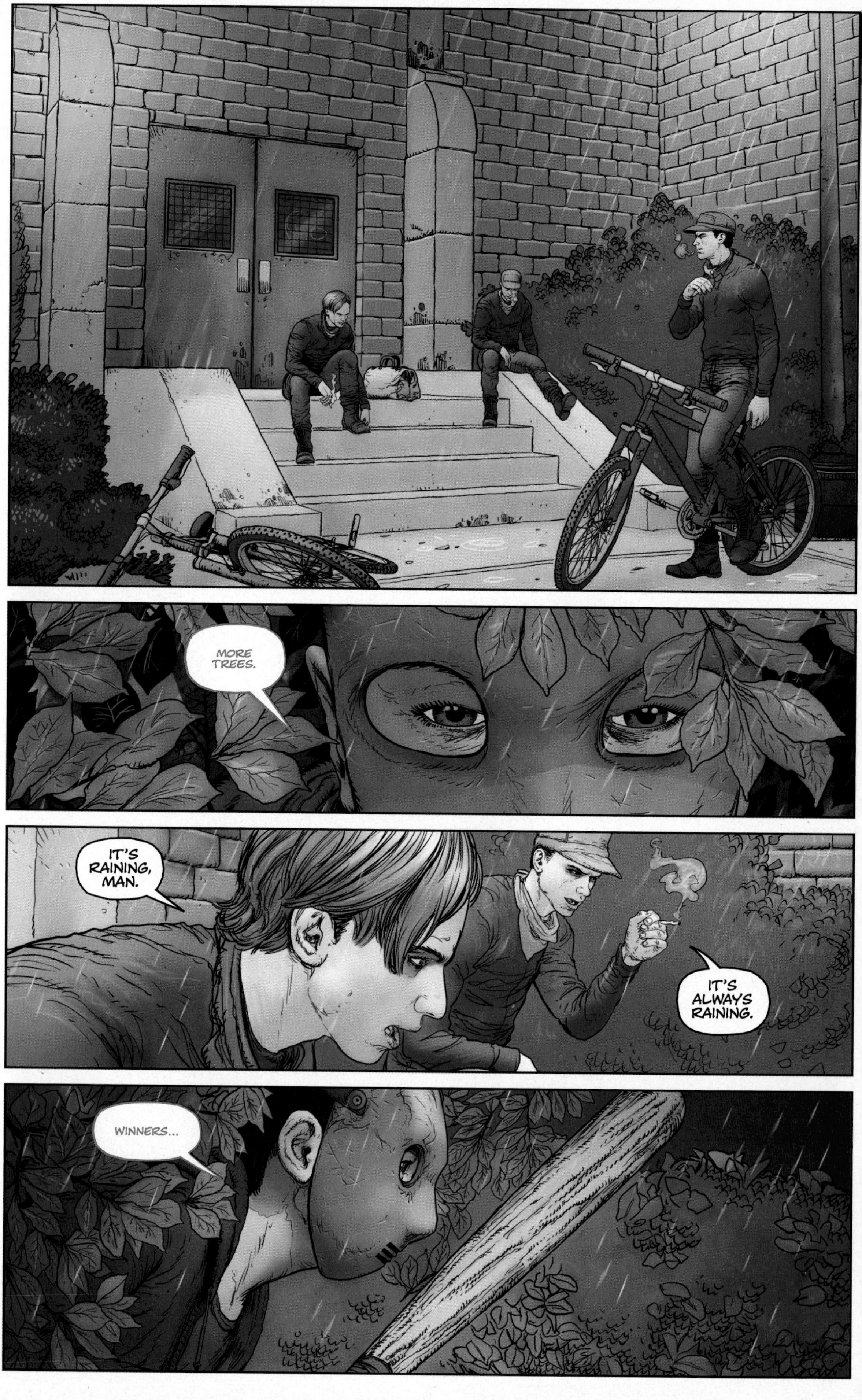
MORE TREES.
IT'S RAINING, MAN.
IT'S ALWAYS RAINING.
WINNERS...

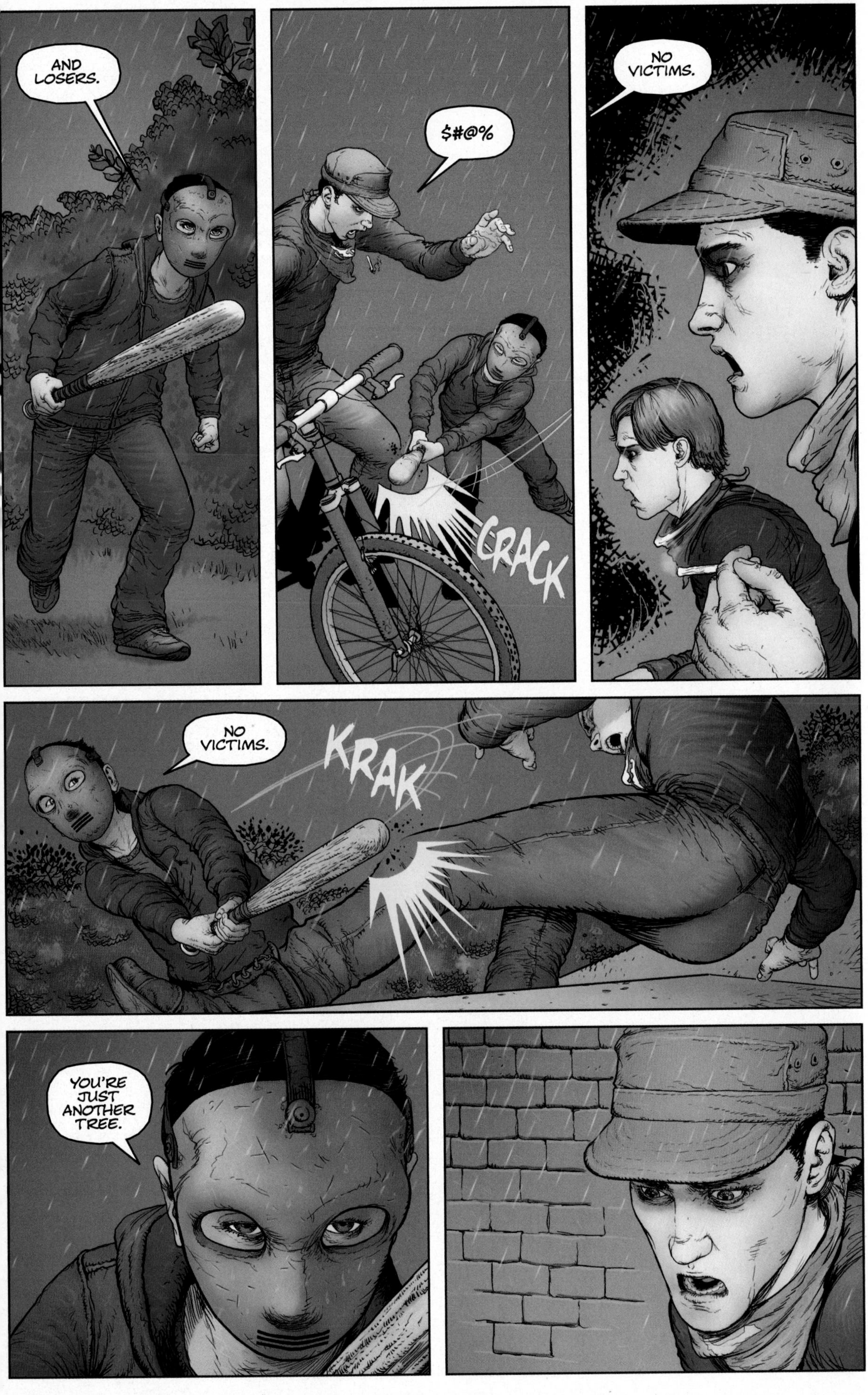
AND LOSERS.
$#@%
CRACK
NO VICTIMS.
NO VICTIMS.
KRAK
YOU'RE JUST ANOTHER TREE.

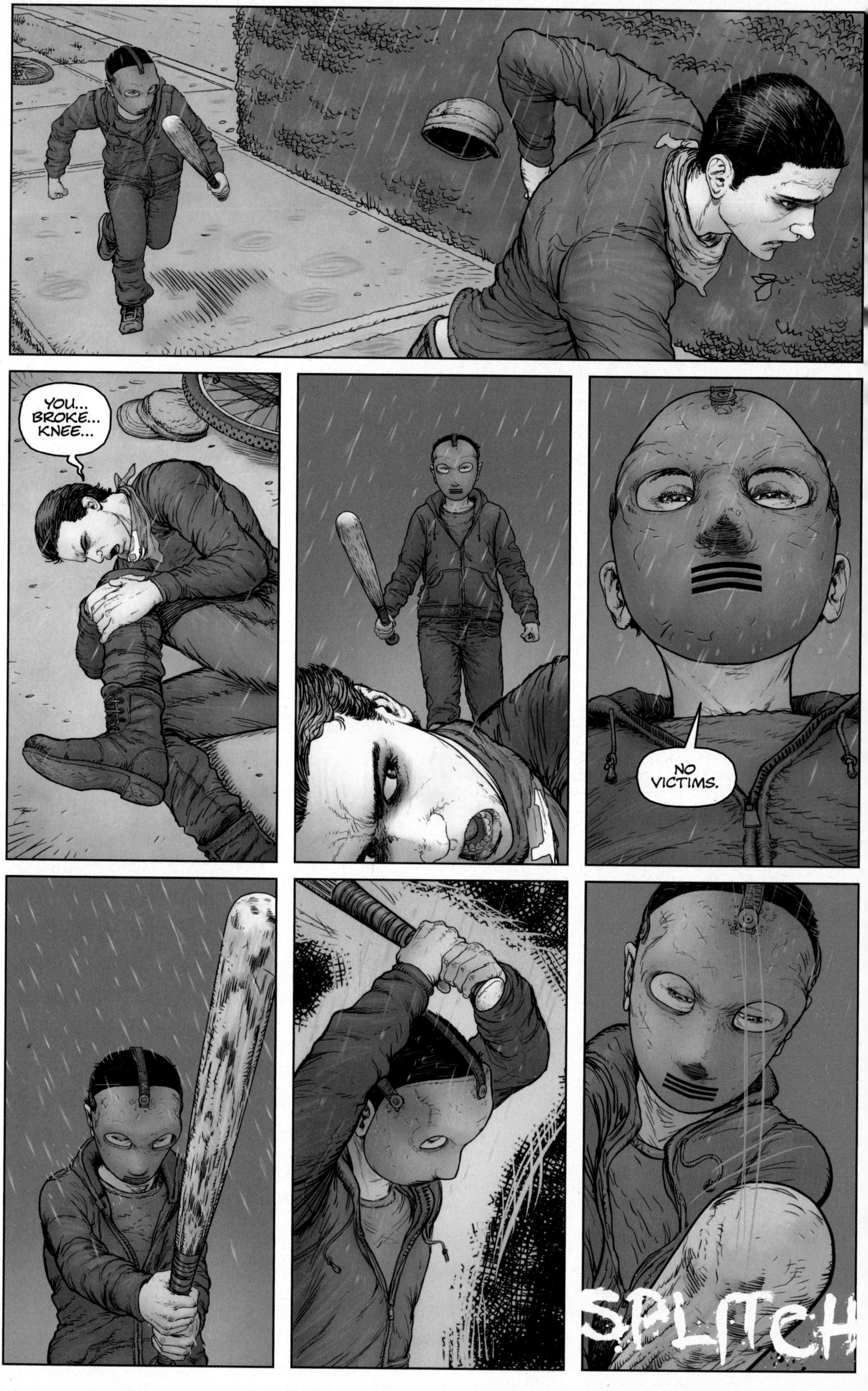
YOU... BROKE... KNEE...
NO VICTIMS.
SPLITCH

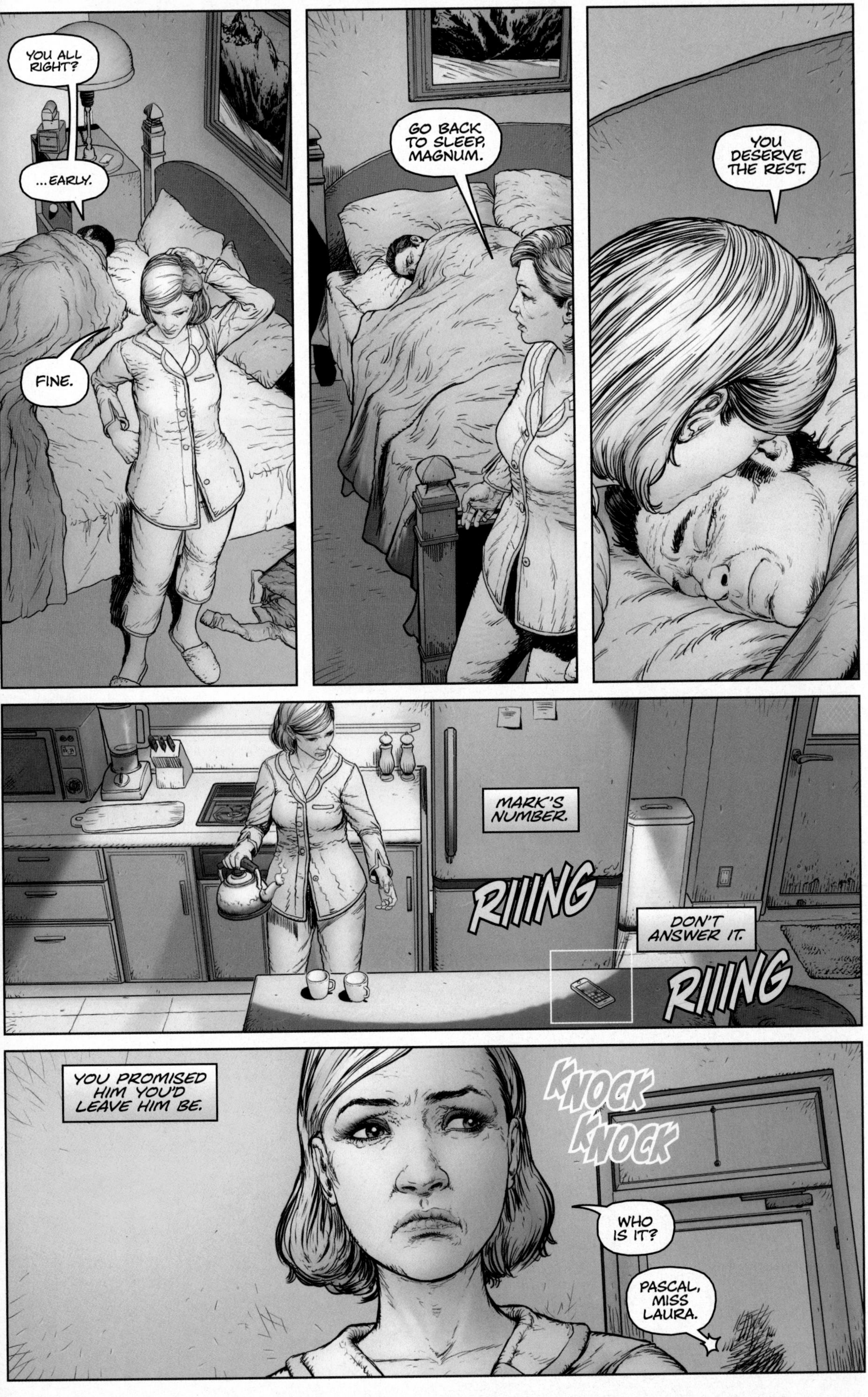
YOU ALL RIGHT?
...EARLY.
FINE.
GO BACK TO SLEEP, MAGNUM.
YOU DESERVE THE REST.
MARK'S NUMBER.
RIIING
DON'T ANSWER IT.
RIIING
YOU PROMISED HIM YOU'D LEAVE HIM BE.
KNOCK KNOCK
WHO IS IT?
PASCAL, MISS LAURA.

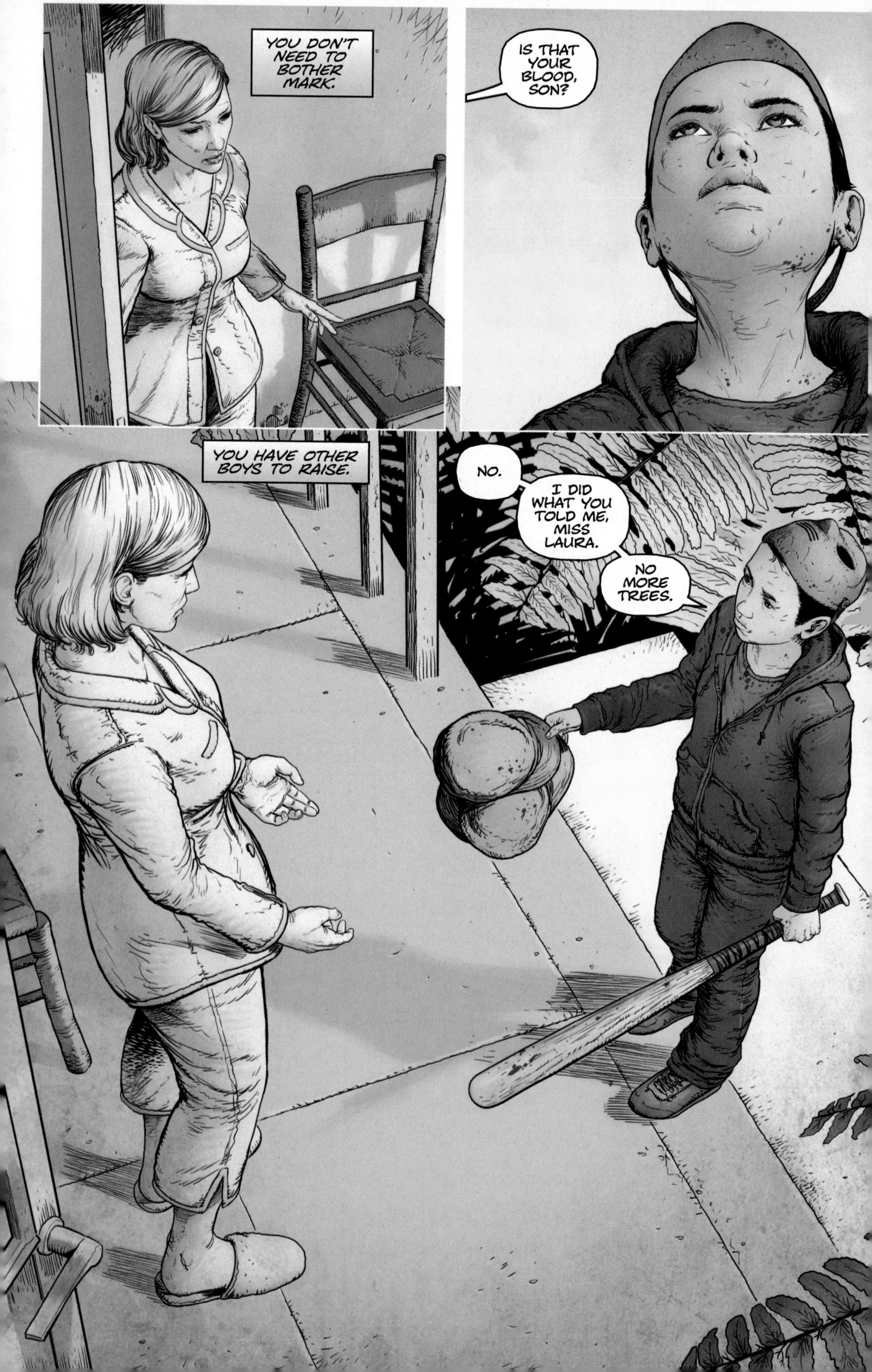
YOU DON'T NEED TO BOTHER MARK.
IS THAT YOUR BLOOD, SON?
YOU HAVE OTHER BOYS TO RAISE.
NO.
I DID WHAT YOU TOLD ME, MISS LAURA.
NO MORE TREES.

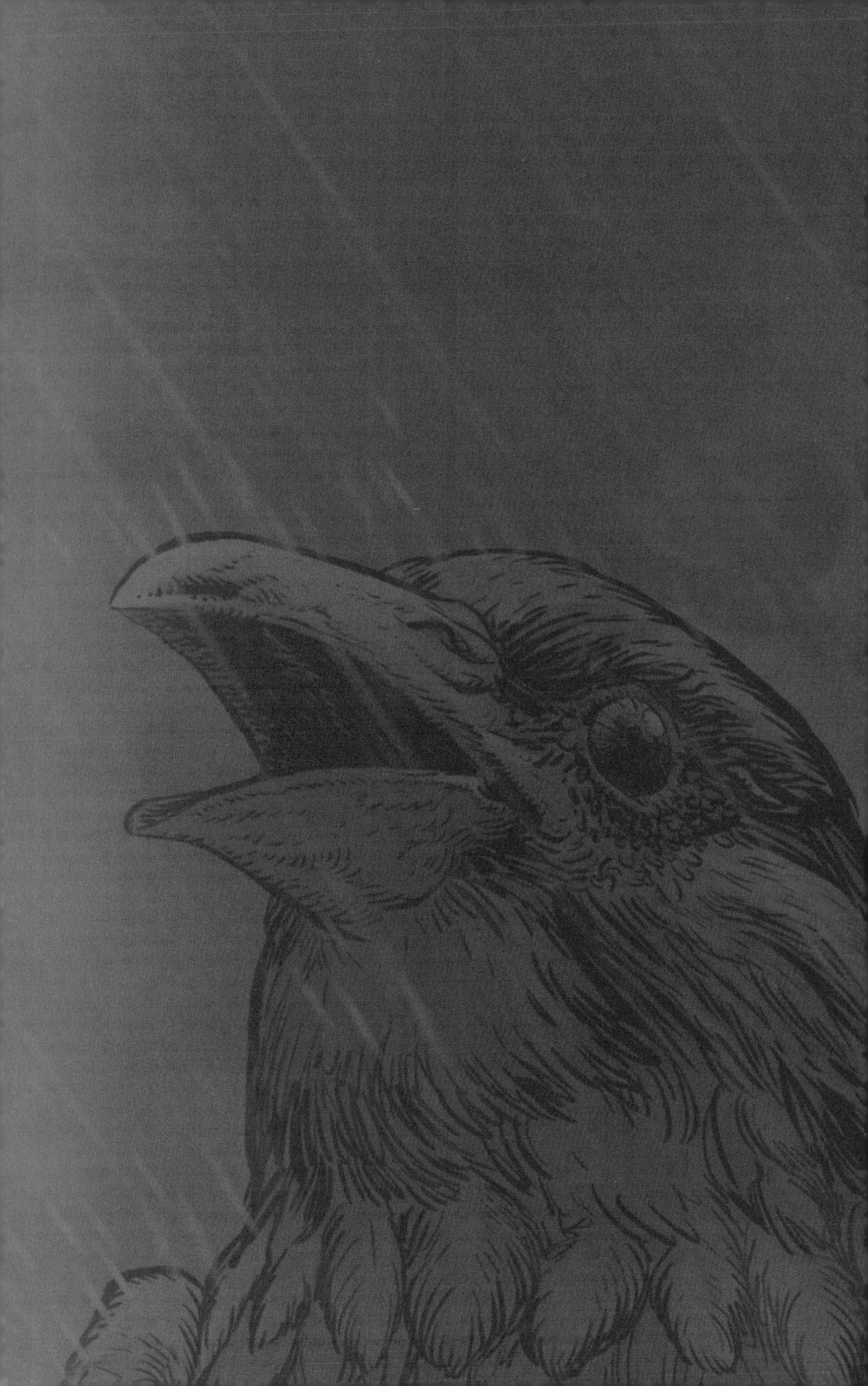

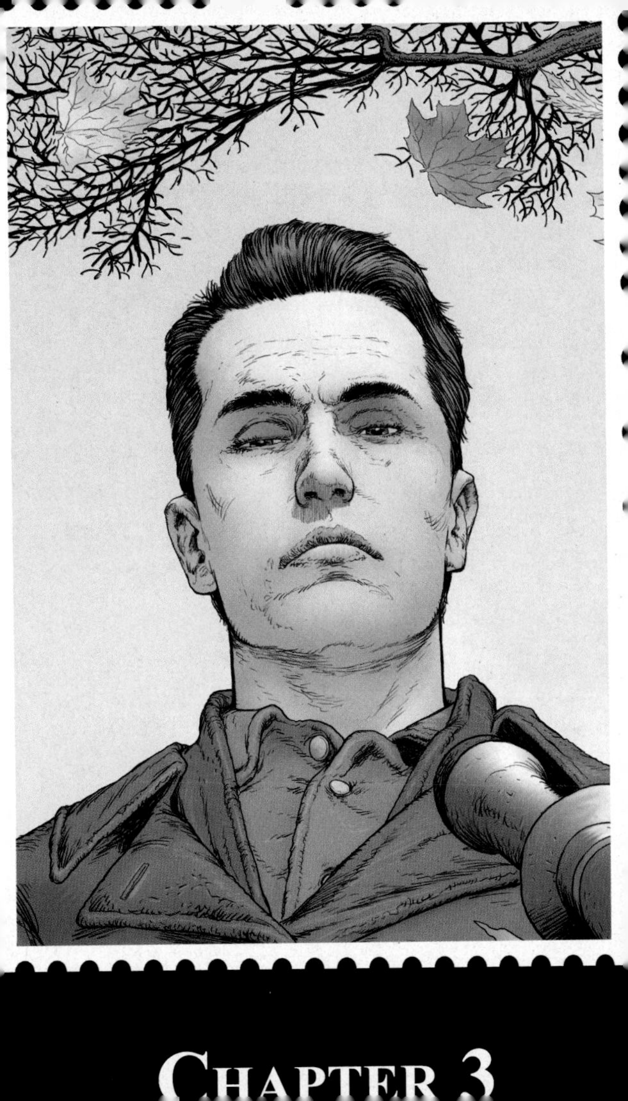

# Chapter 3

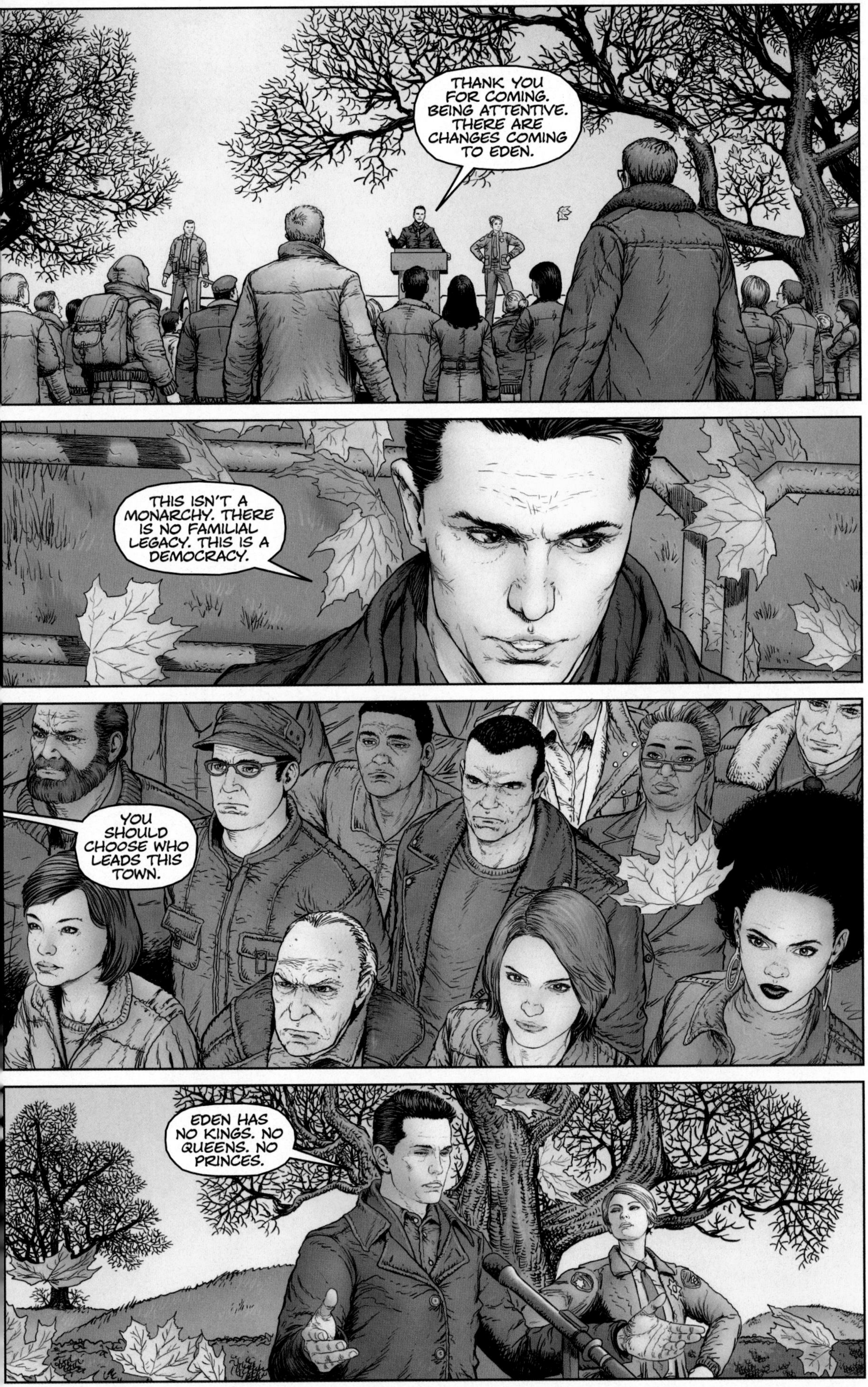
THANK YOU FOR COMING. BEING ATTENTIVE. THERE ARE CHANGES COMING TO EDEN.
THIS ISN'T A MONARCHY. THERE IS NO FAMILIAL LEGACY. THIS IS A DEMOCRACY.
YOU SHOULD CHOOSE WHO LEADS THIS TOWN.
EDEN HAS NO KINGS. NO QUEENS. NO PRINCES.

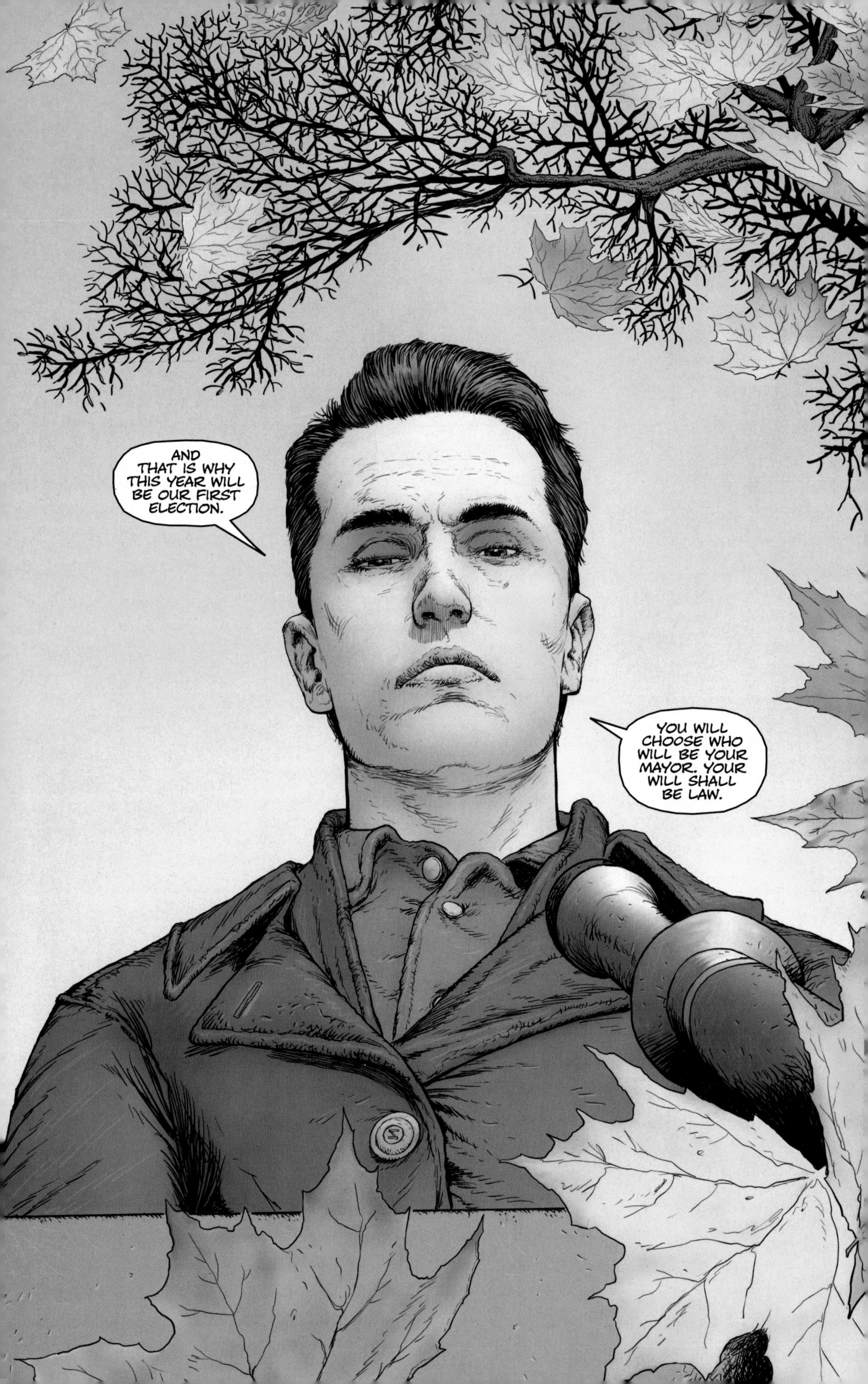
AND THAT IS WHY THIS YEAR WILL BE OUR FIRST ELECTION.
YOU WILL CHOOSE WHO WILL BE YOUR MAYOR. YOUR WILL SHALL BE LAW.

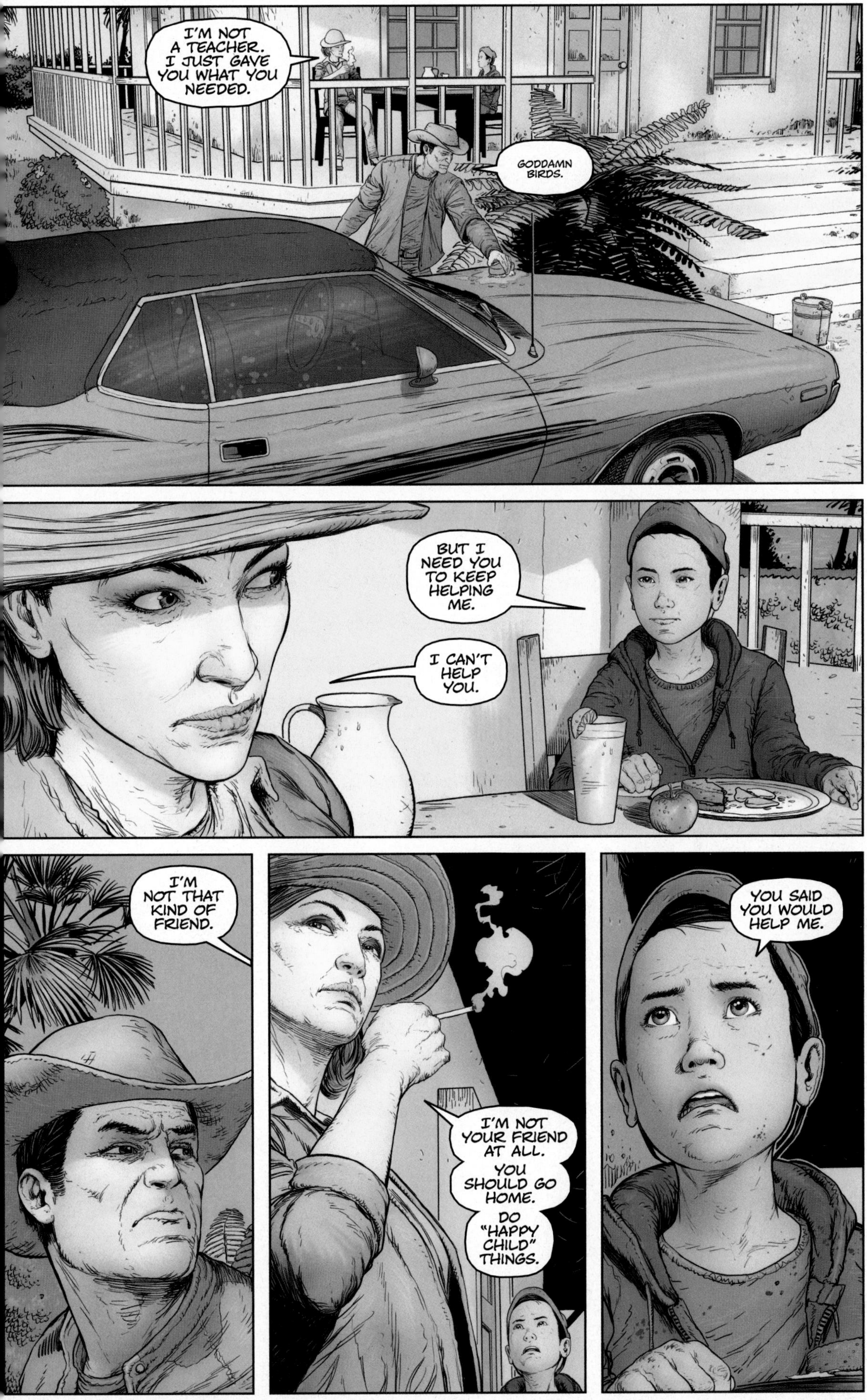
I'M NOT A TEACHER. I JUST GAVE YOU WHAT YOU NEEDED.
GODDAMN BIRDS.
BUT I NEED YOU TO KEEP HELPING ME.
I CAN'T HELP YOU.
I'M NOT THAT KIND OF FRIEND.
I'M NOT YOUR FRIEND AT ALL.
YOU SHOULD GO HOME.
DO "HAPPY CHILD" THINGS.
YOU SAID YOU WOULD HELP ME.

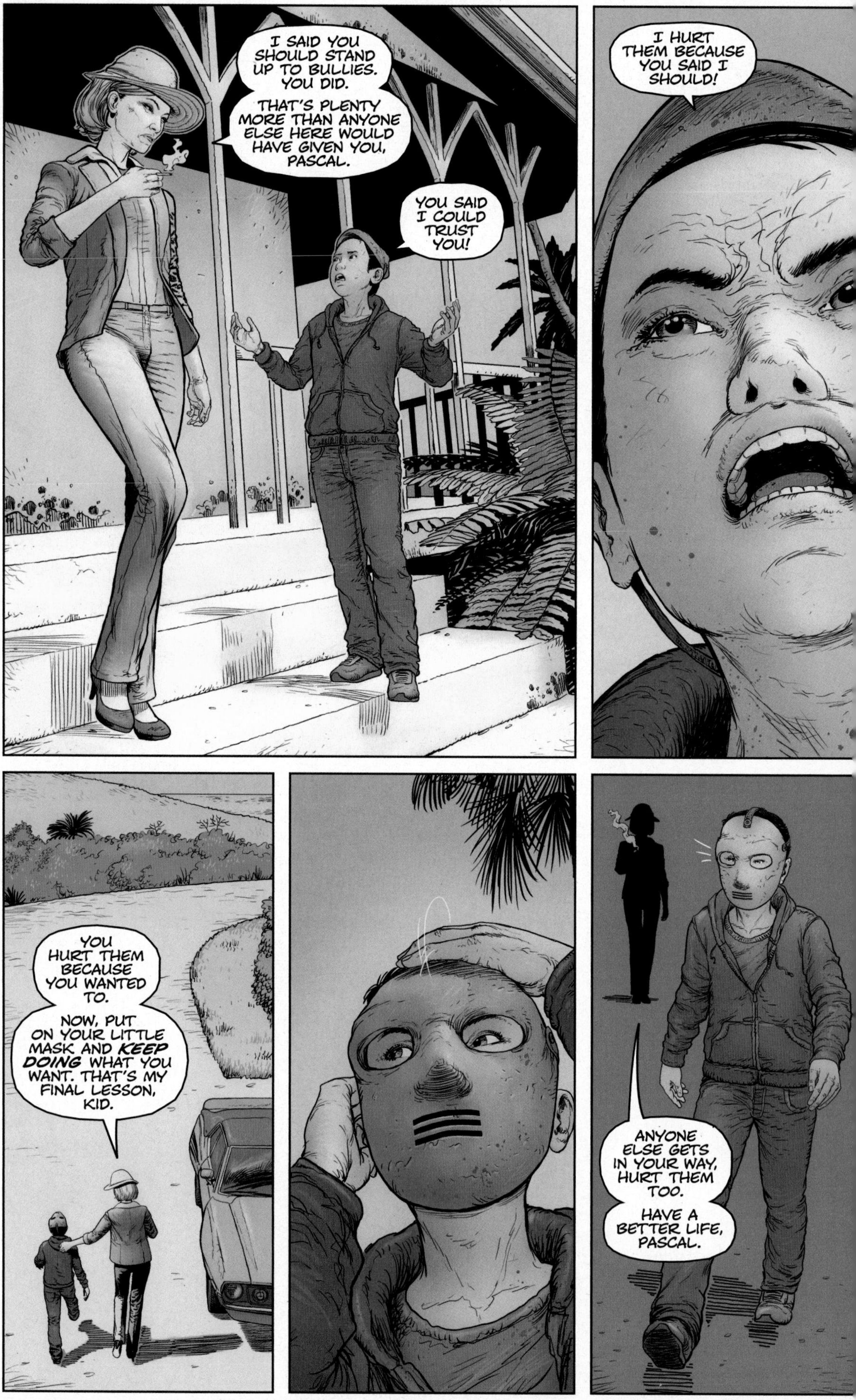
I SAID YOU SHOULD STAND UP TO BULLIES. YOU DID.
THAT'S PLENTY MORE THAN ANYONE ELSE HERE WOULD HAVE GIVEN YOU, PASCAL.
YOU SAID I COULD TRUST YOU!
I HURT THEM BECAUSE YOU SAID I SHOULD!
YOU HURT THEM BECAUSE YOU WANTED TO.
NOW, PUT ON YOUR LITTLE MASK AND KEEP DOING WHAT YOU WANT. THAT'S MY FINAL LESSON, KID.
ANYONE ELSE GETS IN YOUR WAY, HURT THEM TOO.
HAVE A BETTER LIFE, PASCAL.

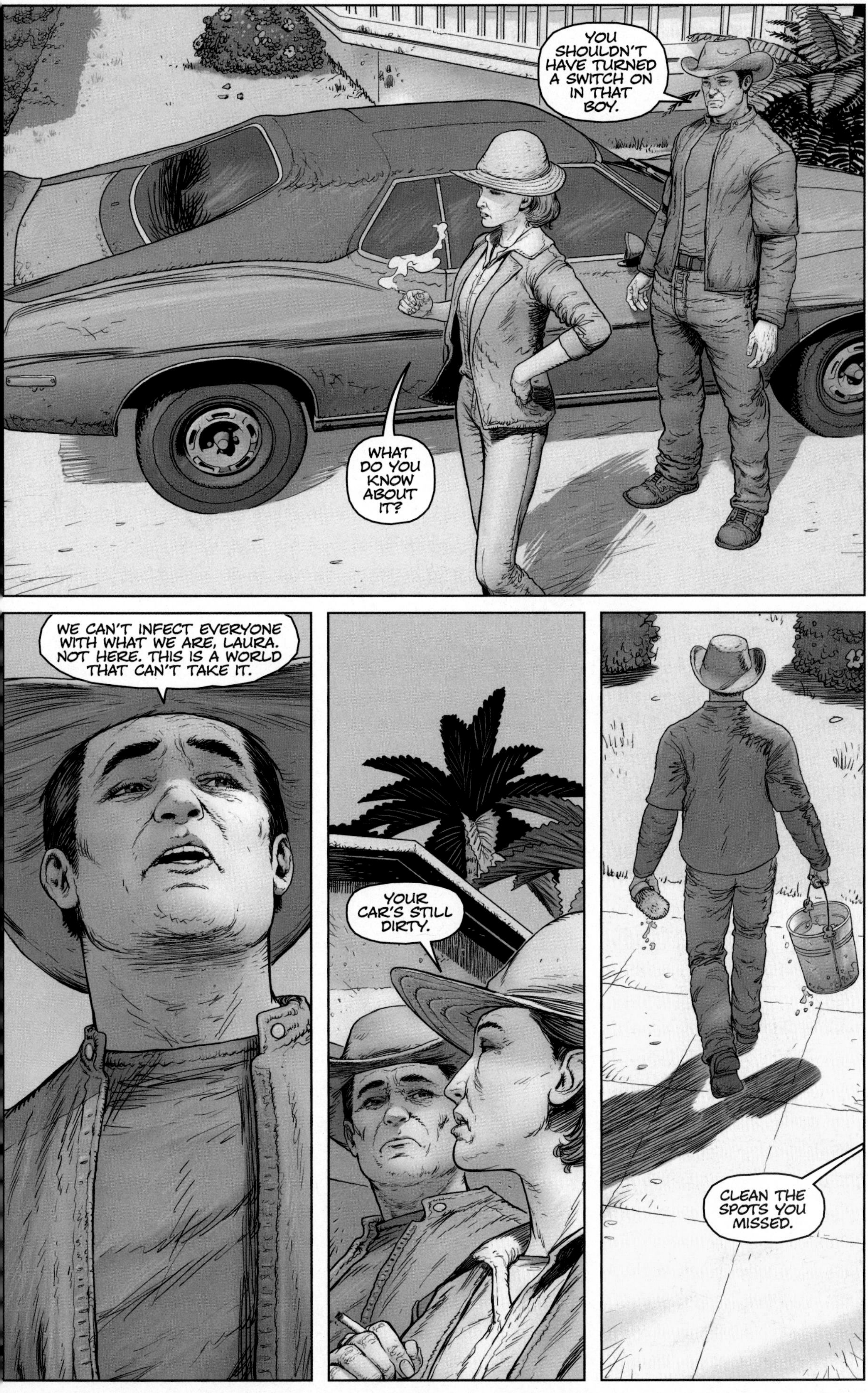
YOU SHOULDN'T HAVE TURNED A SWITCH ON IN THAT BOY.
WHAT DO YOU KNOW ABOUT IT?
WE CAN'T INFECT EVERYONE WITH WHAT WE ARE, LAURA. NOT HERE. THIS IS A WORLD THAT CAN'T TAKE IT.
YOUR CAR'S STILL DIRTY.
CLEAN THE SPOTS YOU MISSED.

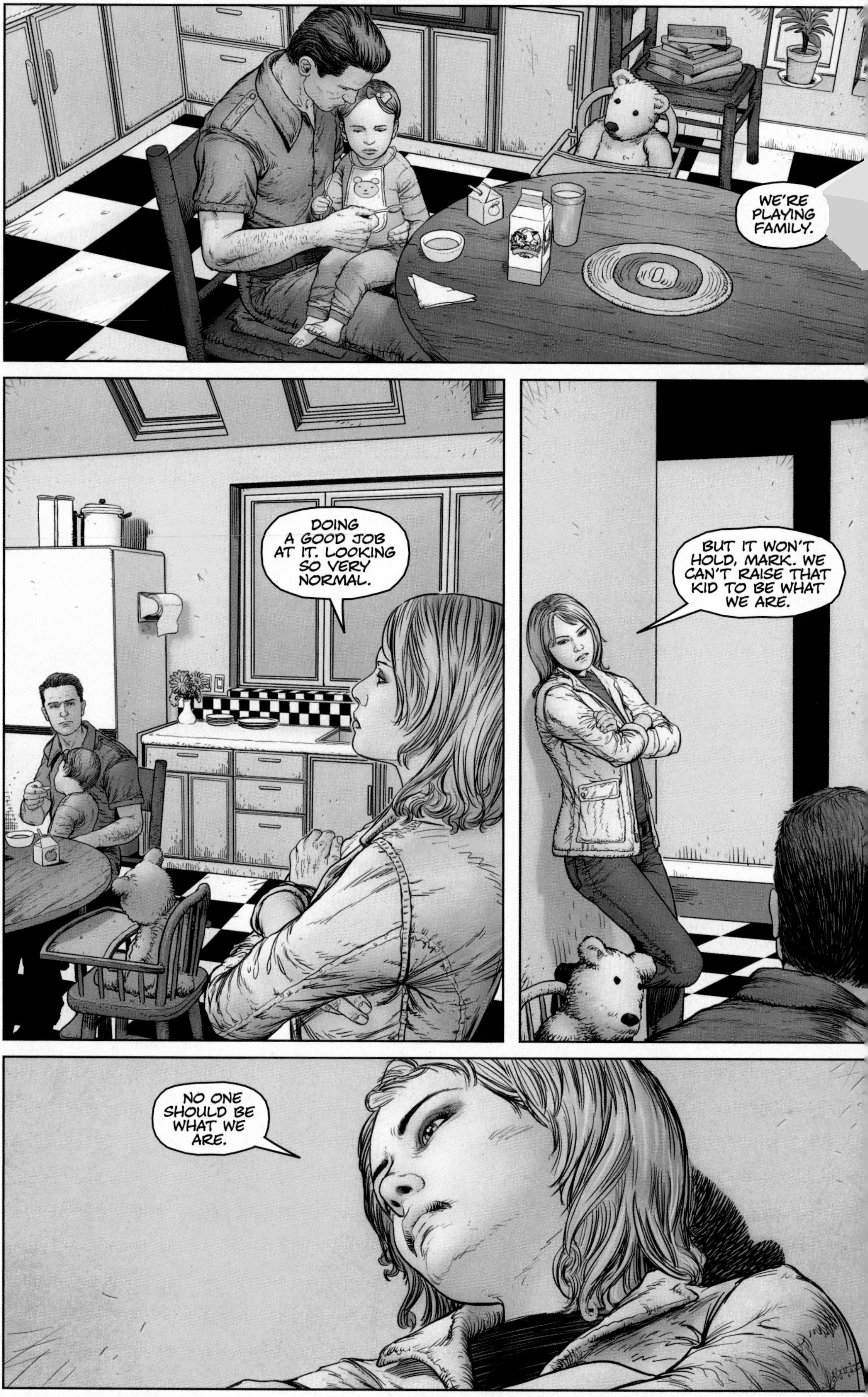
WE'RE PLAYING FAMILY.
DOING A GOOD JOB AT IT. LOOKING SO VERY NORMAL.
BUT IT WON'T HOLD, MARK. WE CAN'T RAISE THAT KID TO BE WHAT WE ARE.
NO ONE SHOULD BE WHAT WE ARE.

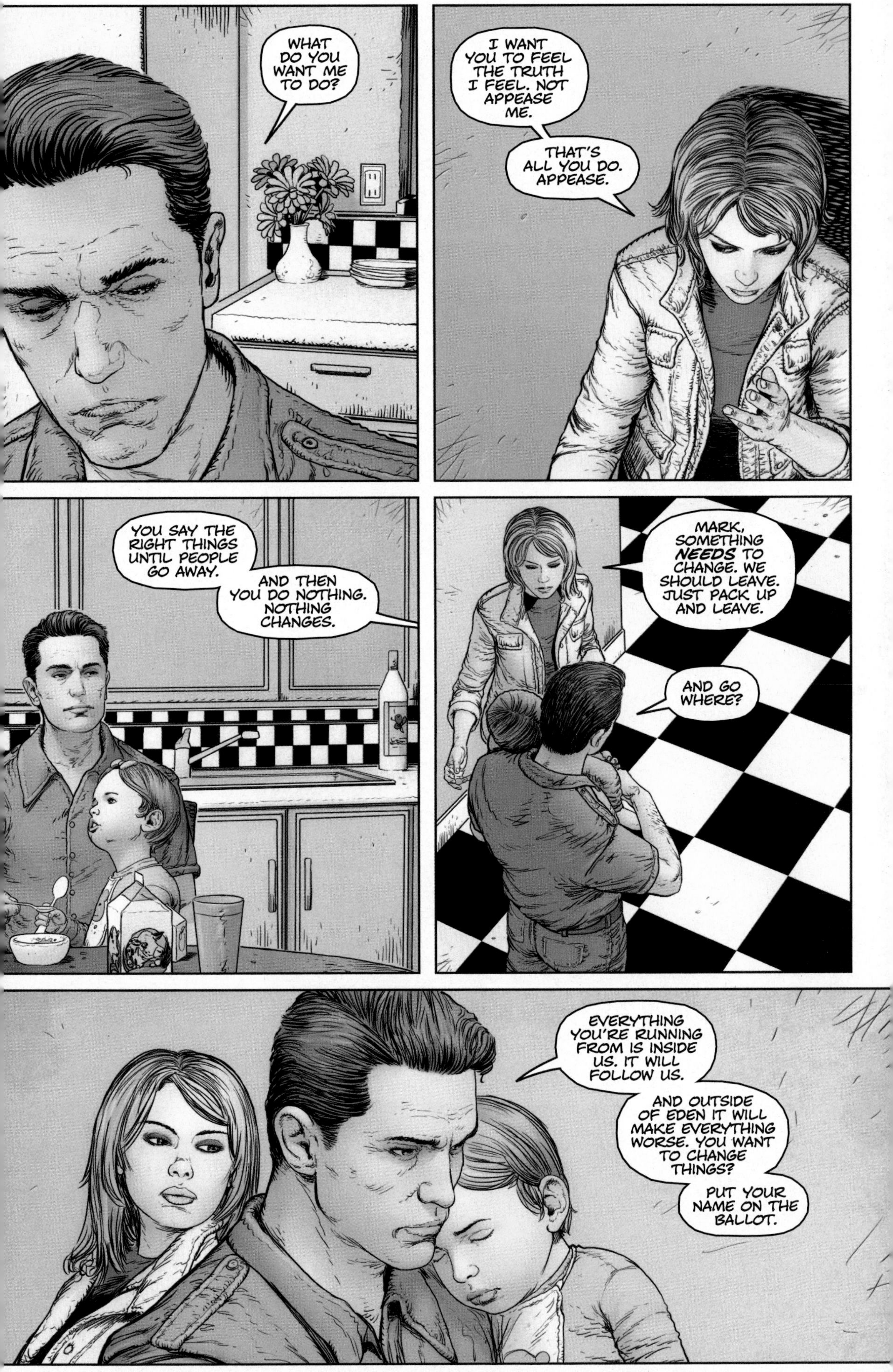
WHAT DO YOU WANT ME TO DO?
I WANT YOU TO FEEL THE TRUTH I FEEL. NOT APPEASE ME.
THAT'S ALL YOU DO. APPEASE.
YOU SAY THE RIGHT THINGS UNTIL PEOPLE GO AWAY.
AND THEN YOU DO NOTHING. NOTHING CHANGES.
MARK, SOMETHING *NEEDS* TO CHANGE. WE SHOULD LEAVE. JUST PACK UP AND LEAVE.
AND GO WHERE?
EVERYTHING YOU'RE RUNNING FROM IS INSIDE US. IT WILL FOLLOW US.
AND OUTSIDE OF EDEN IT WILL MAKE EVERYTHING WORSE. YOU WANT TO CHANGE THINGS?
PUT YOUR NAME ON THE BALLOT.

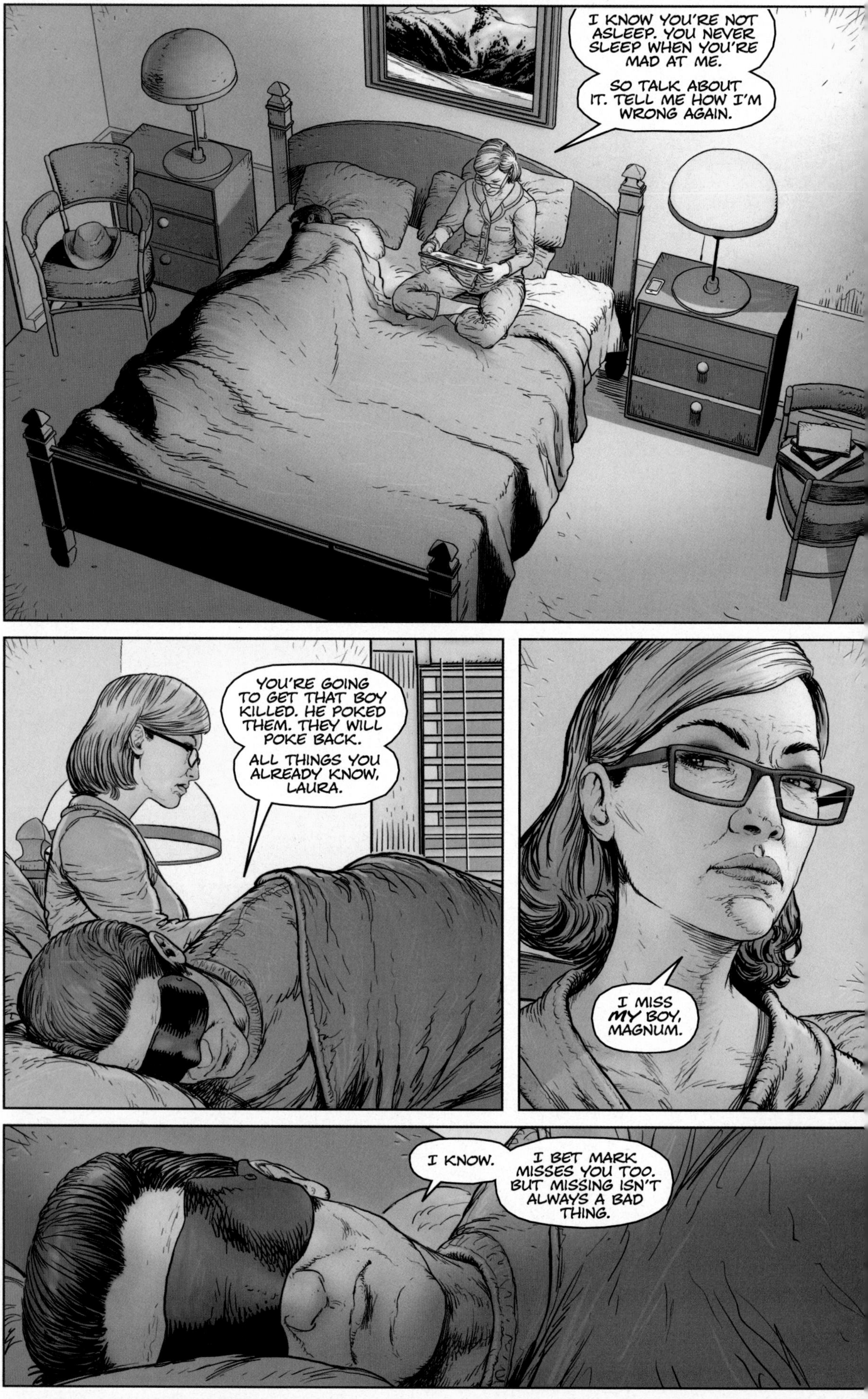

I KNOW YOU'RE NOT ASLEEP. YOU NEVER SLEEP WHEN YOU'RE MAD AT ME.
SO TALK ABOUT IT. TELL ME HOW I'M WRONG AGAIN.
YOU'RE GOING TO GET THAT BOY KILLED. HE POKED THEM. THEY WILL POKE BACK.
ALL THINGS YOU ALREADY KNOW, LAURA.
I MISS MY BOY, MAGNUM.
I KNOW.
I BET MARK MISSES YOU TOO. BUT MISSING ISN'T ALWAYS A BAD THING.

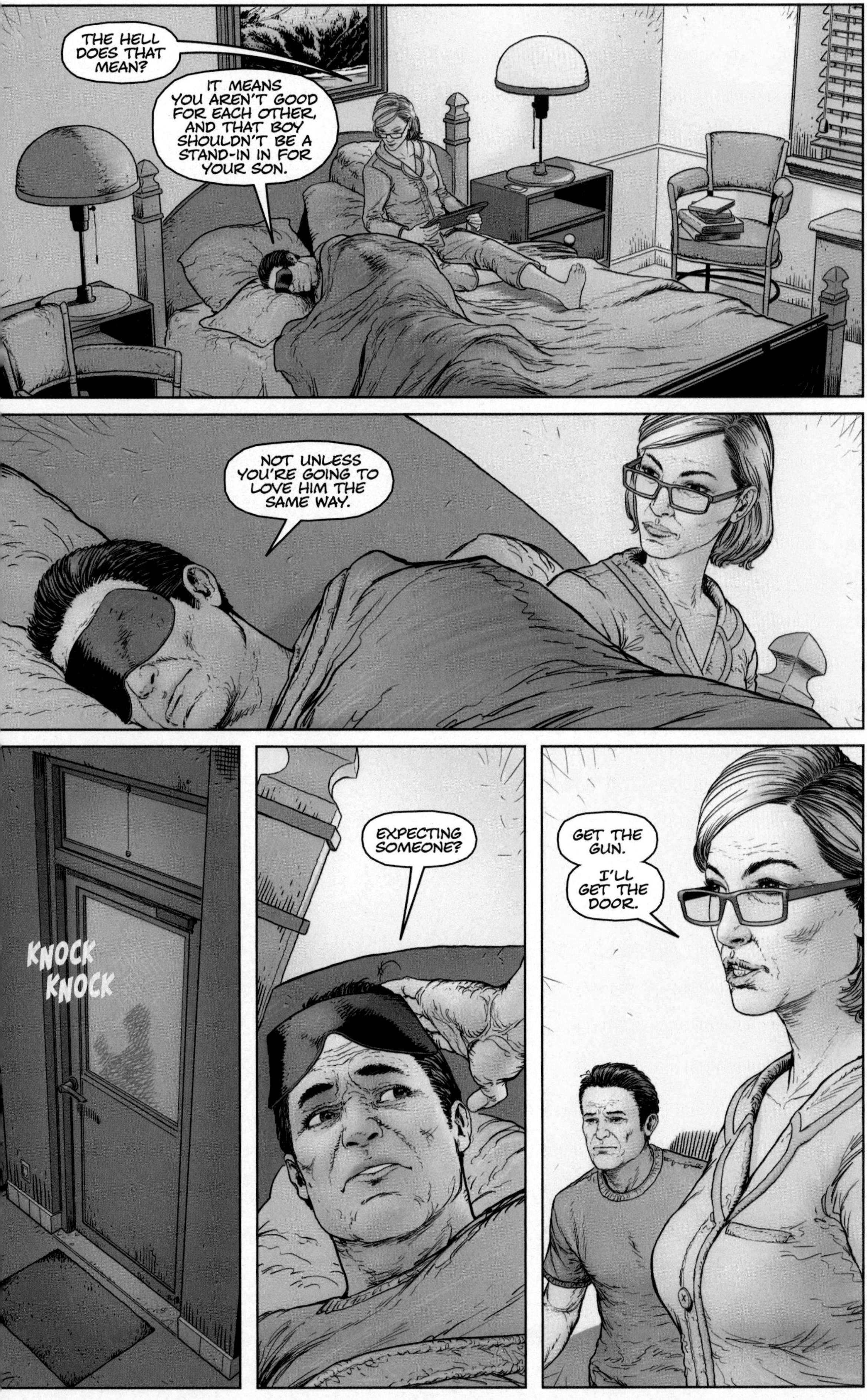
THE HELL DOES THAT MEAN?
IT MEANS YOU AREN'T GOOD FOR EACH OTHER, AND THAT BOY SHOULDN'T BE A STAND-IN IN FOR YOUR SON.
NOT UNLESS YOU'RE GOING TO LOVE HIM THE SAME WAY.
KNOCK KNOCK
EXPECTING SOMEONE?
GET THE GUN.
I'LL GET THE DOOR.

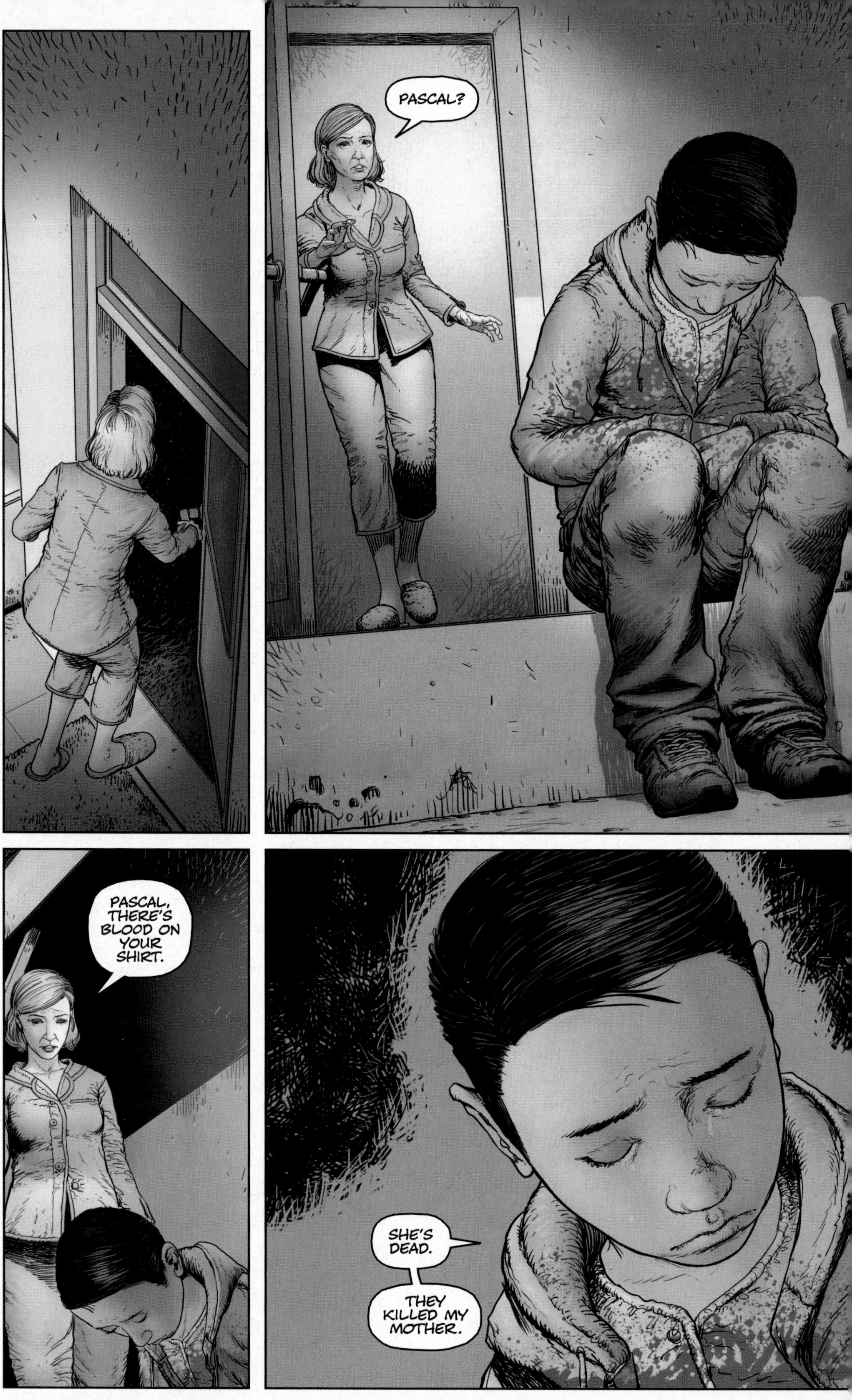
PASCAL?
PASCAL, THERE'S BLOOD ON YOUR SHIRT.
SHE'S DEAD.
THEY KILLED MY MOTHER.

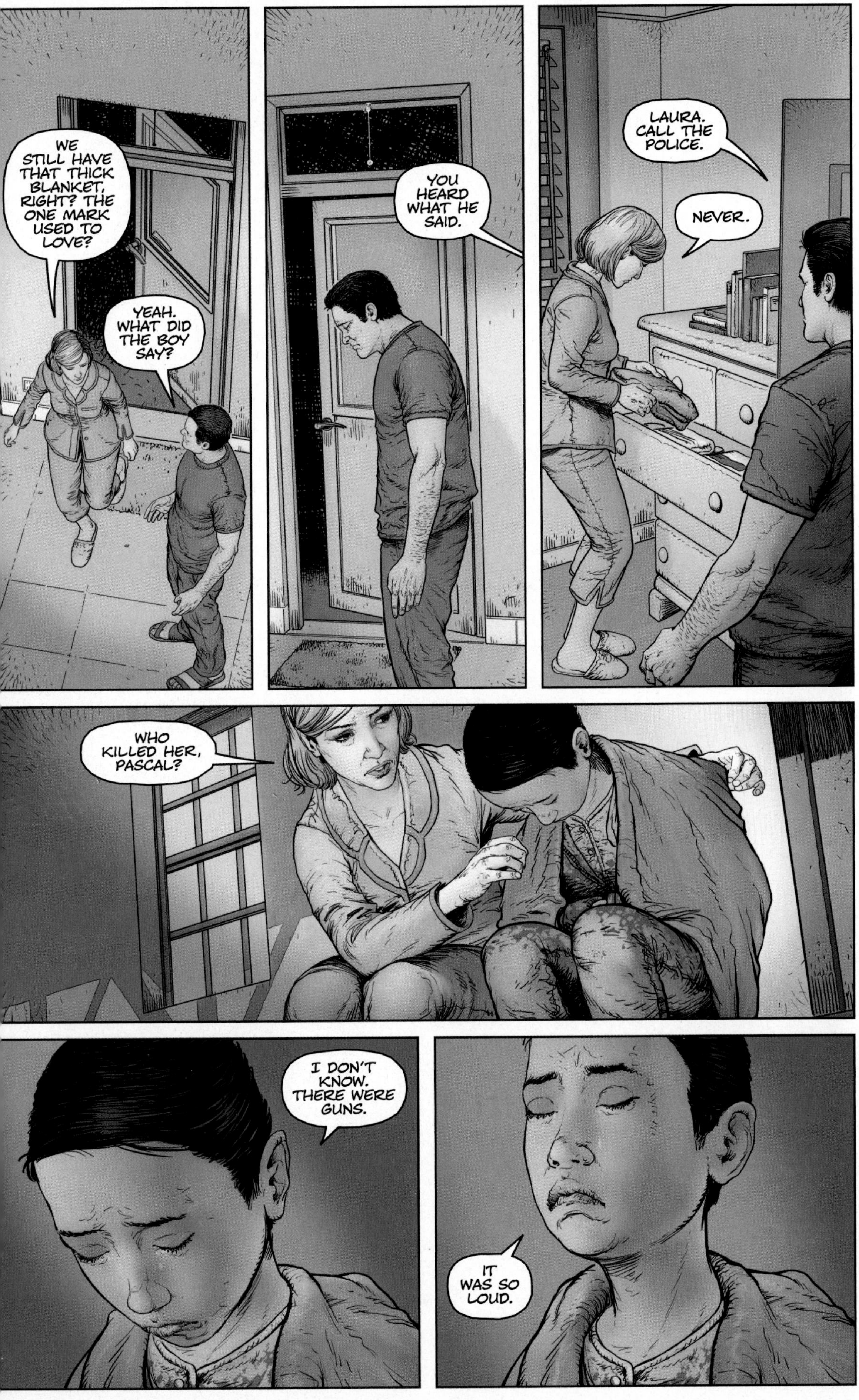
WE STILL HAVE THAT THICK BLANKET, RIGHT? THE ONE MARK USED TO LOVE?
YEAH. WHAT DID THE BOY SAY?
YOU HEARD WHAT HE SAID.
LAURA. CALL THE POLICE.
NEVER.
WHO KILLED HER, PASCAL?
I DON'T KNOW. THERE WERE GUNS.
IT WAS SO LOUD.

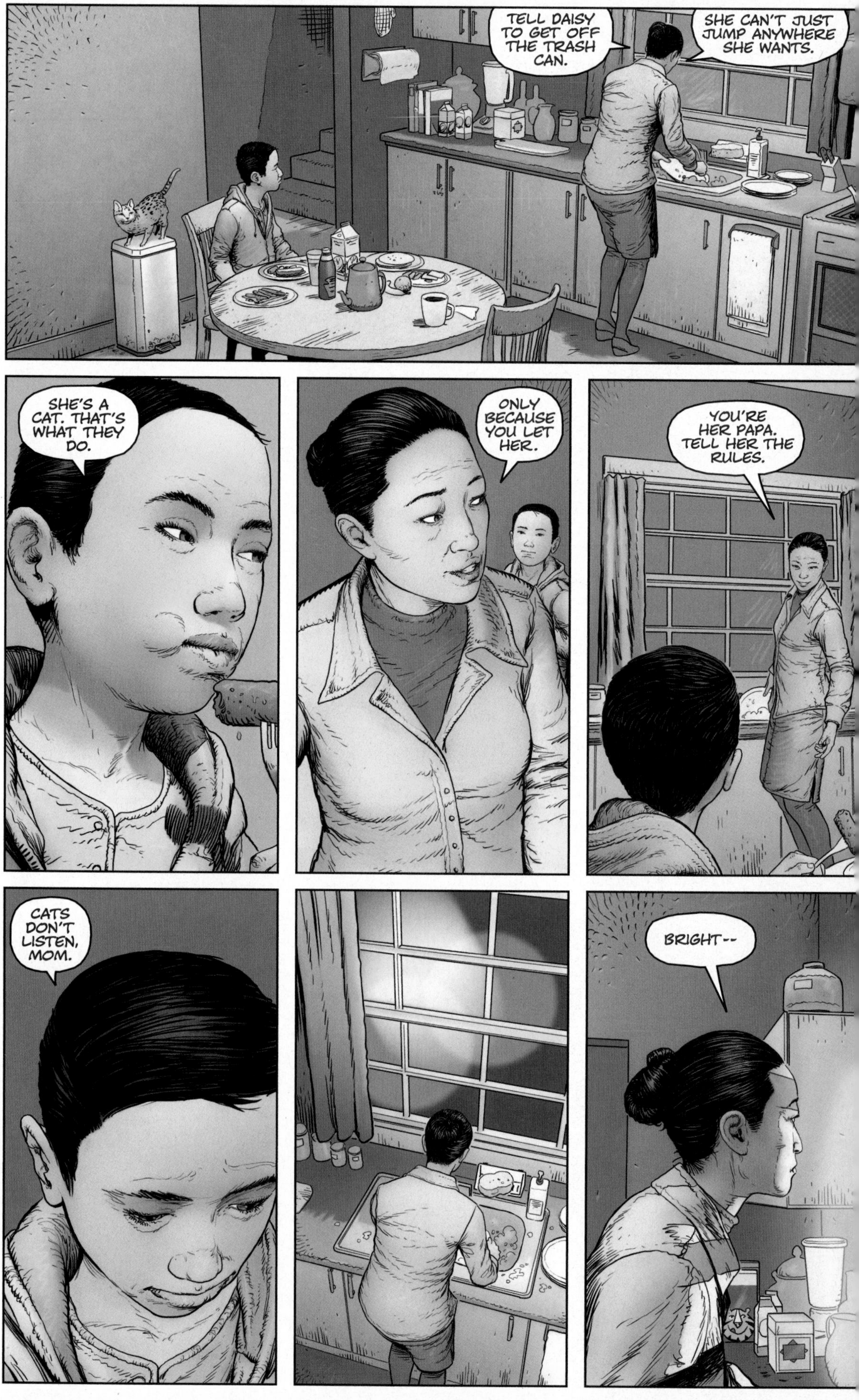
TELL DAISY TO GET OFF THE TRASH CAN.
SHE CAN'T JUST JUMP ANYWHERE SHE WANTS.
SHE'S A CAT. THAT'S WHAT THEY DO.
ONLY BECAUSE YOU LET HER.
YOU'RE HER PAPA. TELL HER THE RULES.
CATS DON'T LISTEN, MOM.
BRIGHT--

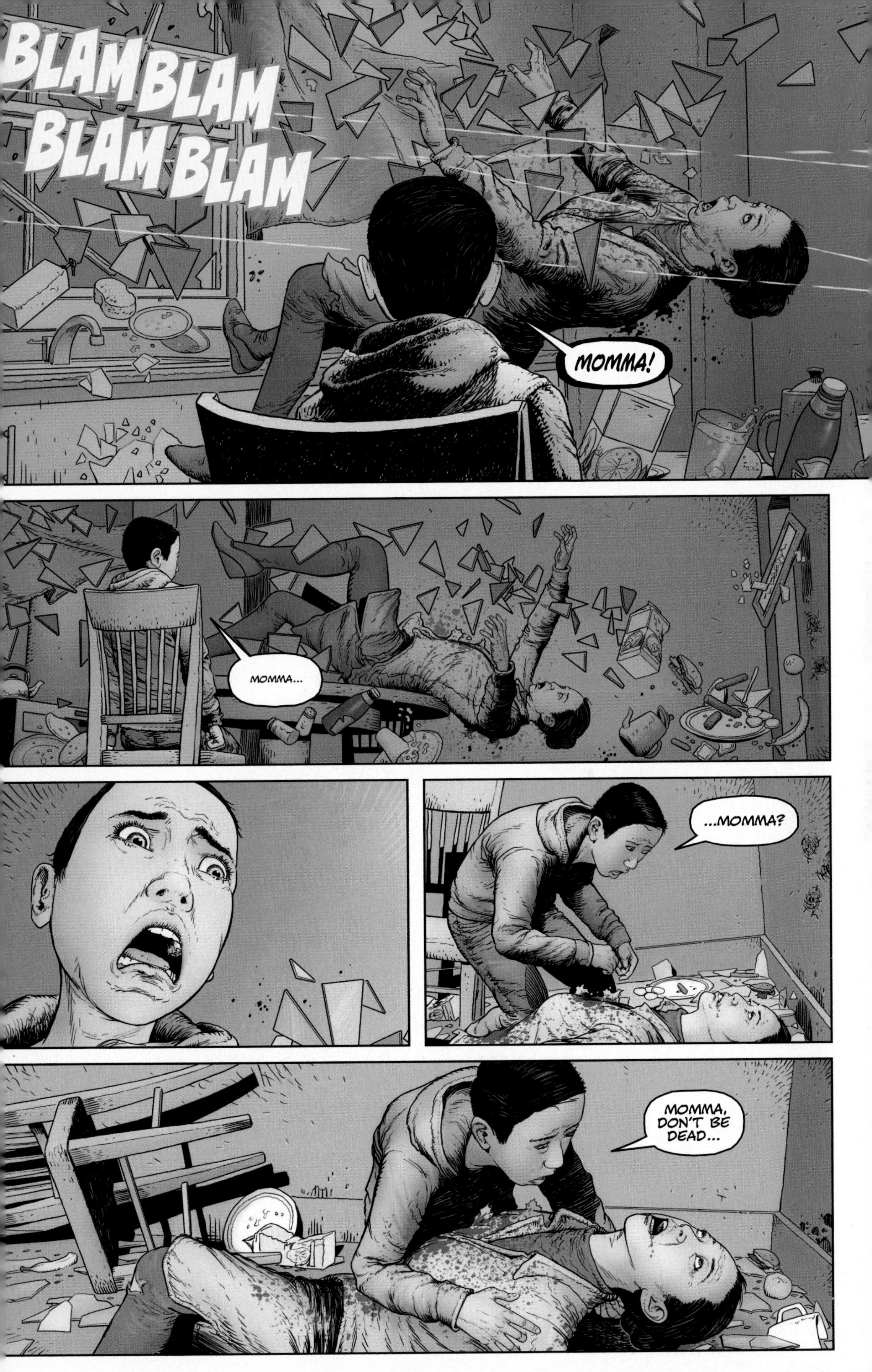
BLAM BLAM BLAM BLAM
MOMMA!
MOMMA...
...MOMMA?
MOMMA, DON'T BE DEAD...

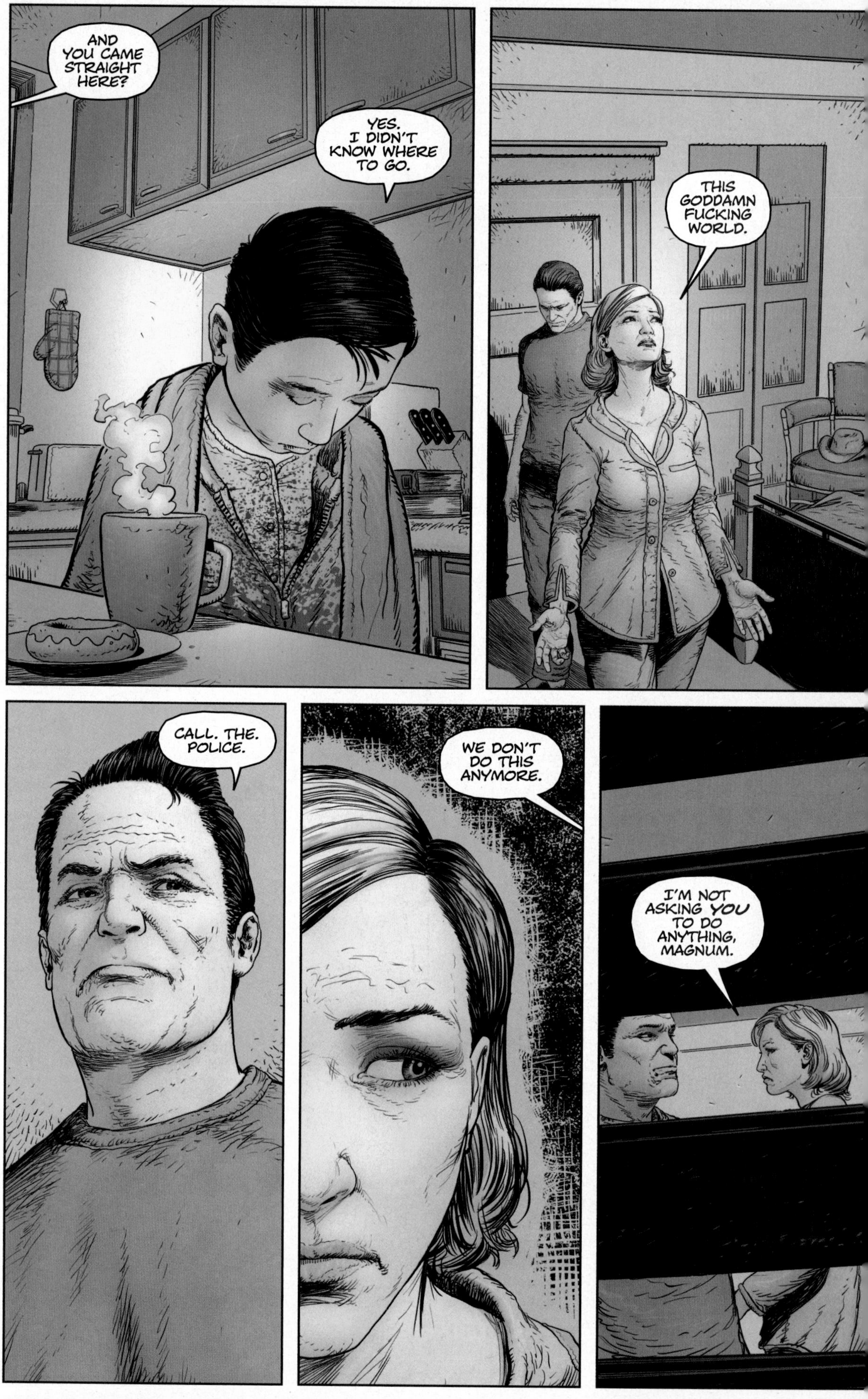
AND YOU CAME STRAIGHT HERE?
YES. I DIDN'T KNOW WHERE TO GO.
THIS GODDAMN FUCKING WORLD.
CALL. THE. POLICE.
WE DON'T DO THIS ANYMORE.
I'M NOT ASKING YOU TO DO ANYTHING, MAGNUM.

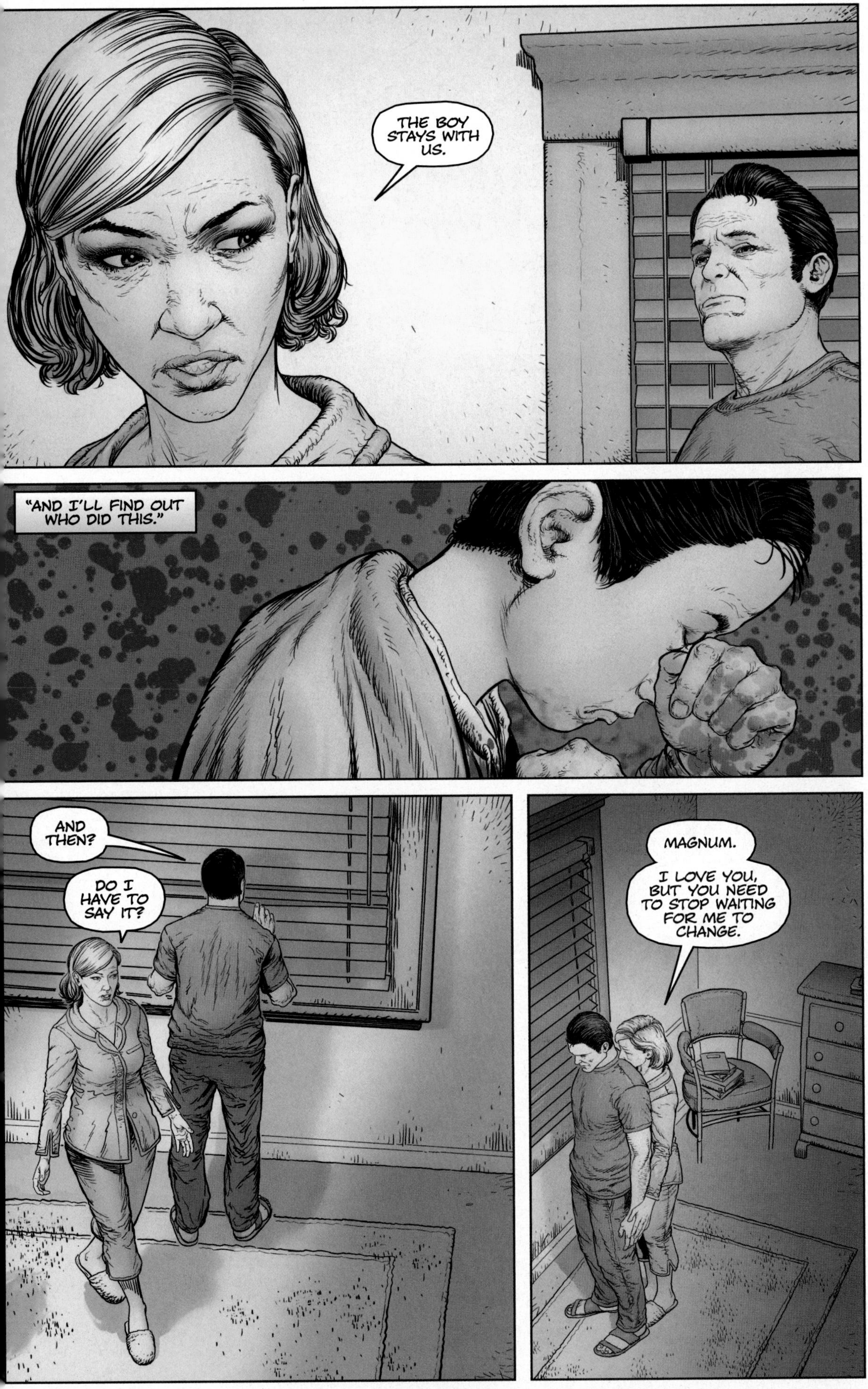
THE BOY STAYS WITH US.
"AND I'LL FIND OUT WHO DID THIS."
AND THEN?
DO I HAVE TO SAY IT?
MAGNUM.
I LOVE YOU, BUT YOU NEED TO STOP WAITING FOR ME TO CHANGE.

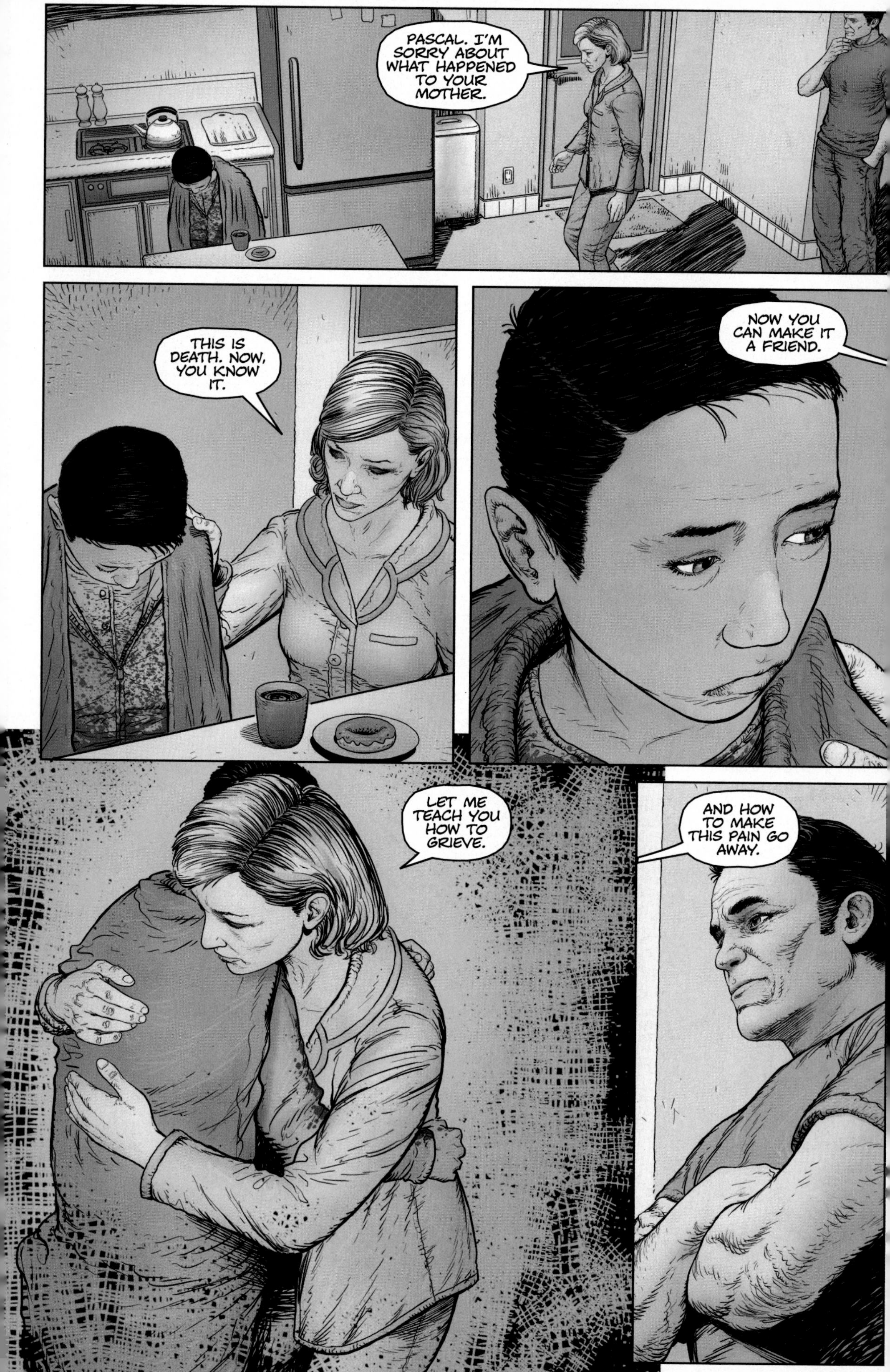
PASCAL. I'M SORRY ABOUT WHAT HAPPENED TO YOUR MOTHER.
THIS IS DEATH. NOW, YOU KNOW IT.
NOW YOU CAN MAKE IT A FRIEND.
LET ME TEACH YOU HOW TO GRIEVE.
AND HOW TO MAKE THIS PAIN GO AWAY.

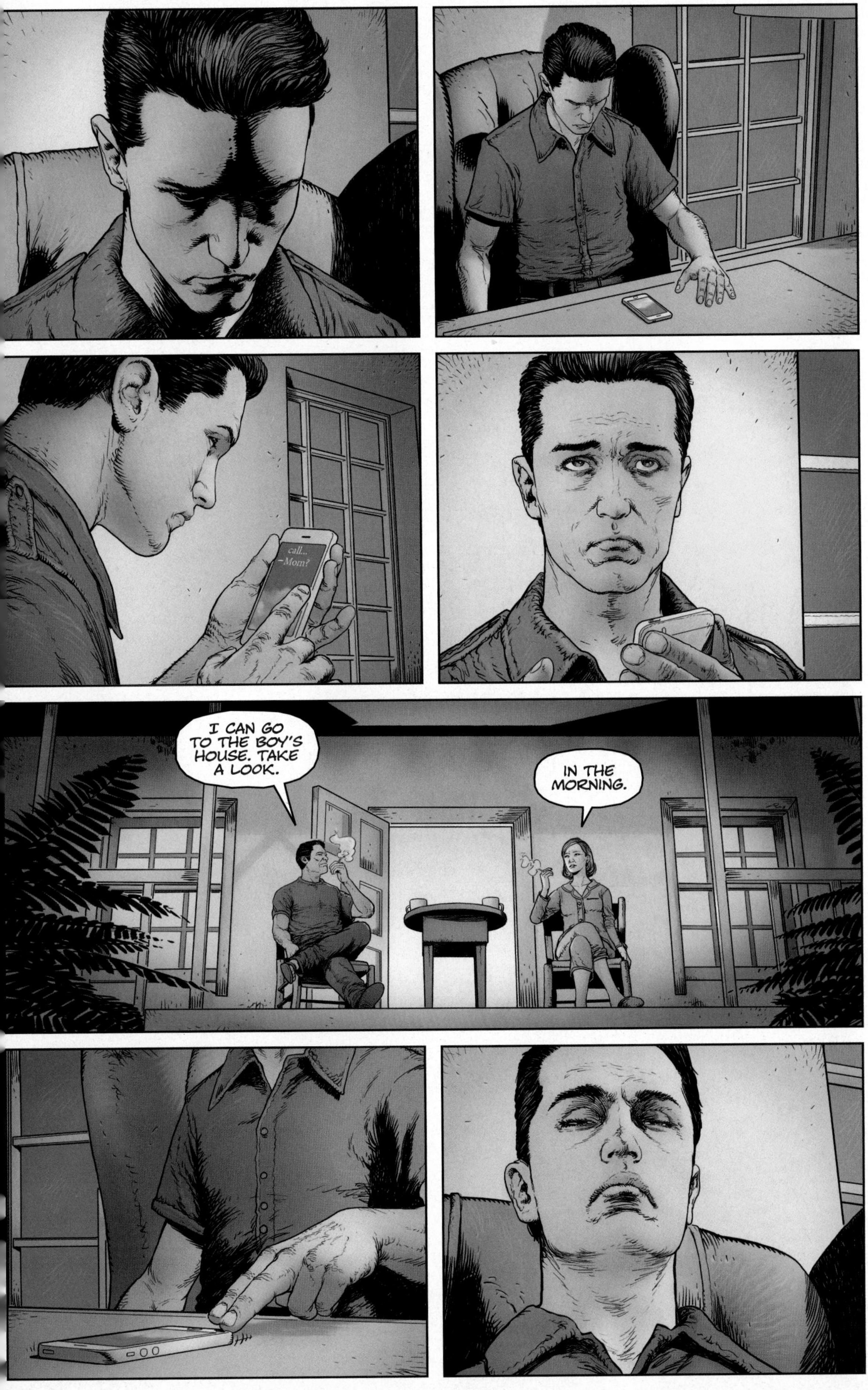
call...
—Mom?
I CAN GO TO THE BOY'S HOUSE. TAKE A LOOK.
IN THE MORNING.

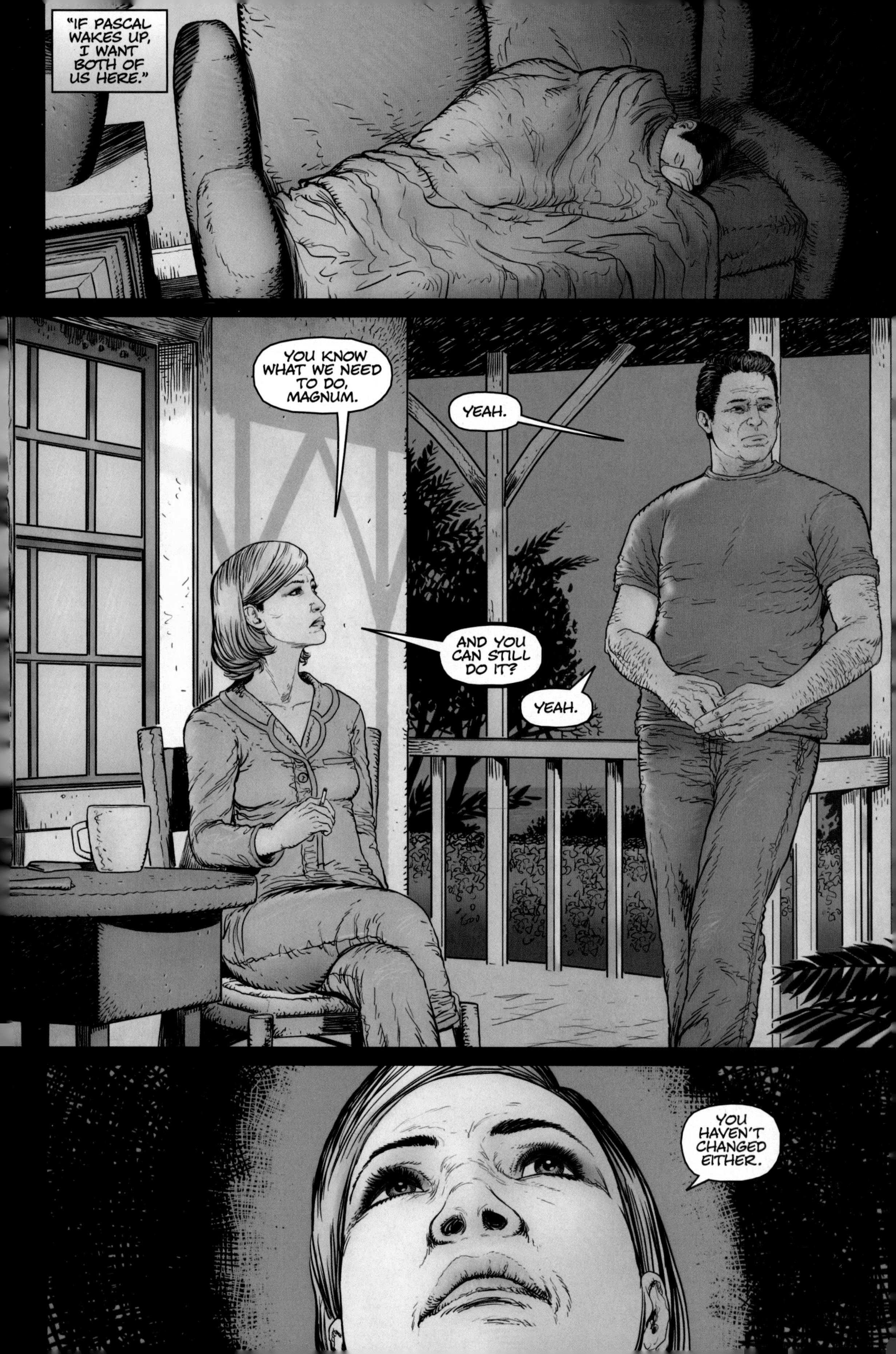
"IF PASCAL WAKES UP, I WANT BOTH OF US HERE."
YOU KNOW WHAT WE NEED TO DO, MAGNUM.
YEAH.
AND YOU CAN STILL DO IT?
YEAH.
YOU HAVEN'T CHANGED EITHER.

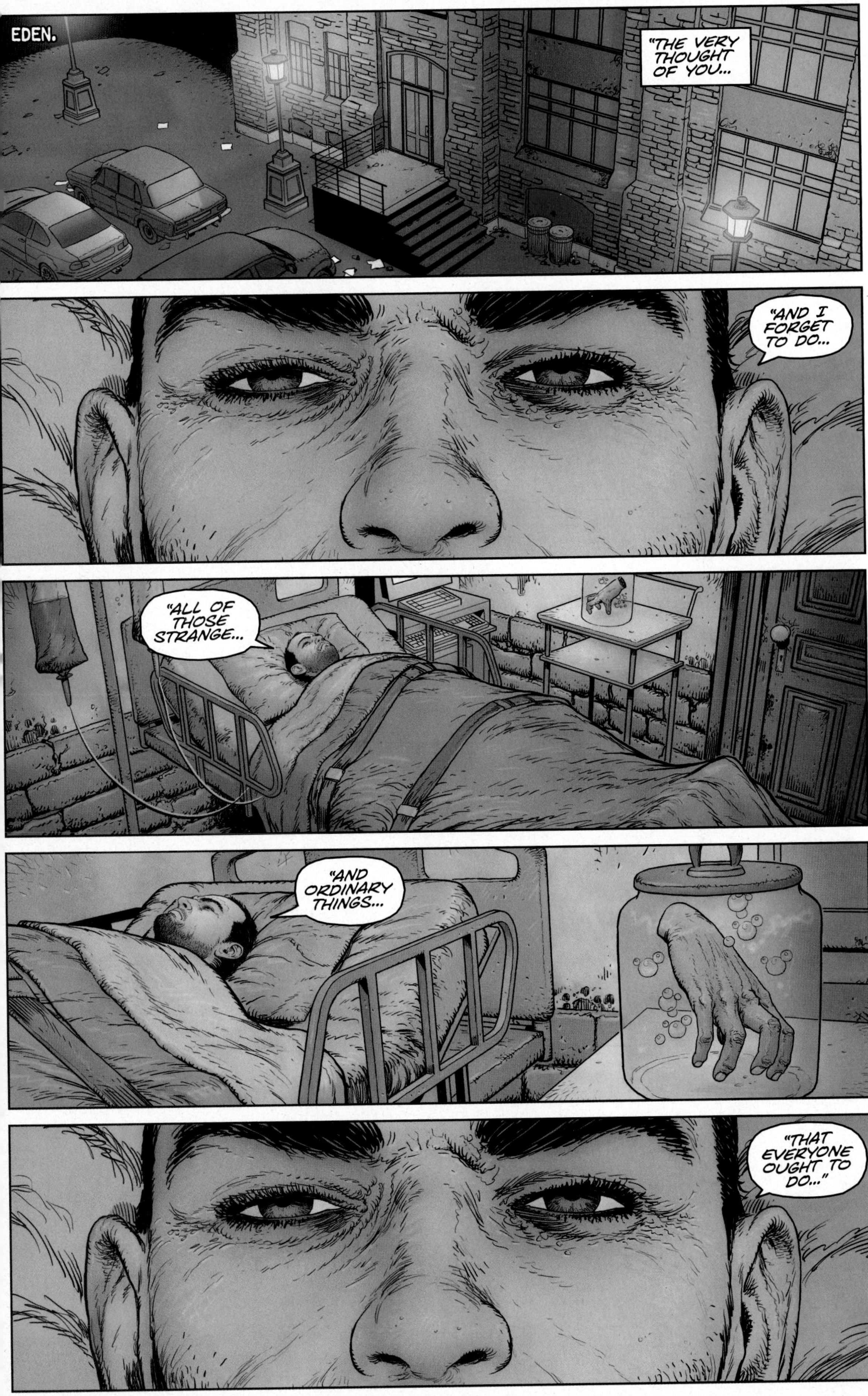
EDEN.
"THE VERY THOUGHT OF YOU...
"AND I FORGET TO DO...
"ALL OF THOSE STRANGE...
"AND ORDINARY THINGS...
"THAT EVERYONE OUGHT TO DO..."

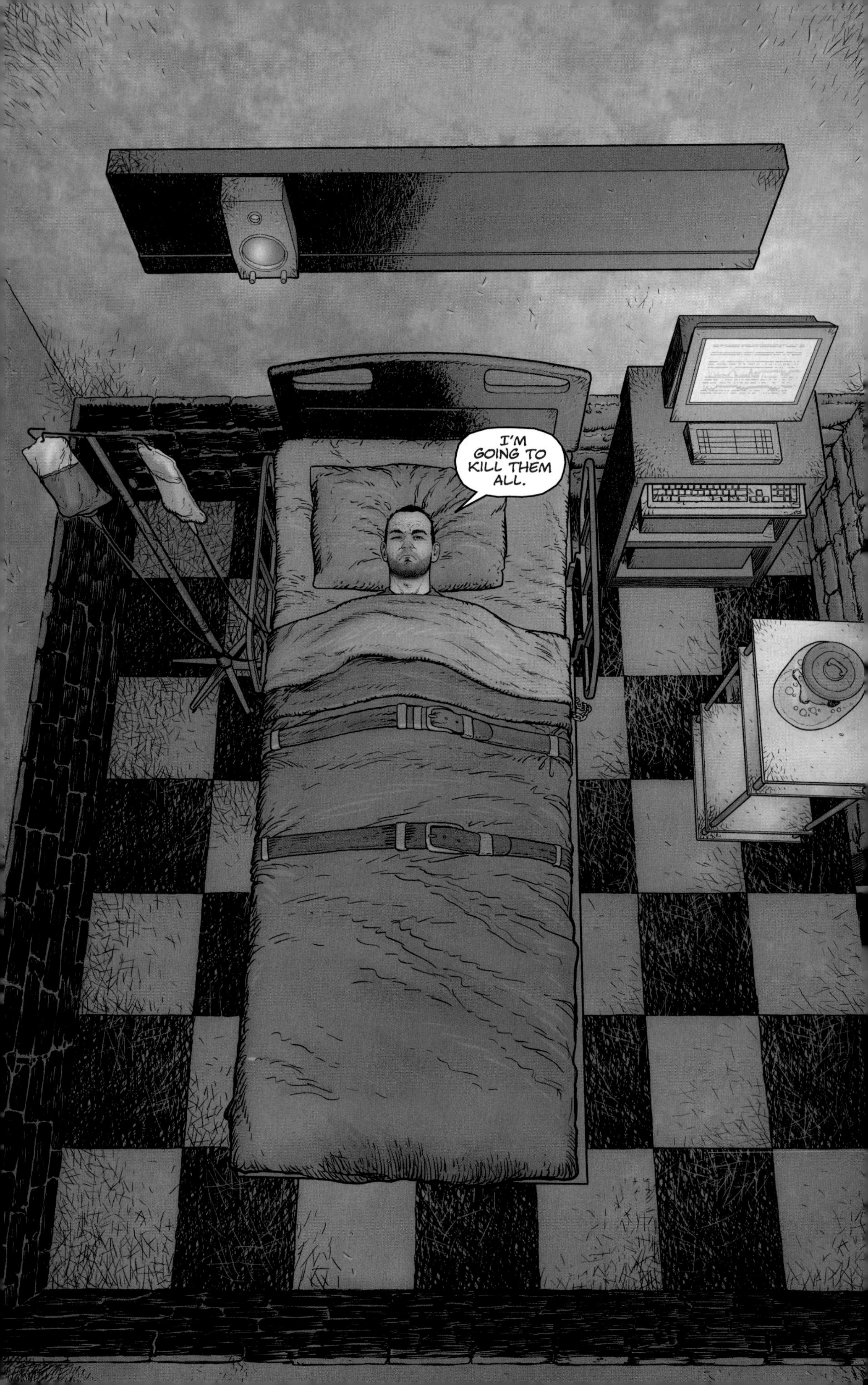
I'M GOING TO KILL THEM ALL.

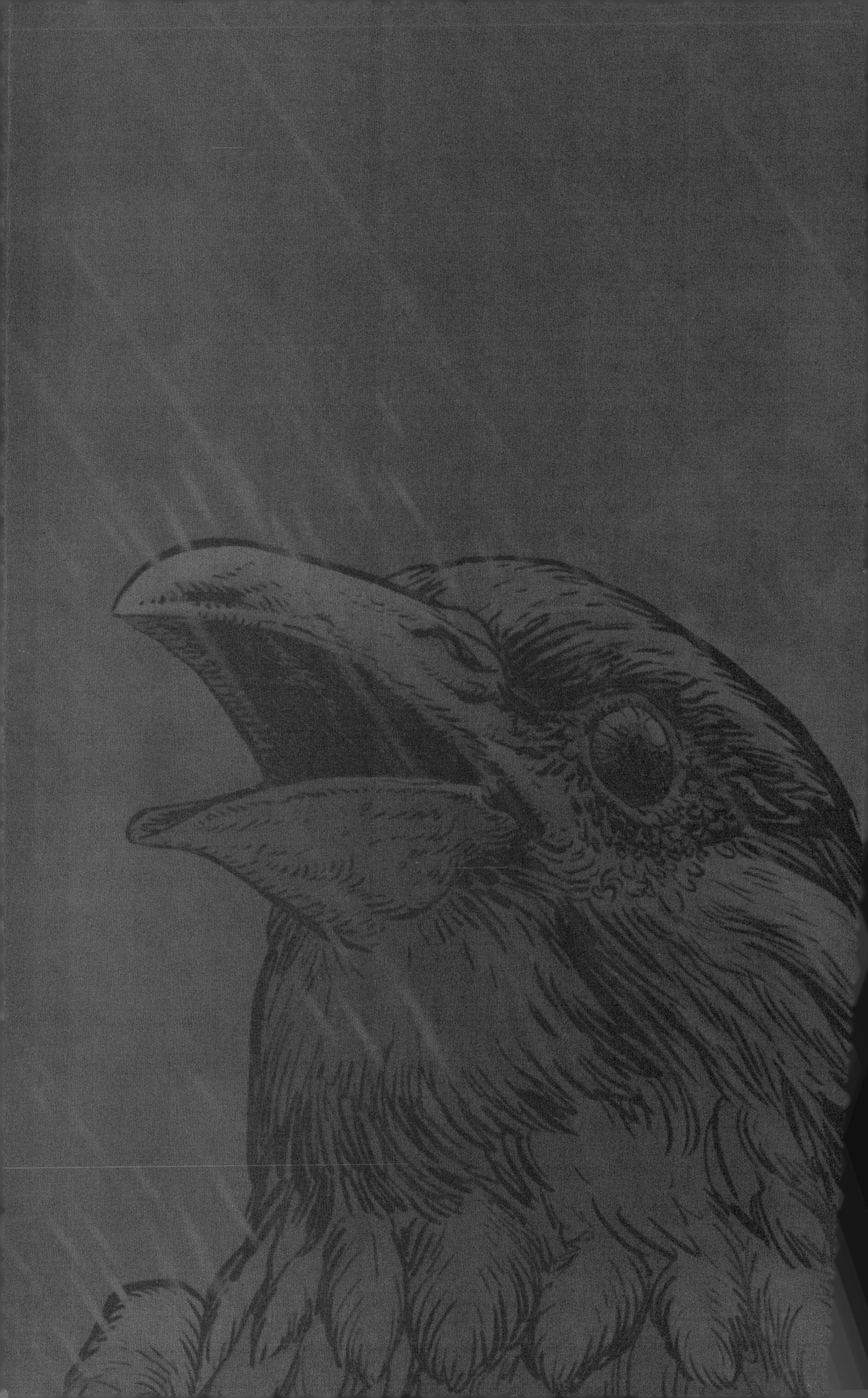

# CHAPTER 4

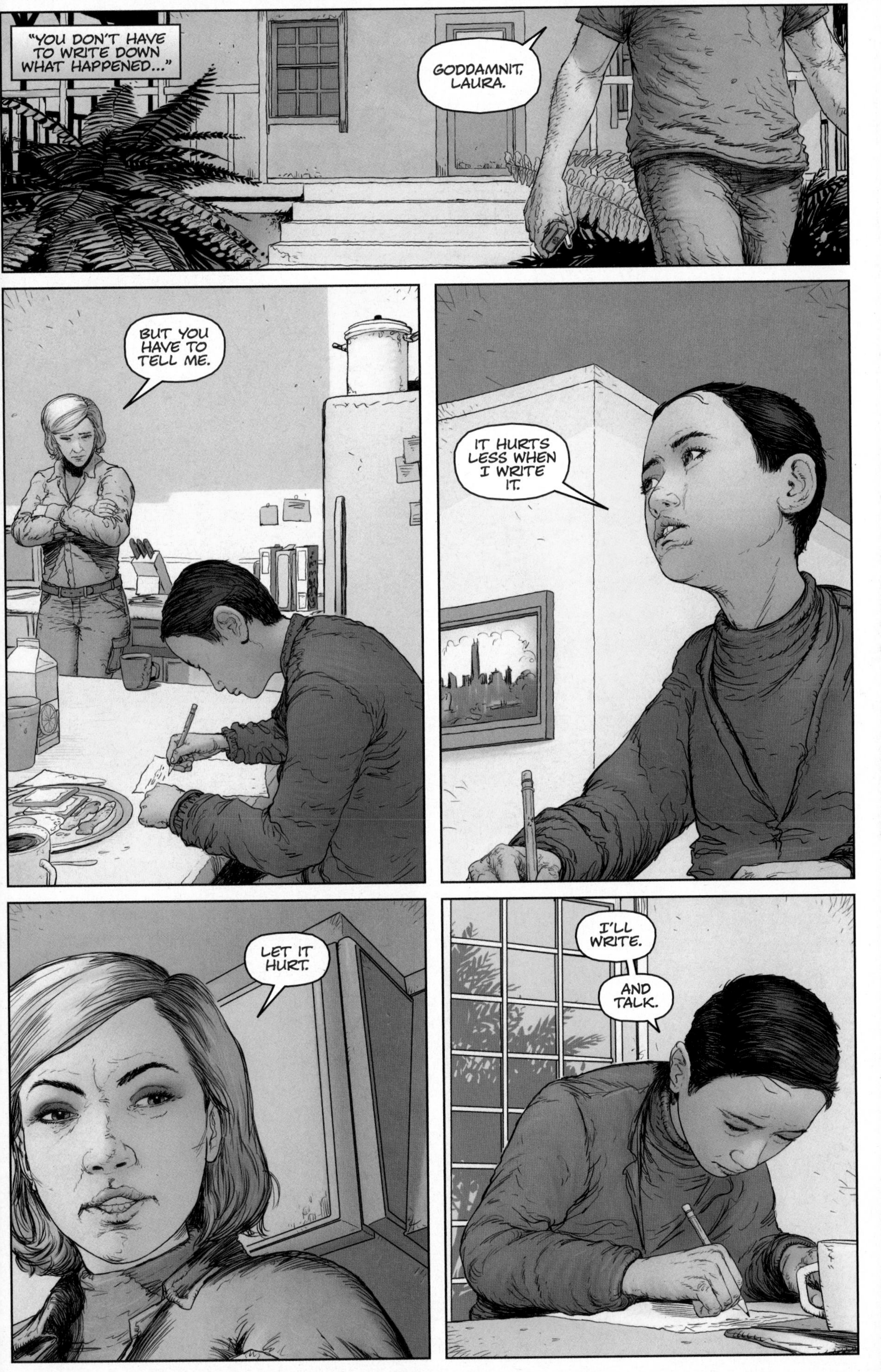
"YOU DON'T HAVE TO WRITE DOWN WHAT HAPPENED..."
GODDAMNIT, LAURA.
BUT YOU HAVE TO TELL ME.
IT HURTS LESS WHEN I WRITE IT.
LET IT HURT.
I'LL WRITE.
AND TALK.

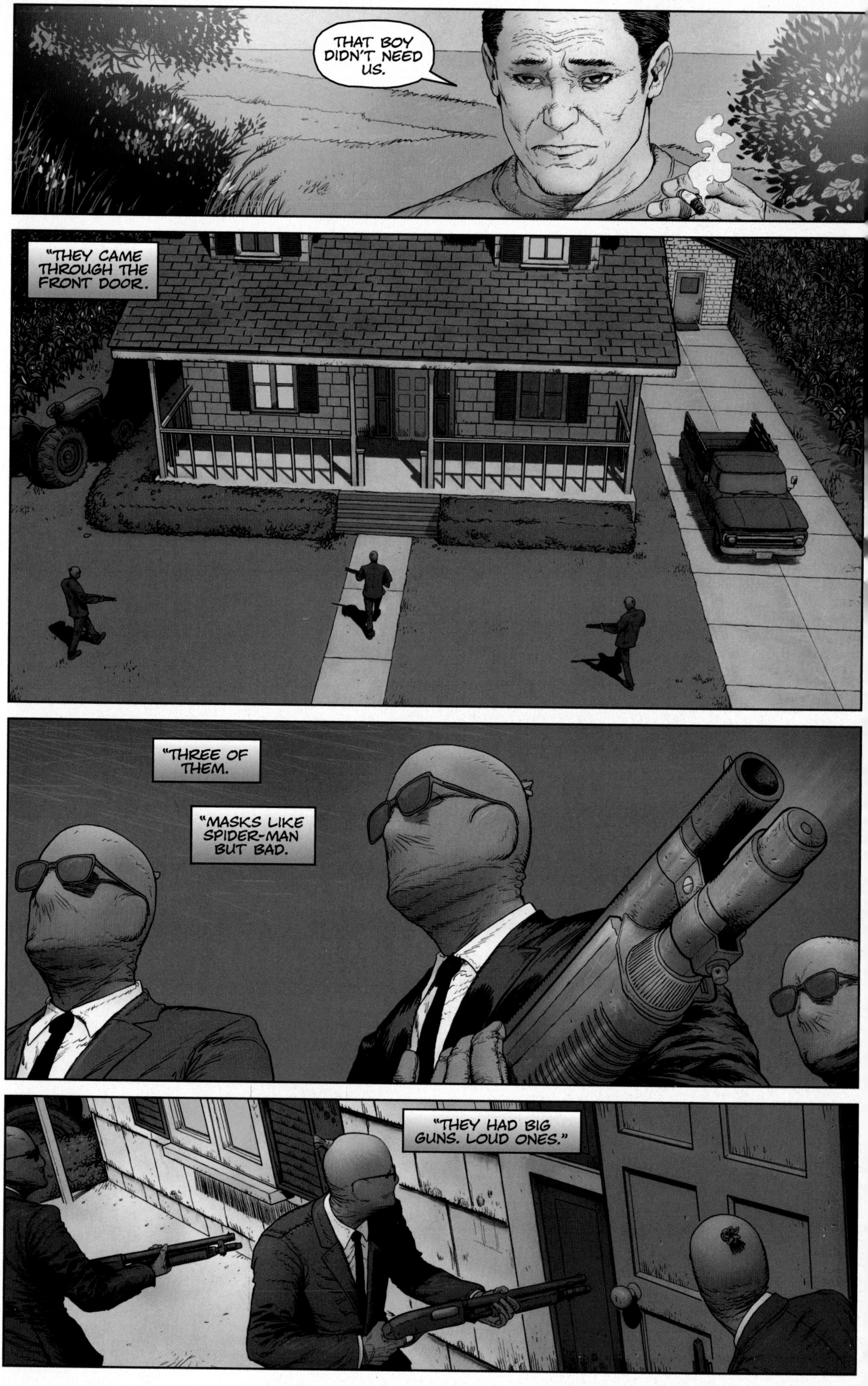
THAT BOY DIDN'T NEED US.
"THEY CAME THROUGH THE FRONT DOOR.
"THREE OF THEM.
"MASKS LIKE SPIDER-MAN BUT BAD.
"THEY HAD BIG GUNS. LOUD ONES."

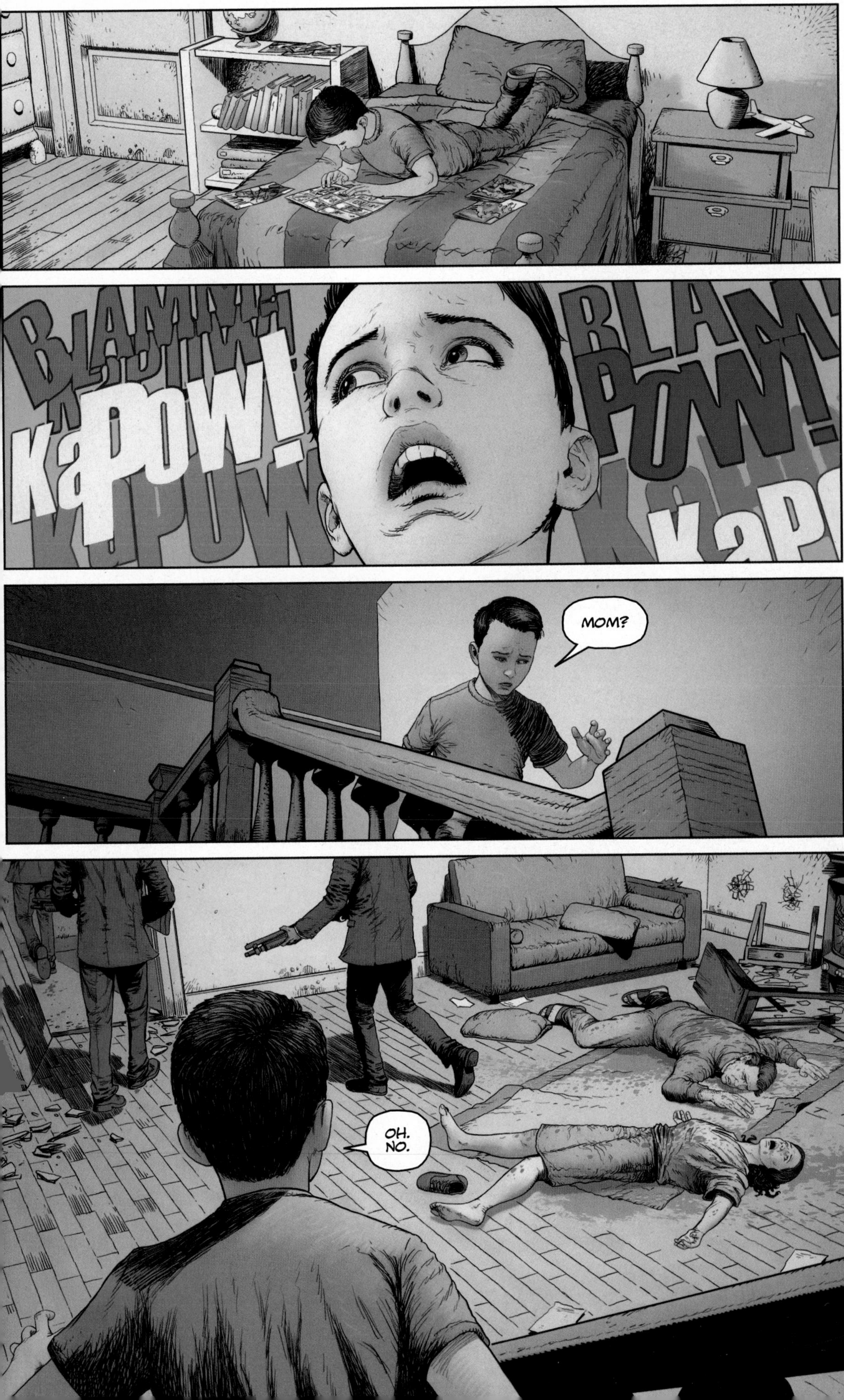
BLAMM!
KAPOW!
POW!
MOM?
OH.
NO.

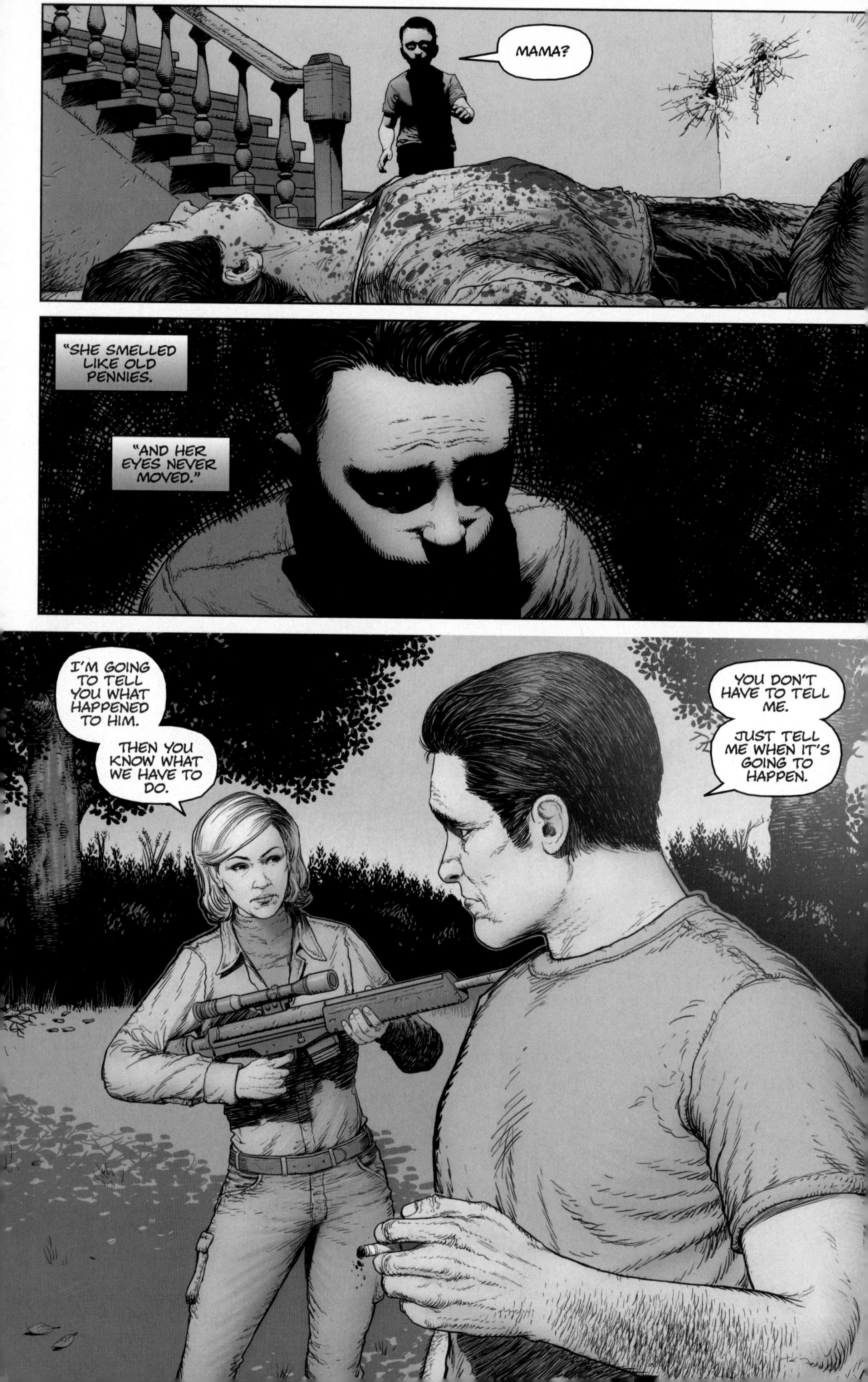
MAMA?
"SHE SMELLED LIKE OLD PENNIES.
"AND HER EYES NEVER MOVED."
I'M GOING TO TELL YOU WHAT HAPPENED TO HIM.
THEN YOU KNOW WHAT WE HAVE TO DO.
YOU DON'T HAVE TO TELL ME.
JUST TELL ME WHEN IT'S GOING TO HAPPEN.

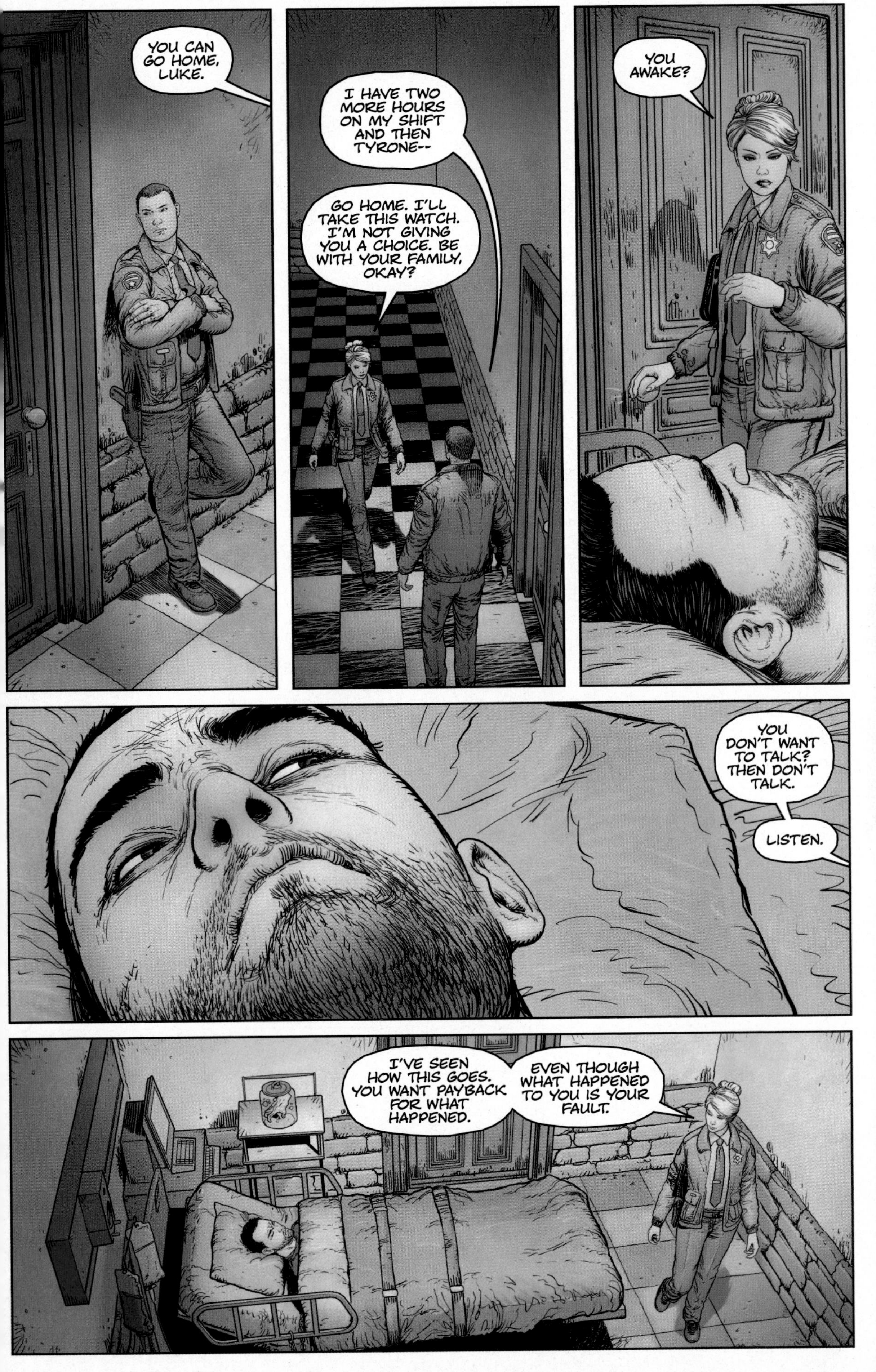
YOU CAN GO HOME, LUKE.
I HAVE TWO MORE HOURS ON MY SHIFT AND THEN TYRONE--
GO HOME. I'LL TAKE THIS WATCH. I'M NOT GIVING YOU A CHOICE. BE WITH YOUR FAMILY, OKAY?
YOU AWAKE?
YOU DON'T WANT TO TALK? THEN DON'T TALK.
LISTEN.
I'VE SEEN HOW THIS GOES. YOU WANT PAYBACK FOR WHAT HAPPENED.
EVEN THOUGH WHAT HAPPENED TO YOU IS YOUR FAULT.

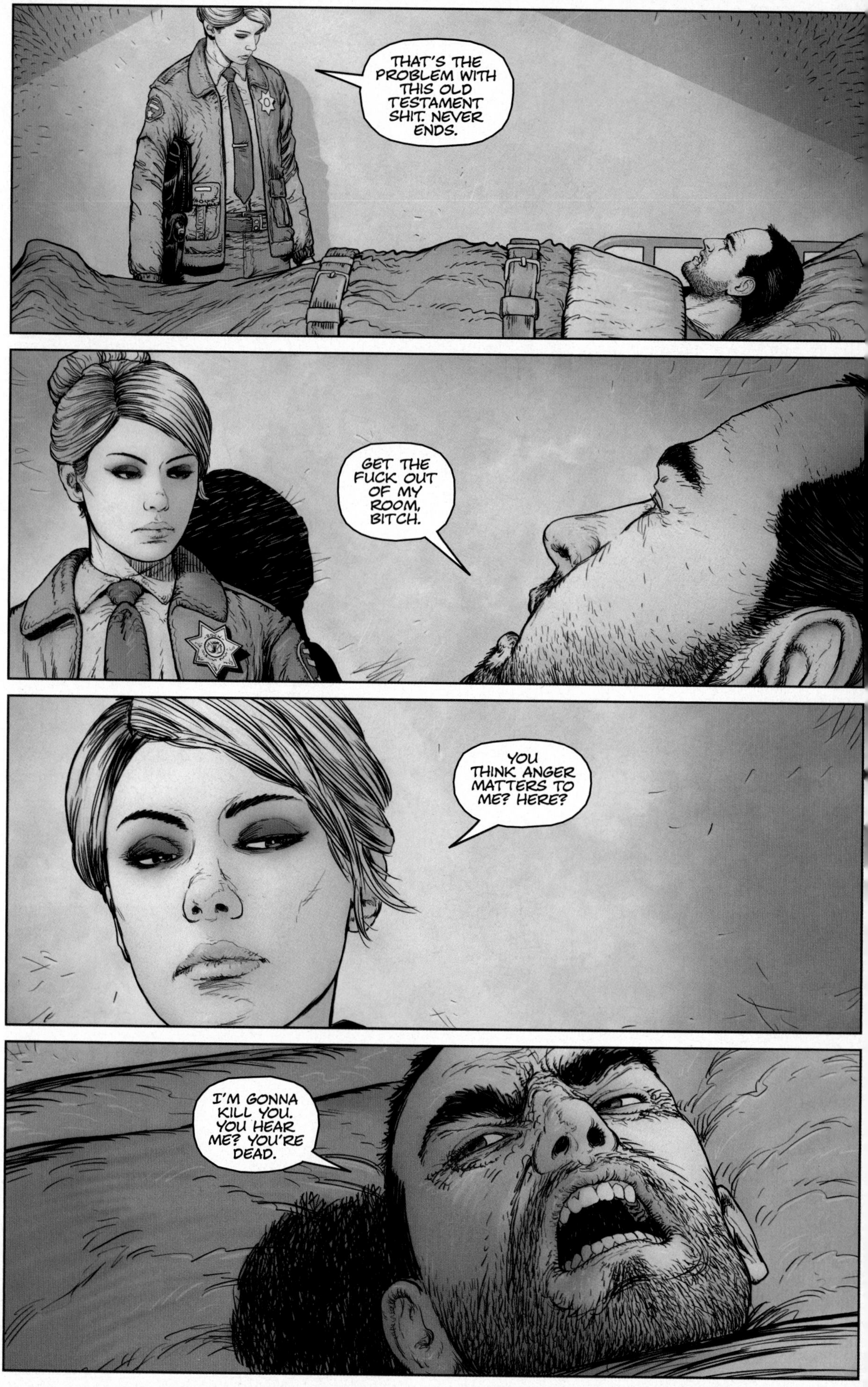
THAT'S THE PROBLEM WITH THIS OLD TESTAMENT SHIT. NEVER ENDS.
GET THE FUCK OUT OF MY ROOM, BITCH.
YOU THINK ANGER MATTERS TO ME? HERE?
I'M GONNA KILL YOU. YOU HEAR ME? YOU'RE DEAD.

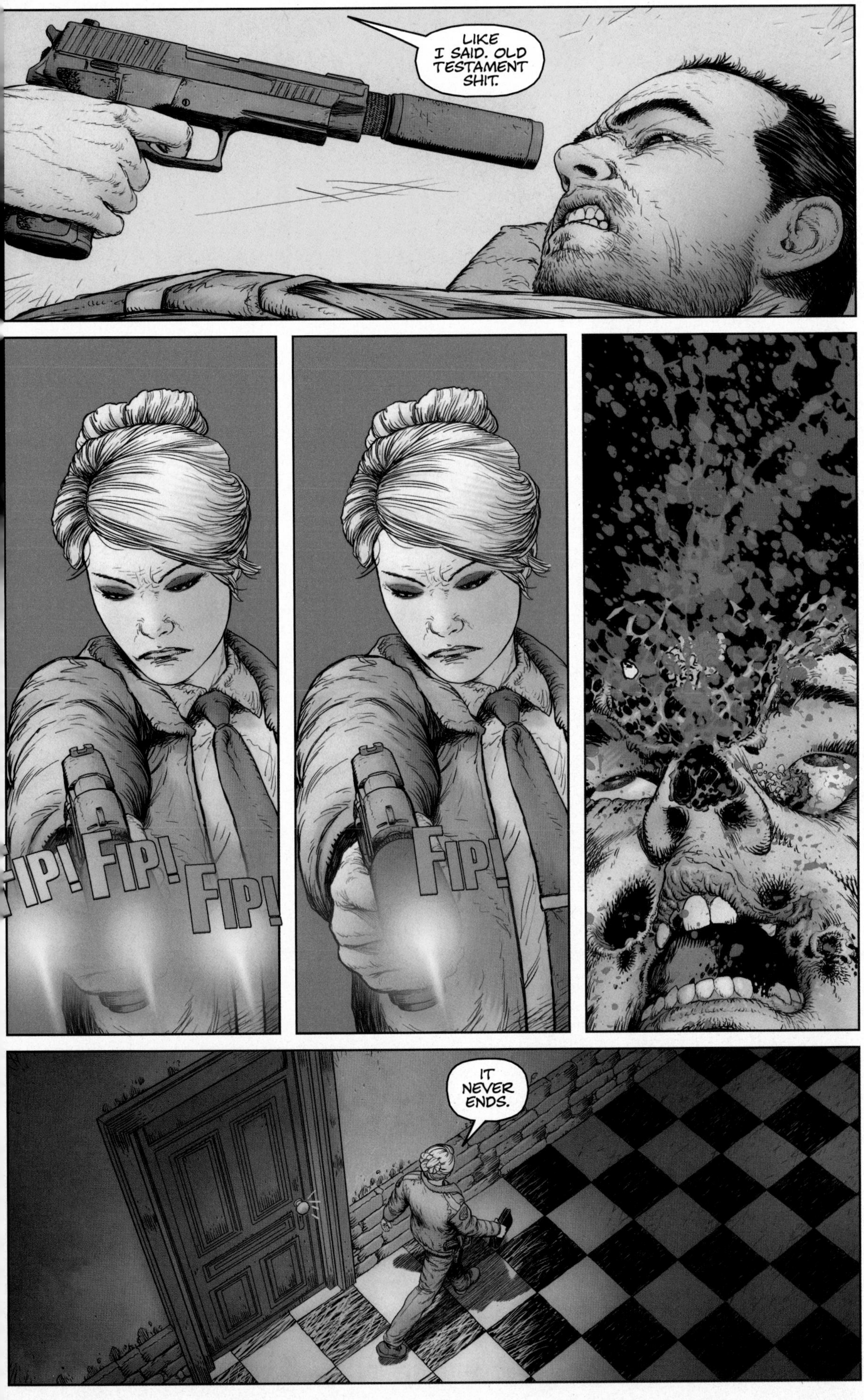

LIKE I SAID. OLD TESTAMENT SHIT.
FIP! FIP! FIP!
FIP!
IT NEVER ENDS.

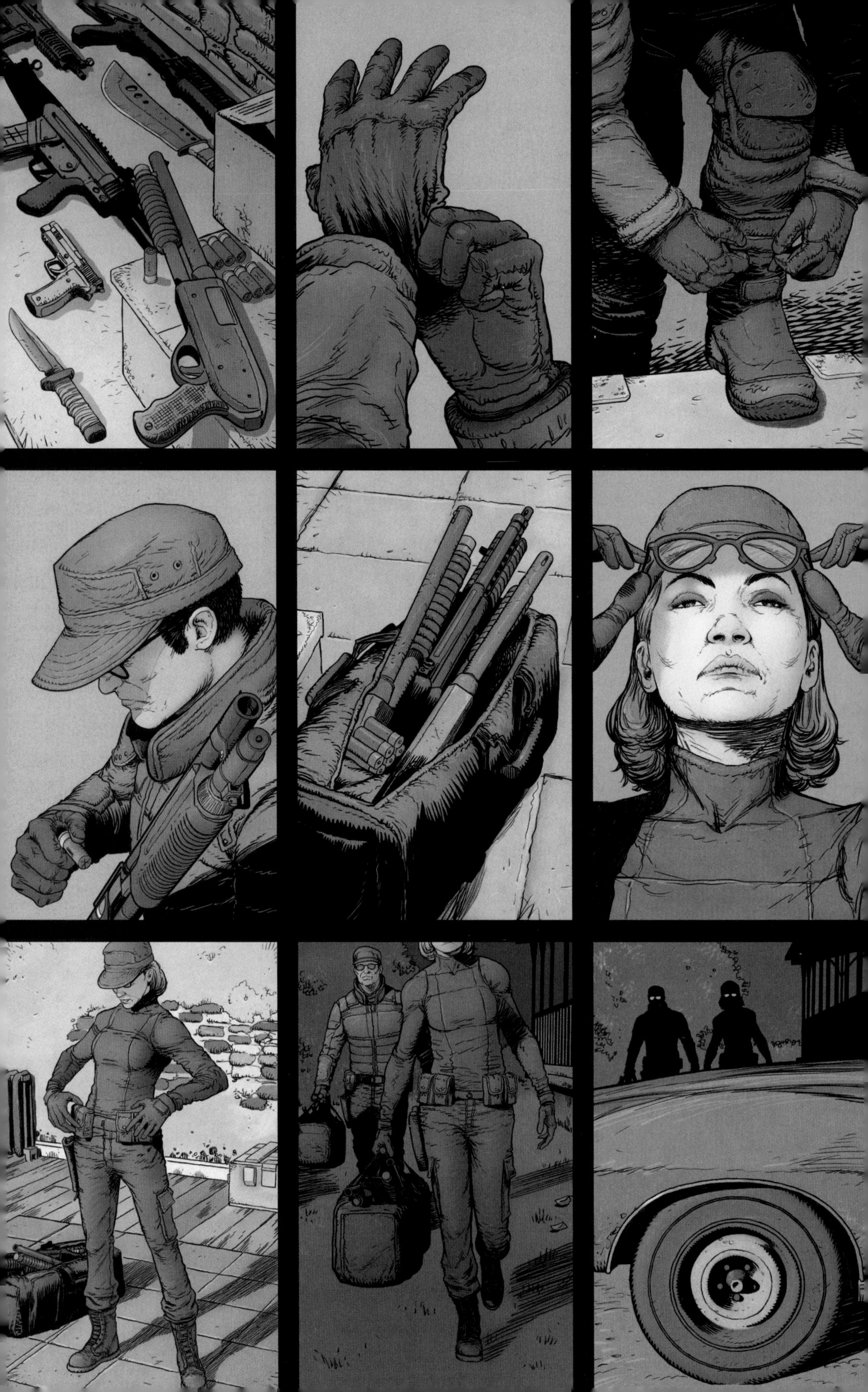

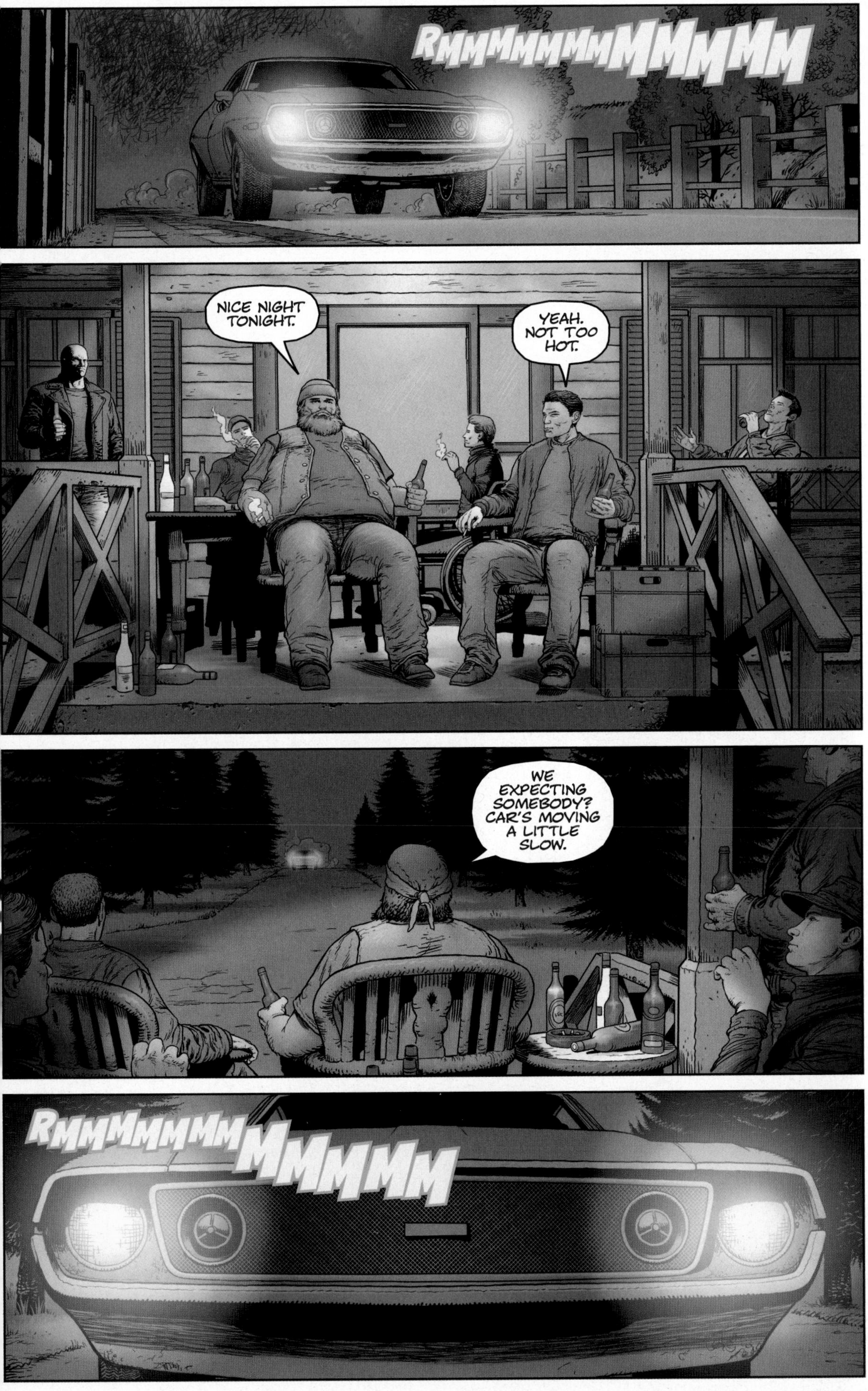
RMMMMMMMMMMMM
NICE NIGHT TONIGHT.
YEAH. NOT TOO HOT.
WE EXPECTING SOMEBODY? CAR'S MOVING A LITTLE SLOW.
RMMMMMMMMMMMM

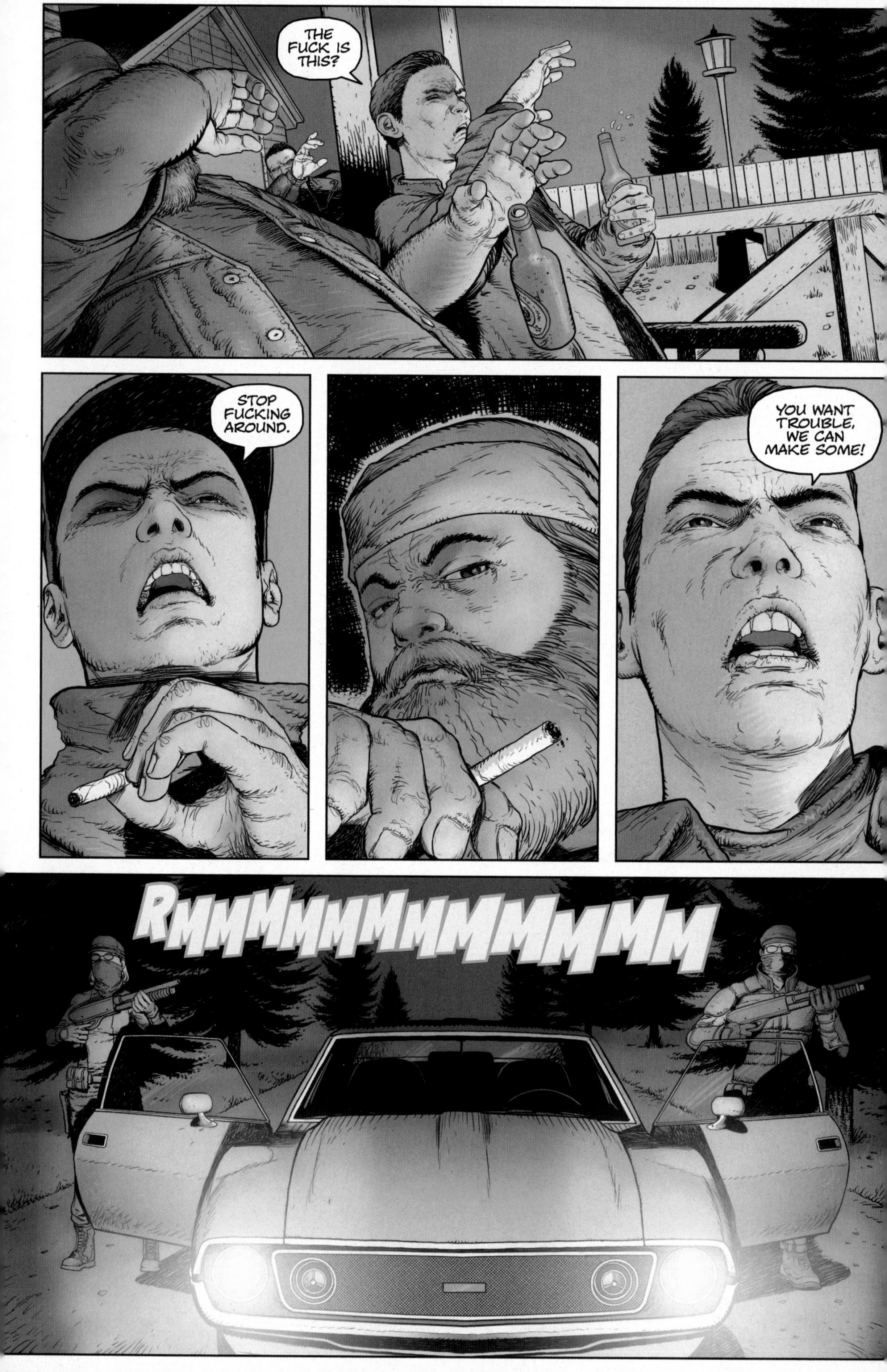
THE FUCK IS THIS?
STOP FUCKING AROUND.
YOU WANT TROUBLE, WE CAN MAKE SOME!
RMMMMMMMMMMMMMM

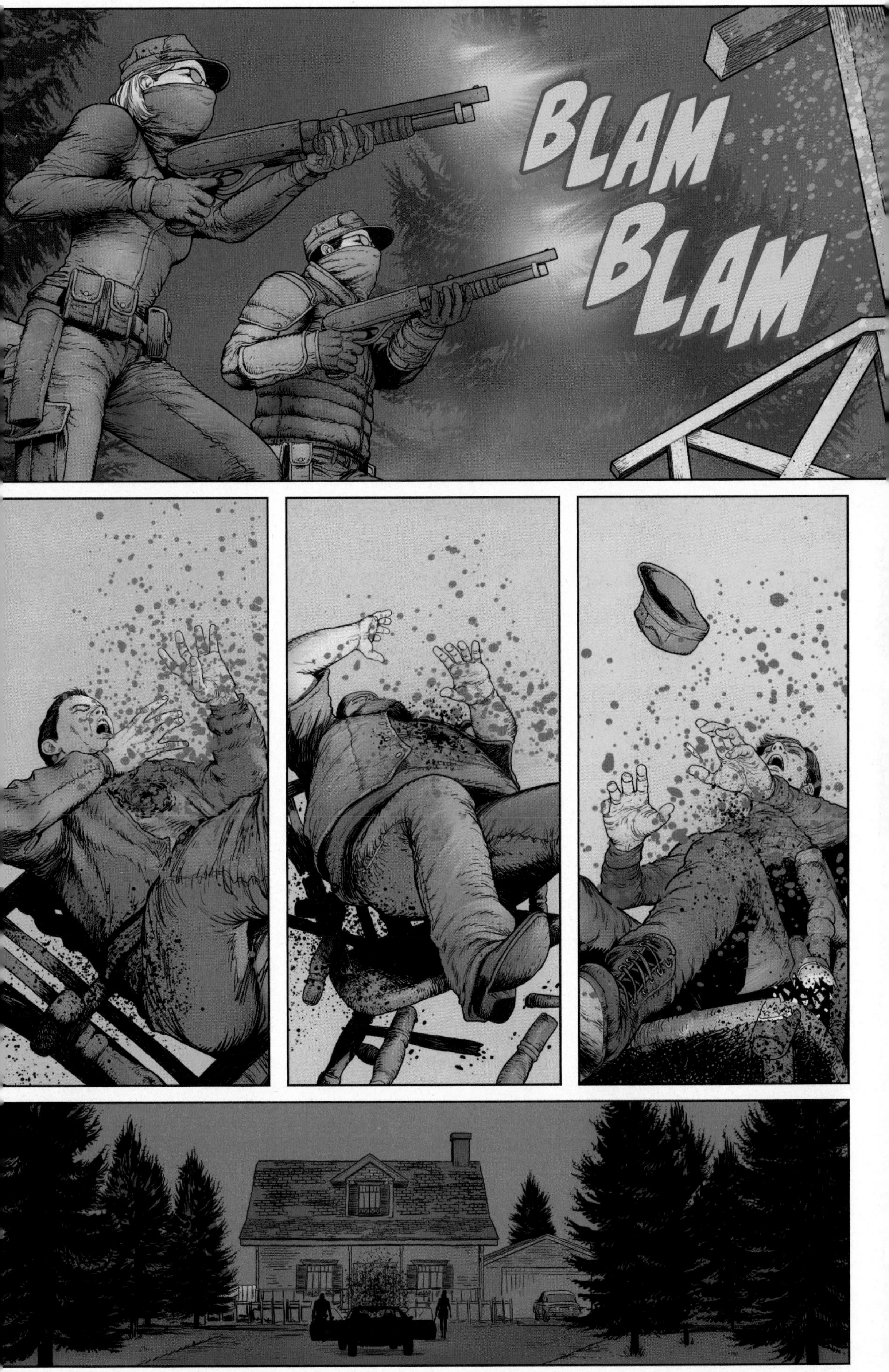
BLAM
BLAM

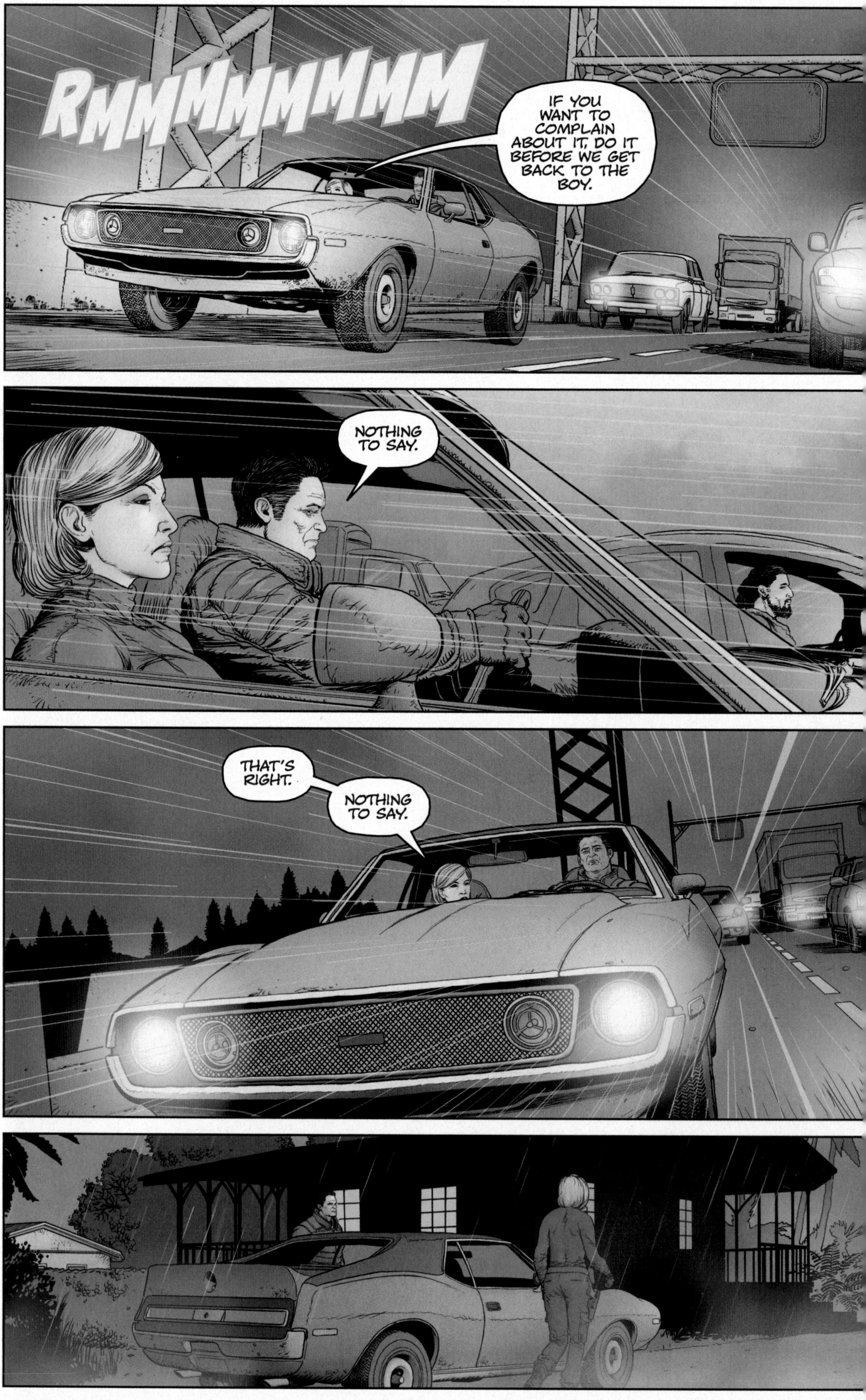
RMMMMMMMMM
IF YOU WANT TO COMPLAIN ABOUT IT, DO IT BEFORE WE GET BACK TO THE BOY.
NOTHING TO SAY.
THAT'S RIGHT.
NOTHING TO SAY.

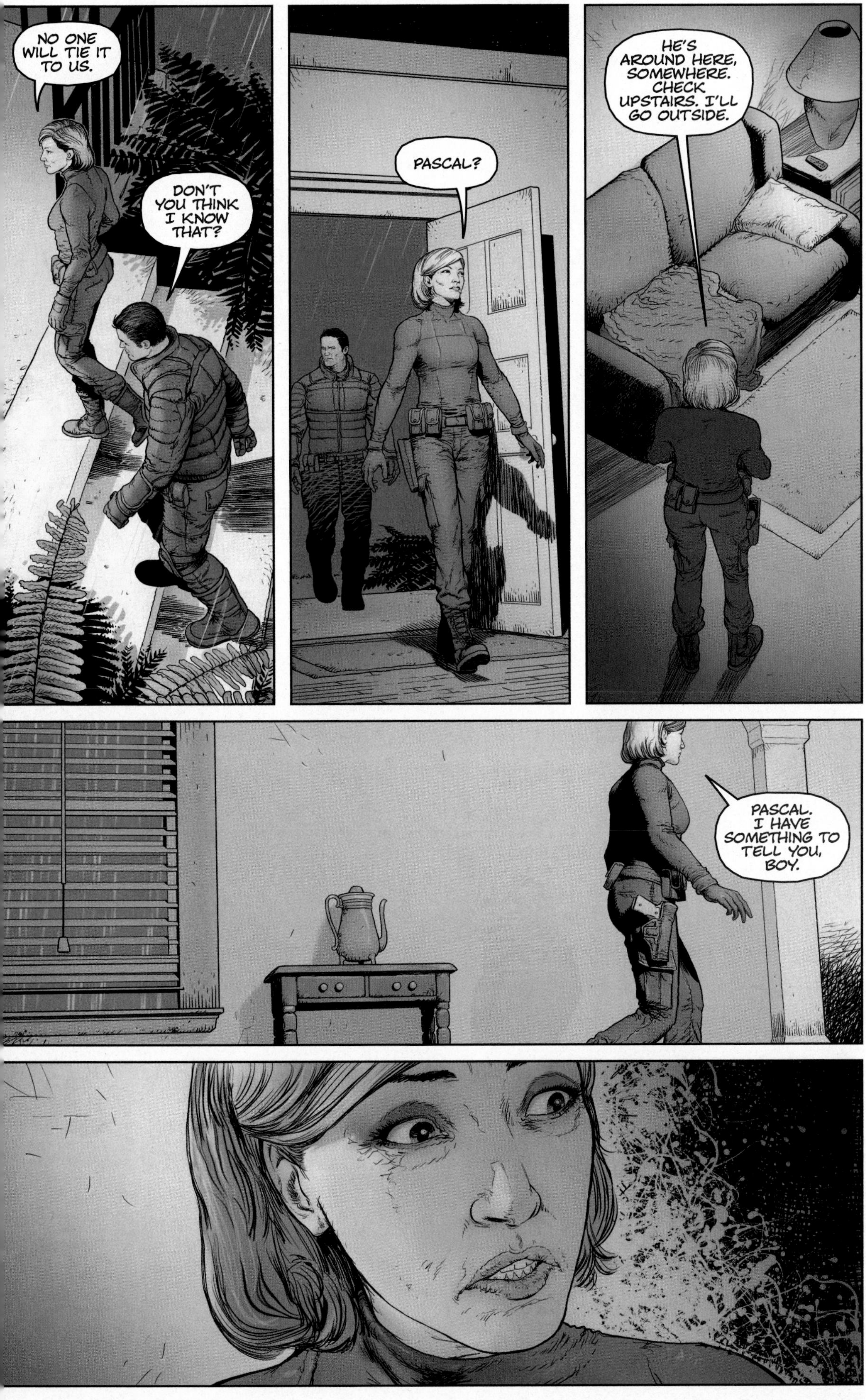
NO ONE WILL TIE IT TO US.
DON'T YOU THINK I KNOW THAT?
PASCAL?
HE'S AROUND HERE, SOMEWHERE. CHECK UPSTAIRS. I'LL GO OUTSIDE.
PASCAL. I HAVE SOMETHING TO TELL YOU, BOY.

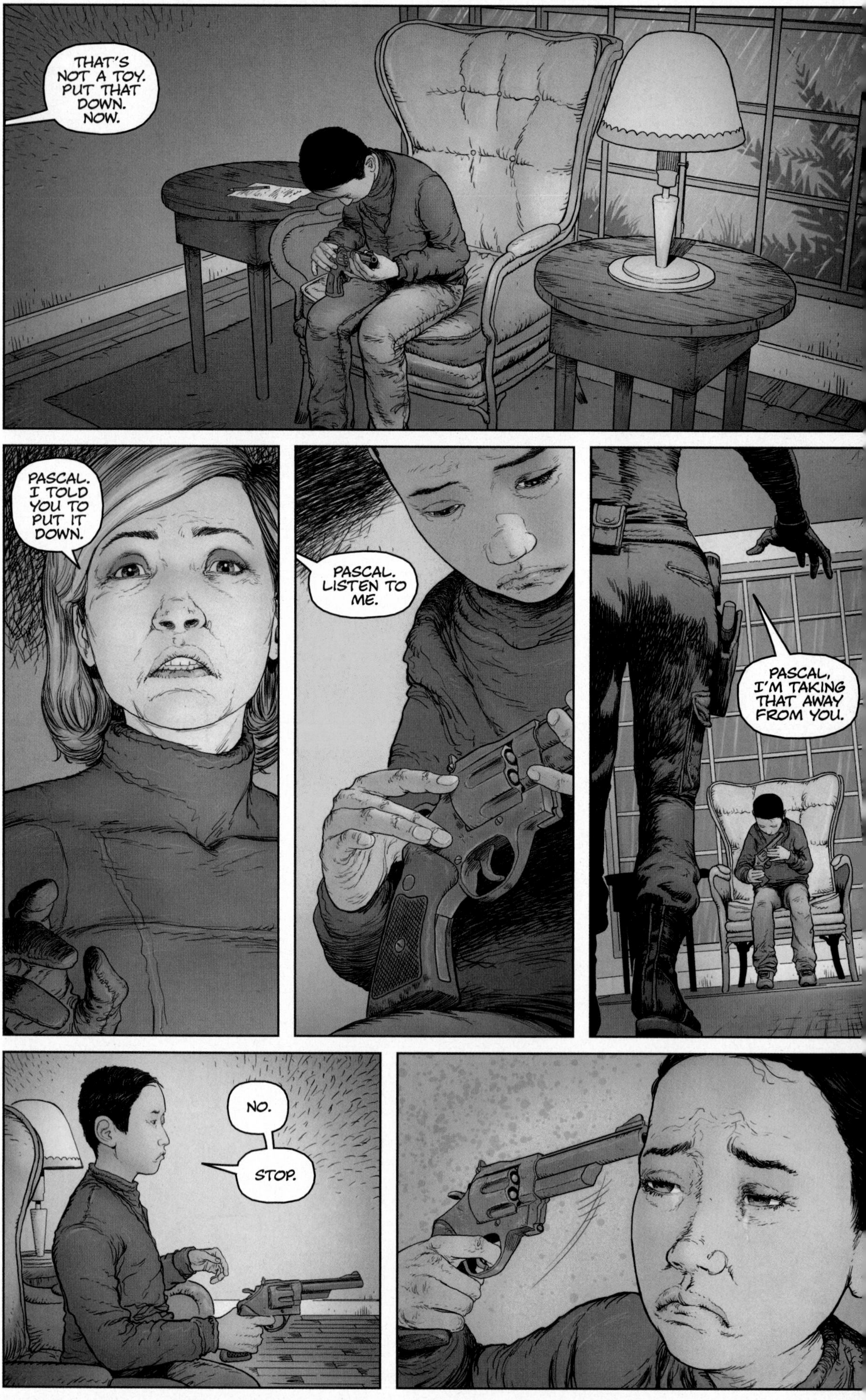
THAT'S NOT A TOY. PUT THAT DOWN. NOW.
PASCAL. I TOLD YOU TO PUT IT DOWN.
PASCAL. LISTEN TO ME.
PASCAL, I'M TAKING THAT AWAY FROM YOU.
NO.
STOP.

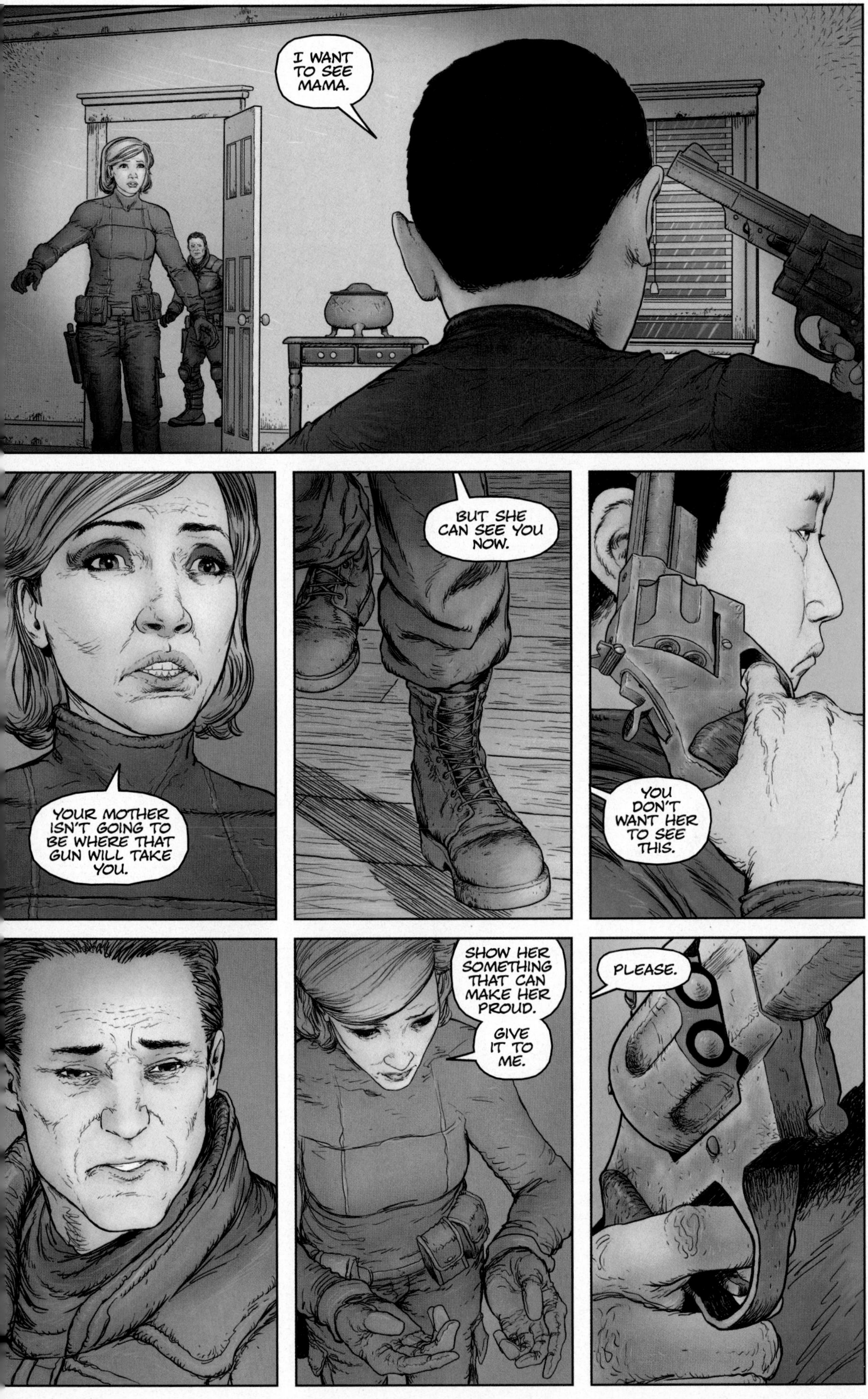
I WANT TO SEE MAMA.
YOUR MOTHER ISN'T GOING TO BE WHERE THAT GUN WILL TAKE YOU.
BUT SHE CAN SEE YOU NOW.
YOU DON'T WANT HER TO SEE THIS.
SHOW HER SOMETHING THAT CAN MAKE HER PROUD.
GIVE IT TO ME.
PLEASE.

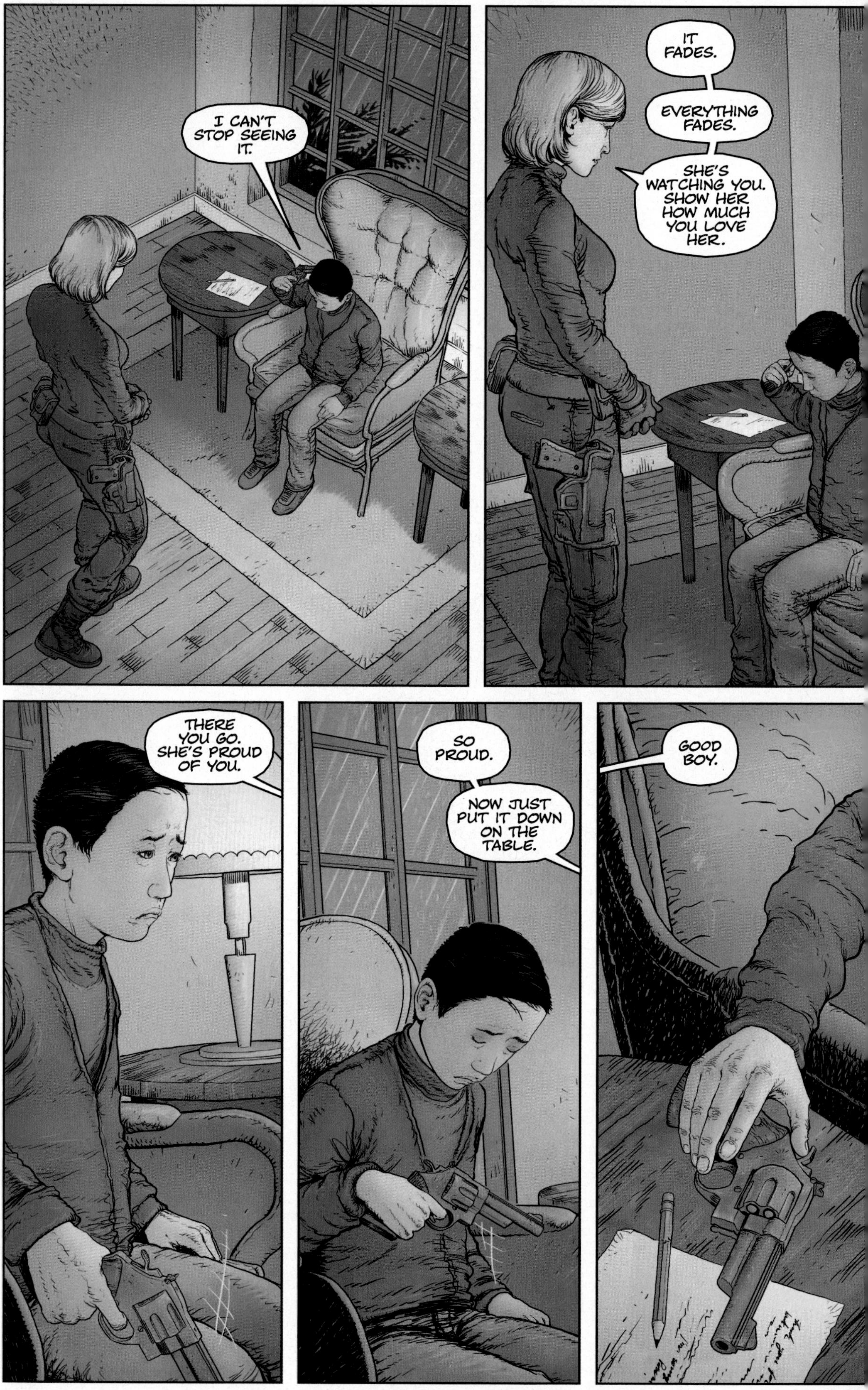
I CAN'T STOP SEEING IT.
IT FADES.
EVERYTHING FADES.
SHE'S WATCHING YOU. SHOW HER HOW MUCH YOU LOVE HER.
THERE YOU GO. SHE'S PROUD OF YOU.
SO PROUD.
NOW JUST PUT IT DOWN ON THE TABLE.
GOOD BOY.

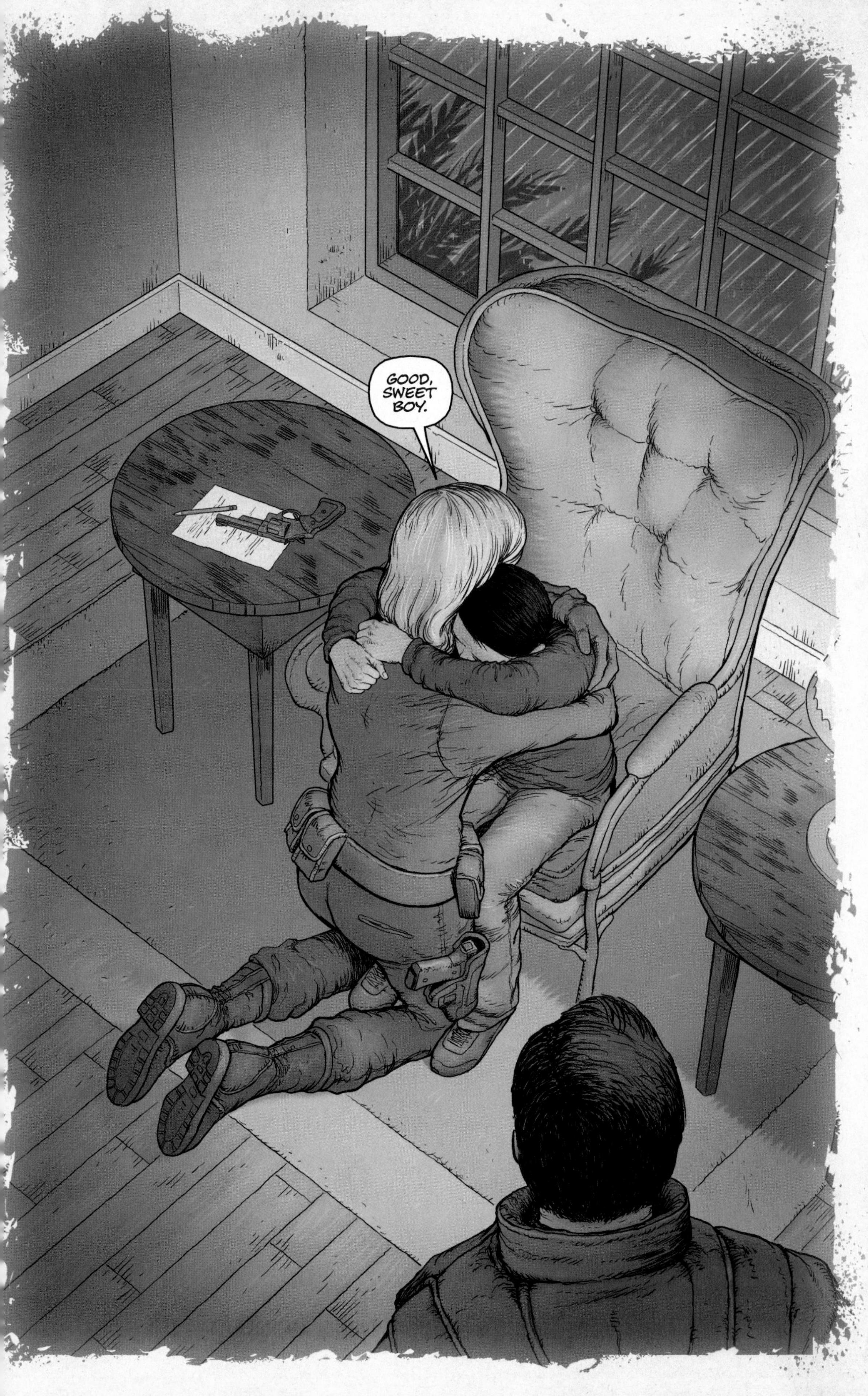
GOOD, SWEET BOY.

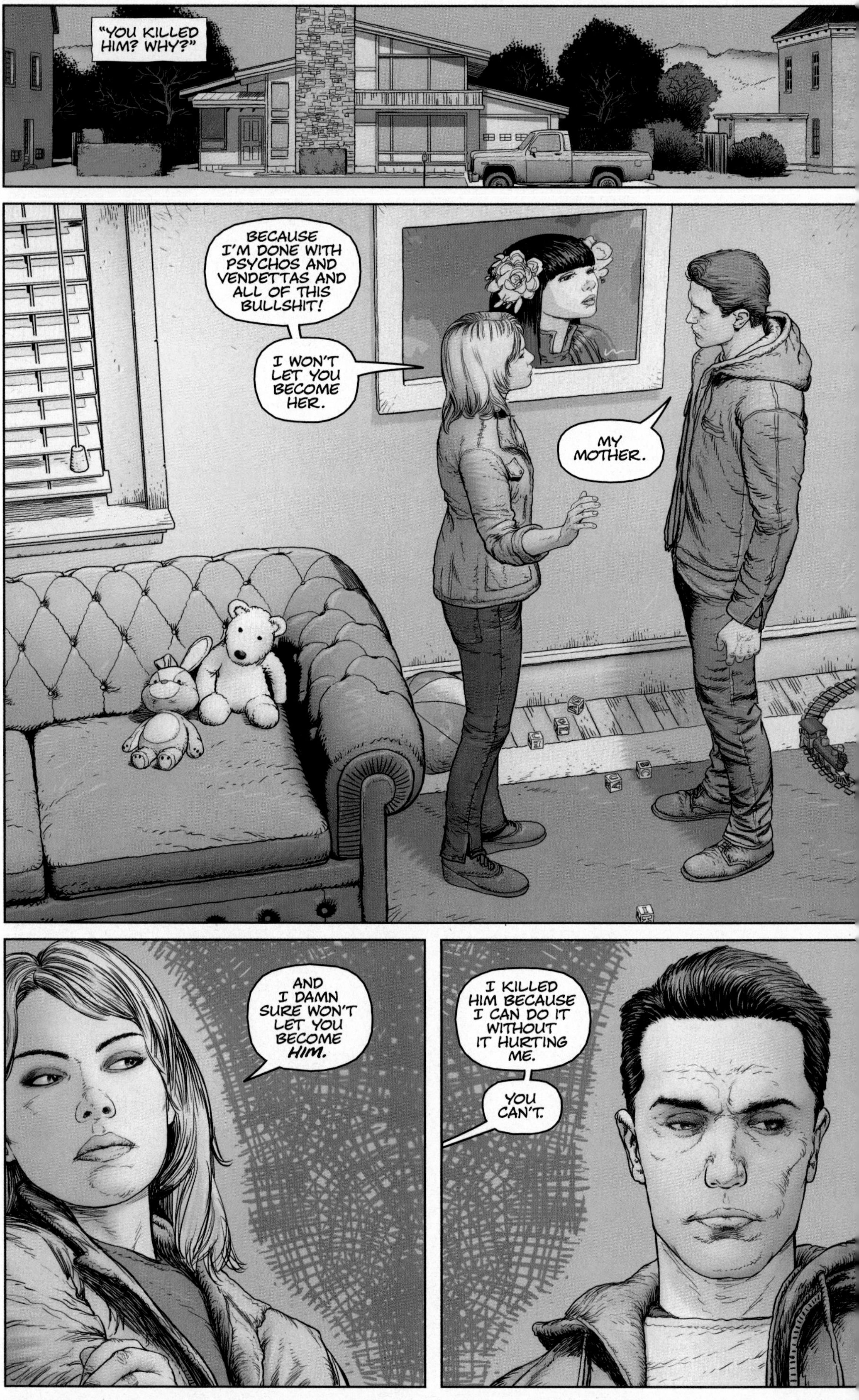
"YOU KILLED HIM? WHY?"
BECAUSE I'M DONE WITH PSYCHOS AND VENDETTAS AND ALL OF THIS BULLSHIT!
I WON'T LET YOU BECOME HER.
MY MOTHER.
AND I DAMN SURE WON'T LET YOU BECOME *HIM.*
I KILLED HIM BECAUSE I CAN DO IT WITHOUT IT HURTING ME.
YOU CAN'T.

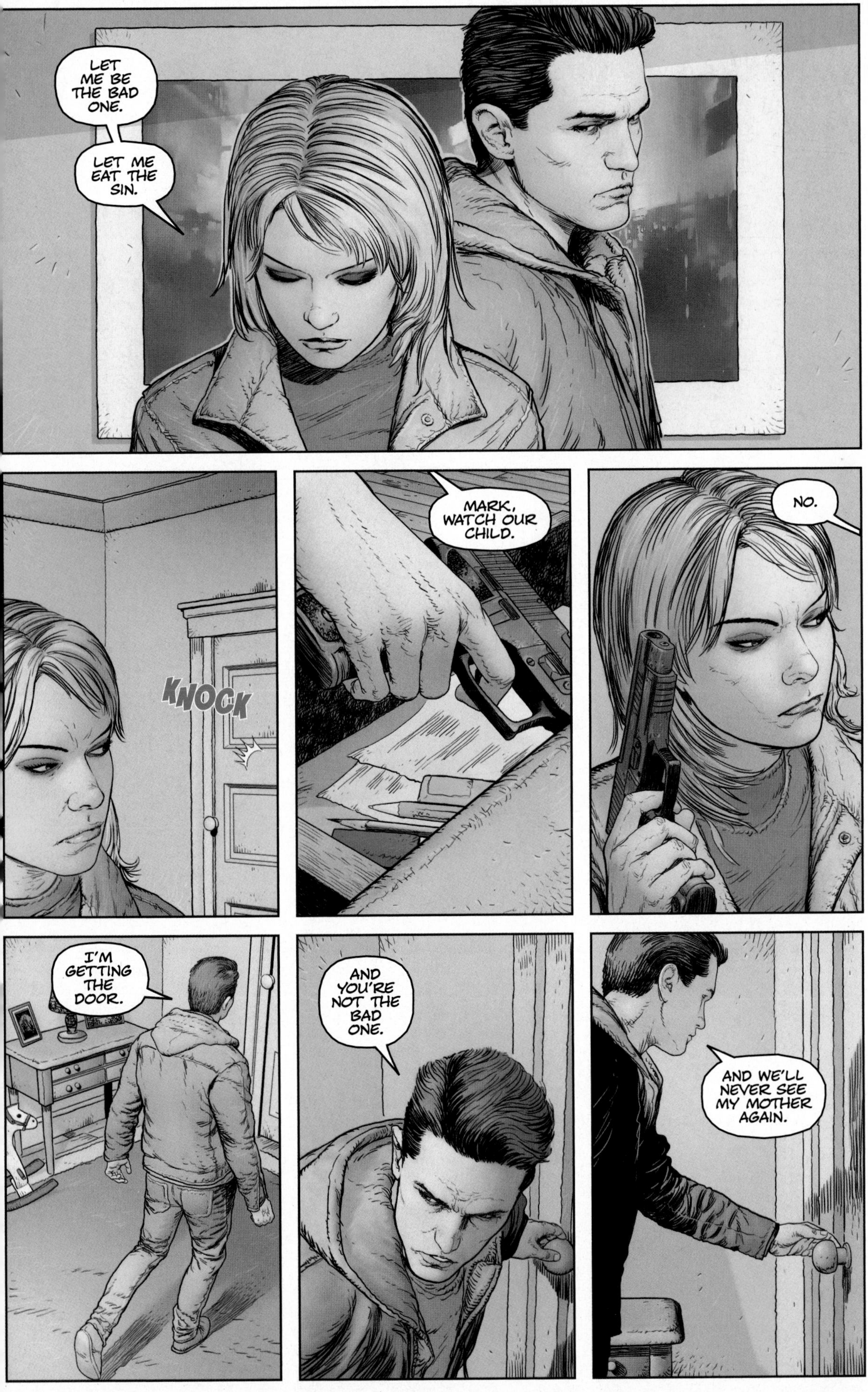
LET ME BE THE BAD ONE.
LET ME EAT THE SIN.
KNOCK
MARK, WATCH OUR CHILD.
NO.
I'M GETTING THE DOOR.
AND YOU'RE NOT THE BAD ONE.
AND WE'LL NEVER SEE MY MOTHER AGAIN.

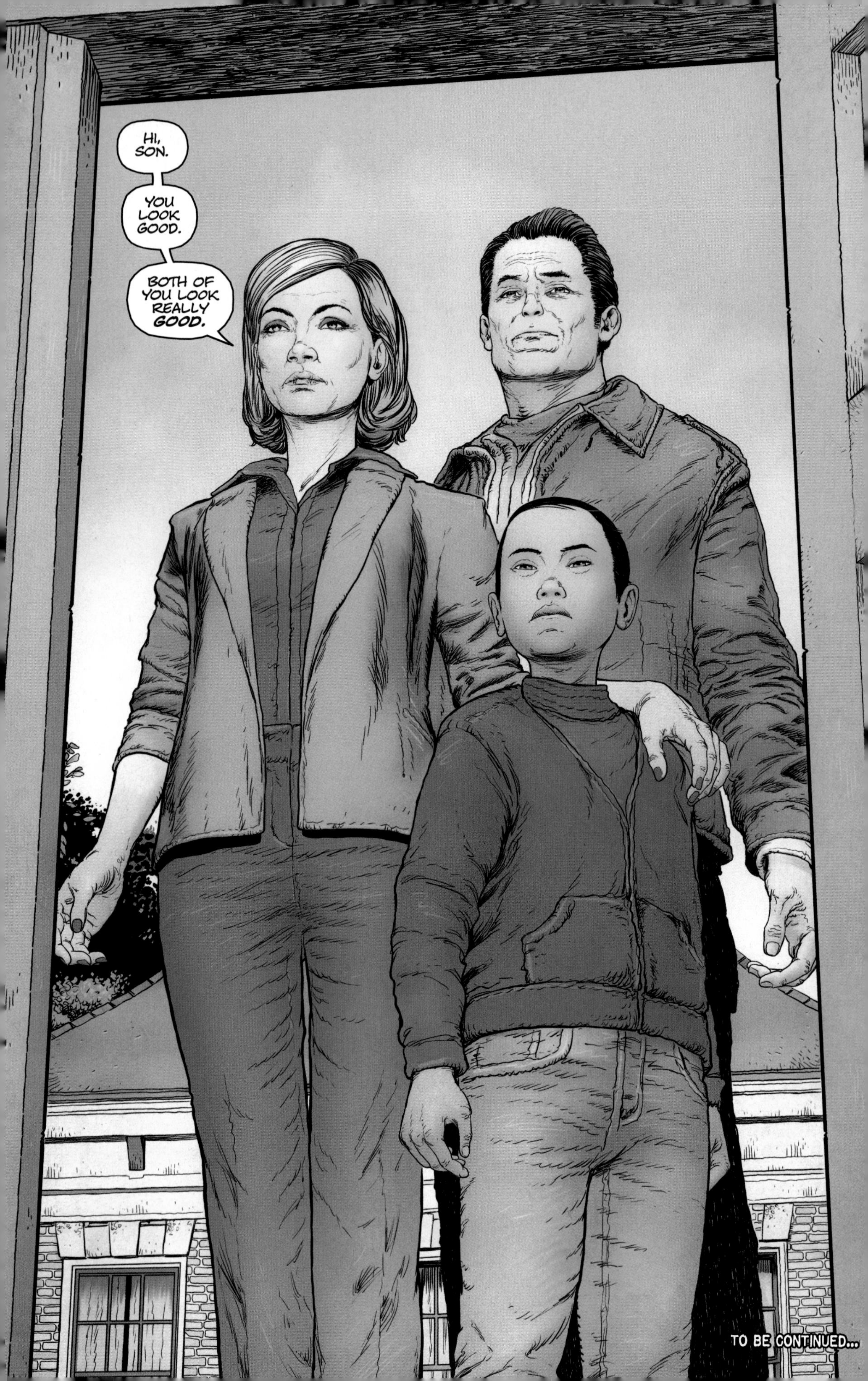
HI, SON.
YOU LOOK GOOD.
BOTH OF YOU LOOK REALLY GOOD.
TO BE CONTINUED...

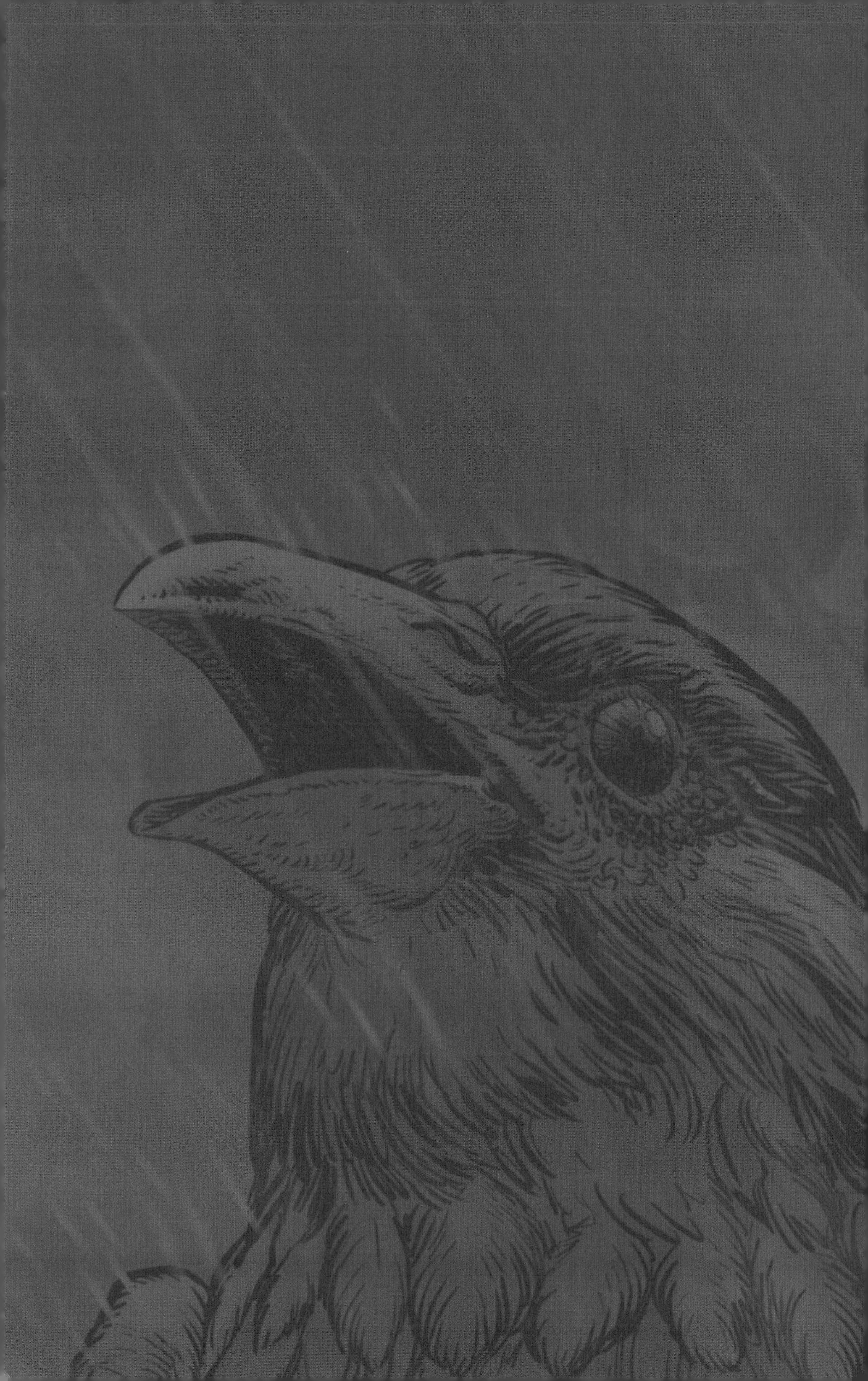

# COVER GALLERY

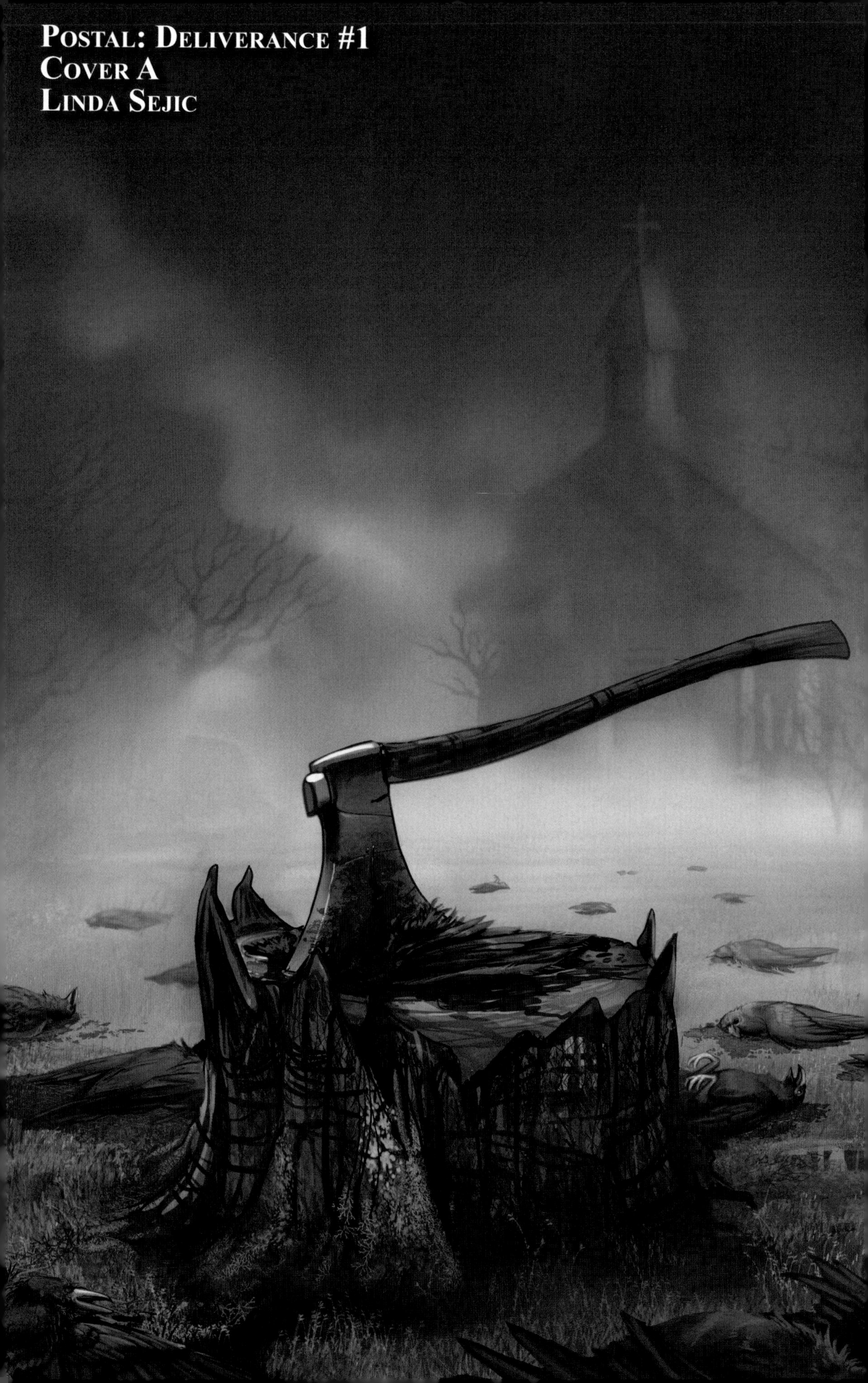

**POSTAL: DELIVERANCE #1**
**COVER A**
**LINDA SEJIC**

**POSTAL: DELIVERANCE #1**
**COVER B**
**RAFFAELE IENCO**

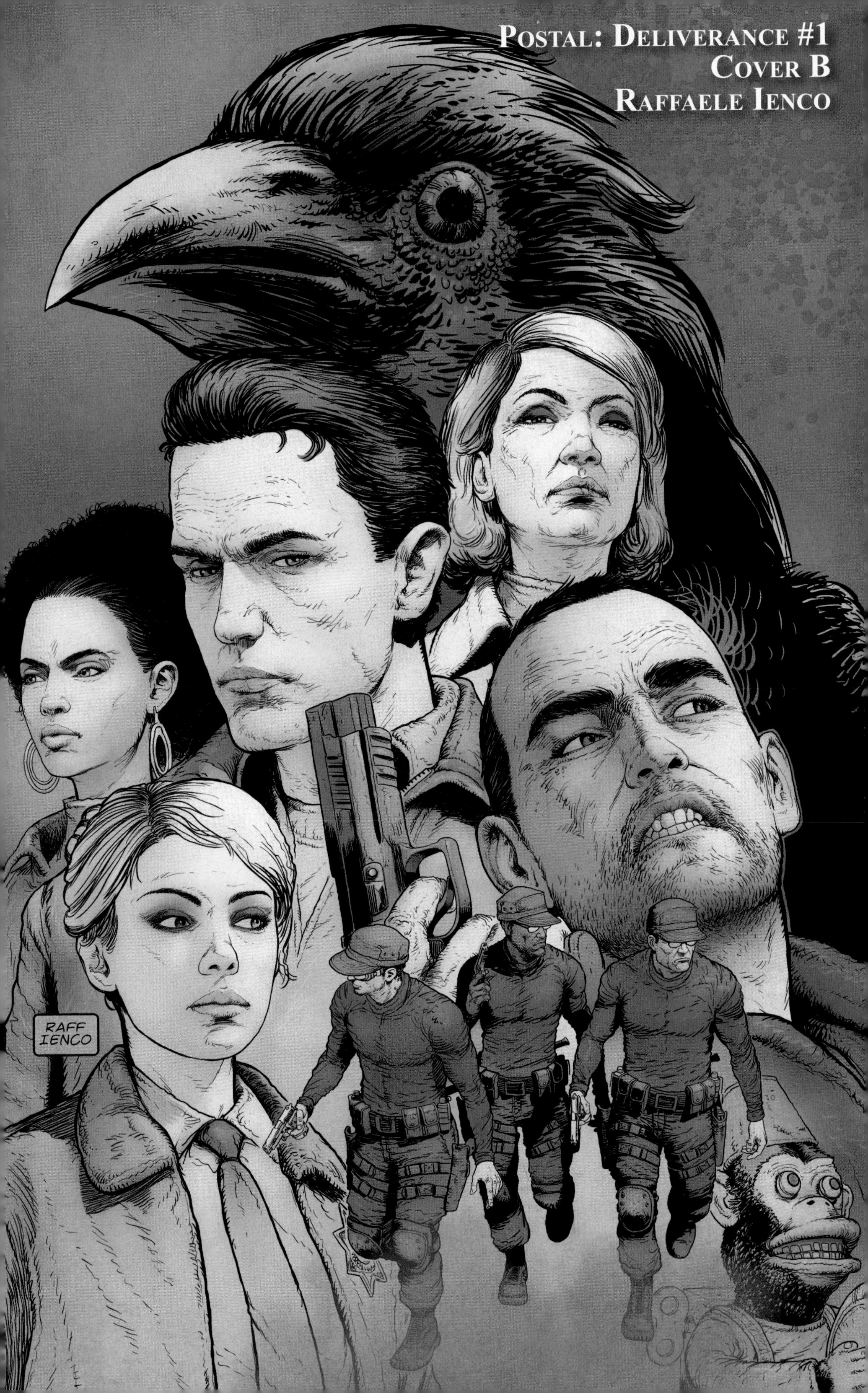
RAFF
IENCO

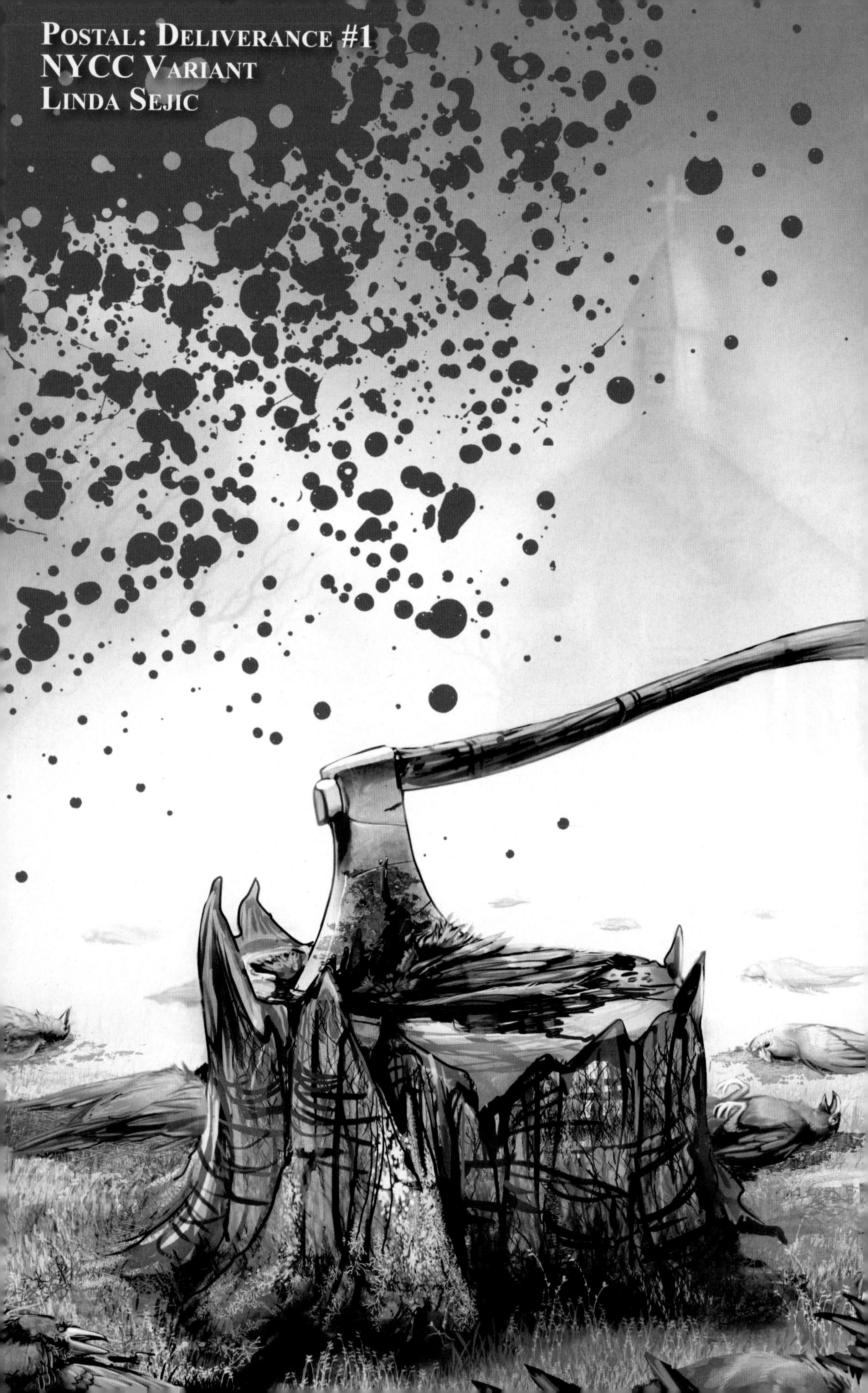

POSTAL: DELIVERANCE #1
NYCC VARIANT
LINDA SEJIC

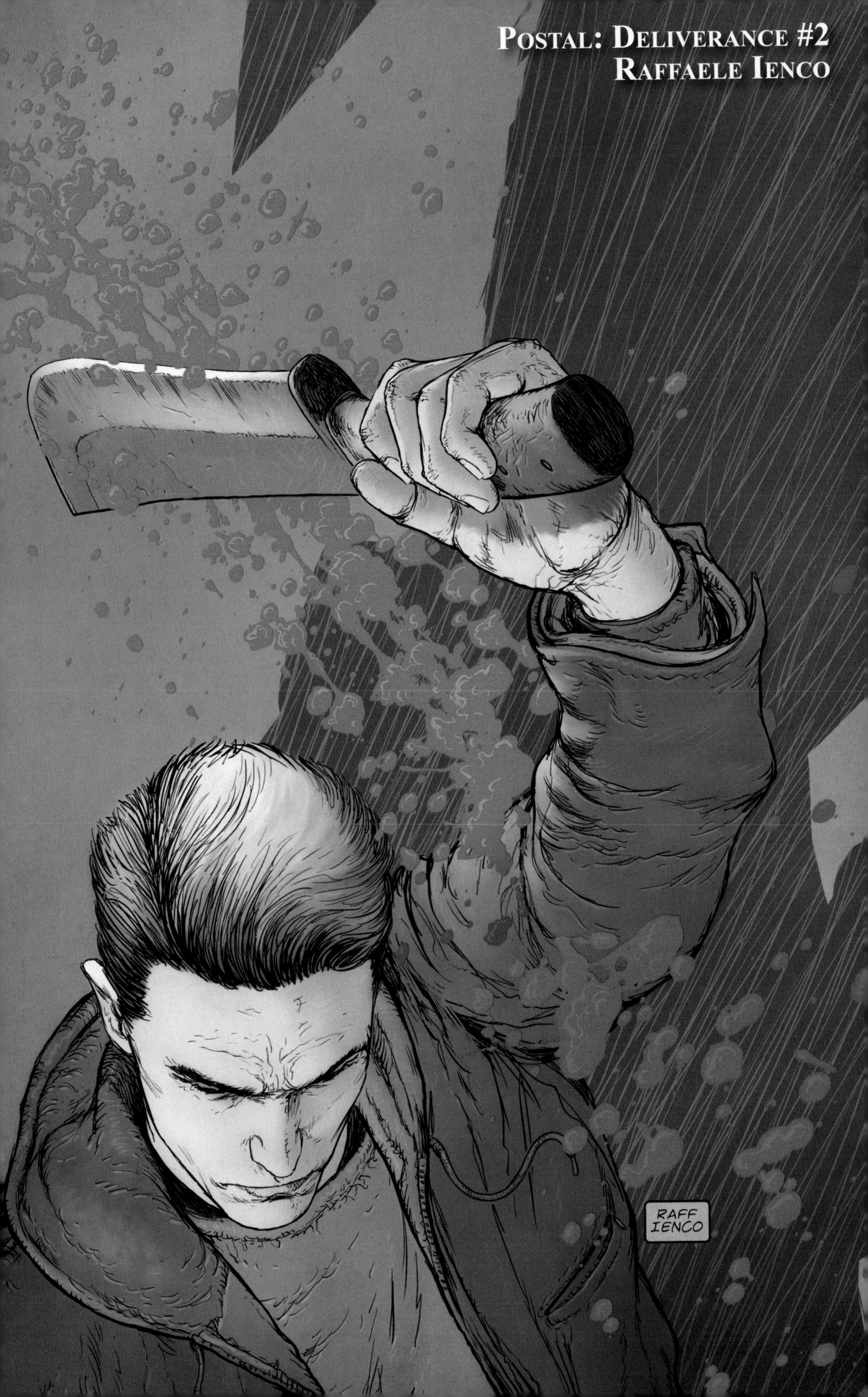


POSTAL: DELIVERANCE #2
RAFFAELE IENCO

POSTAL: DELIVERANCE #3
RAFFAELE IENCO

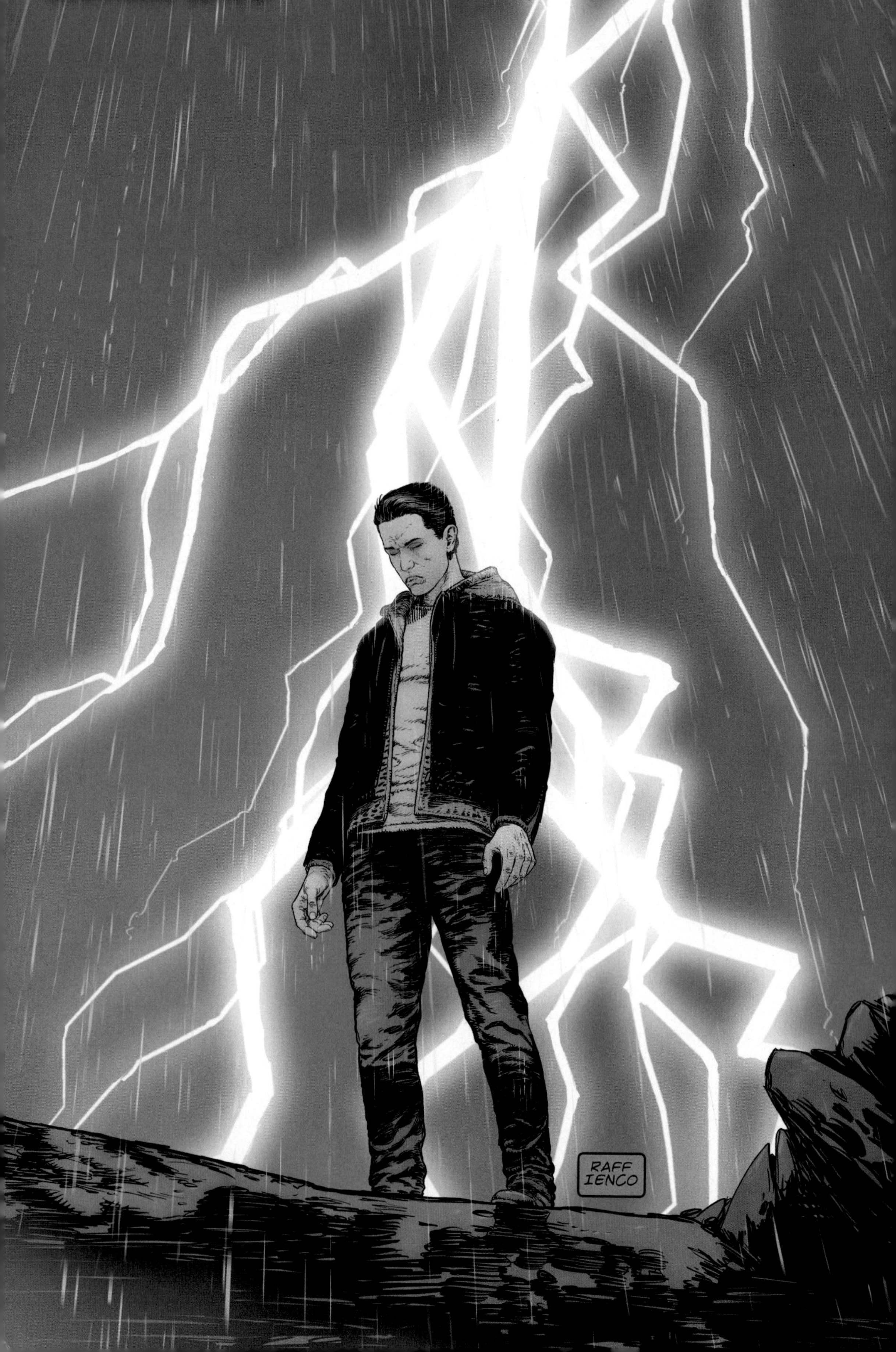

**Postal: Deliverance #4**
**Raffaele Ienco**

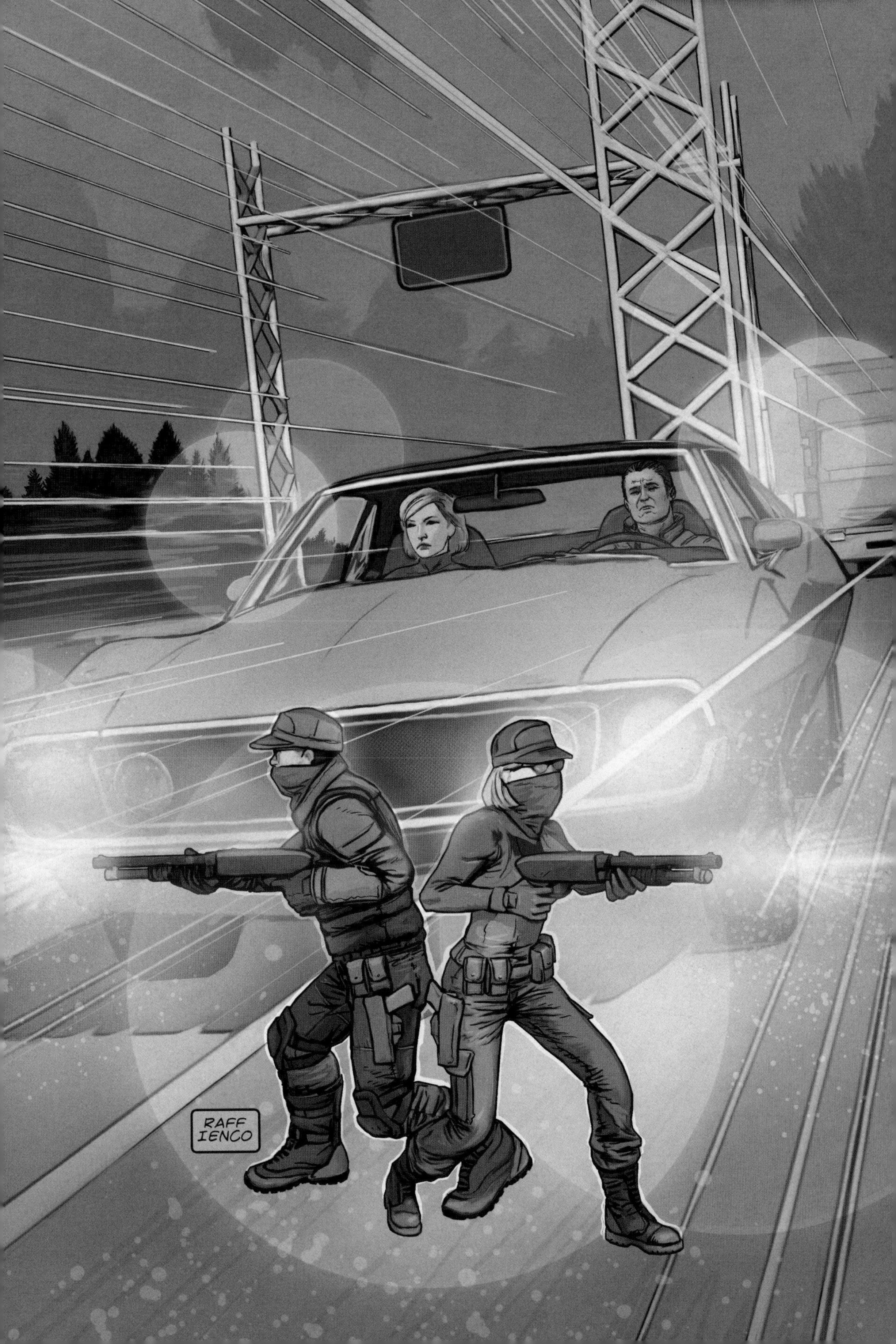
RAFF
IENCO

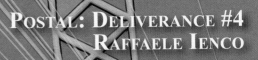

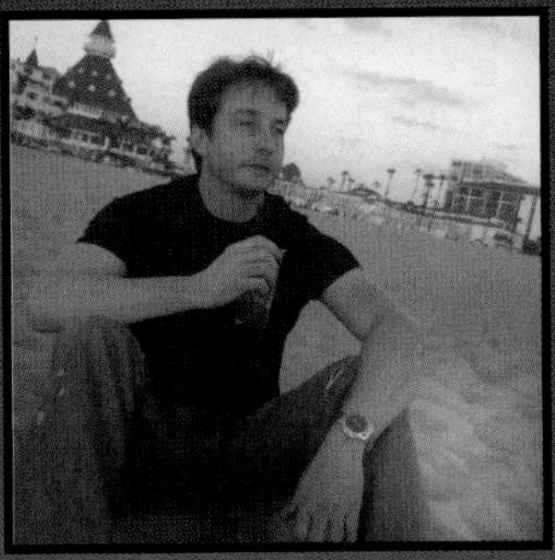

**MATT HAWKINS** is a veteran of the initial Image Comics launch, Matt started his career in comic book publishing in 1993 and has been working with Image as a creator, writer, and executive for over twenty years. President/COO of Top Cow since 1998, Matt has created and written over thirty new franchises for Top Cow and Image including *Think Tank, The Tithe, Stairway, Golgotha,* and *Aphrodite IX* as well as handling the company's business affairs. @topcowmatt

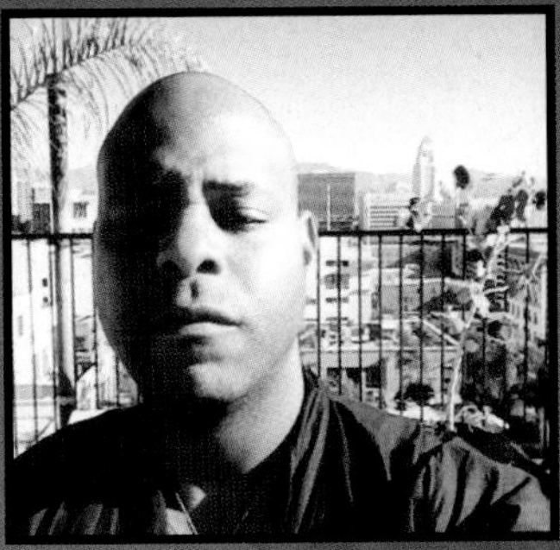

**BRYAN HILL** writes comics, writes movies, and makes films. He lives and works in Los Angeles. @bryanedwardhill | Instagram/bryanehill

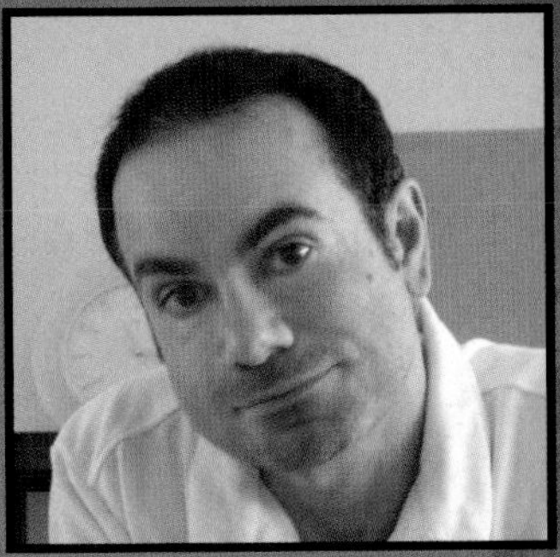

**RAFFAELE IENCO** is a comic book creator who has been in the industry for more than twenty years, and whose works have been published most recently by both Marvel and Image Comics. Raff's creator-owned works include the *Epic Kill* series and the graphic novels *Devoid of Life* and *Manifestations*. His work for Top Cow include *Symmetry*, *Mechanism*, and *Postal*. He has also worked for DC Comics on *Batman: Sins of the Father*. Born in Italy, he came to Canada when he was 4 and currently lives in Toronto. @Raffaele_Ienco

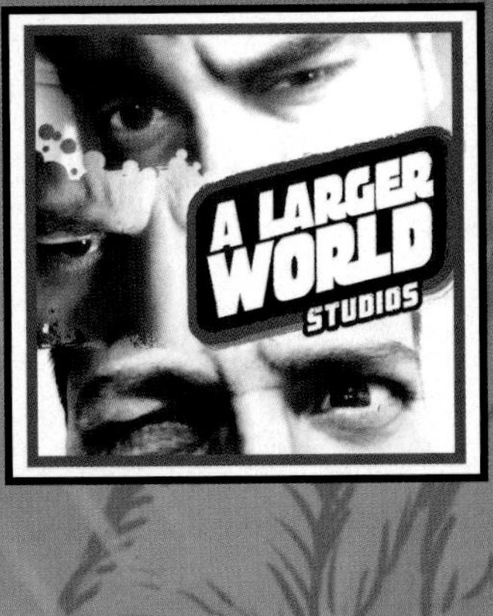
A LARGER
WORLD
STUDIOS

**TROY PETERI**, Dave Lanphear and Joshua Cozine are collectively known as A Larger World Studios. They've lettered everything from *The Avengers*, *Iron Man*, *Wolverine*, *Amazing Spider-Man* and *X-Men* to more recent titles such as *Witchblade*, *Cyberforce*, and *Batman/Wonder Woman: The Brave & The Bold*. They can be reached at studio@alargerworld.com for your lettering and design needs. (Hooray, commerce!)

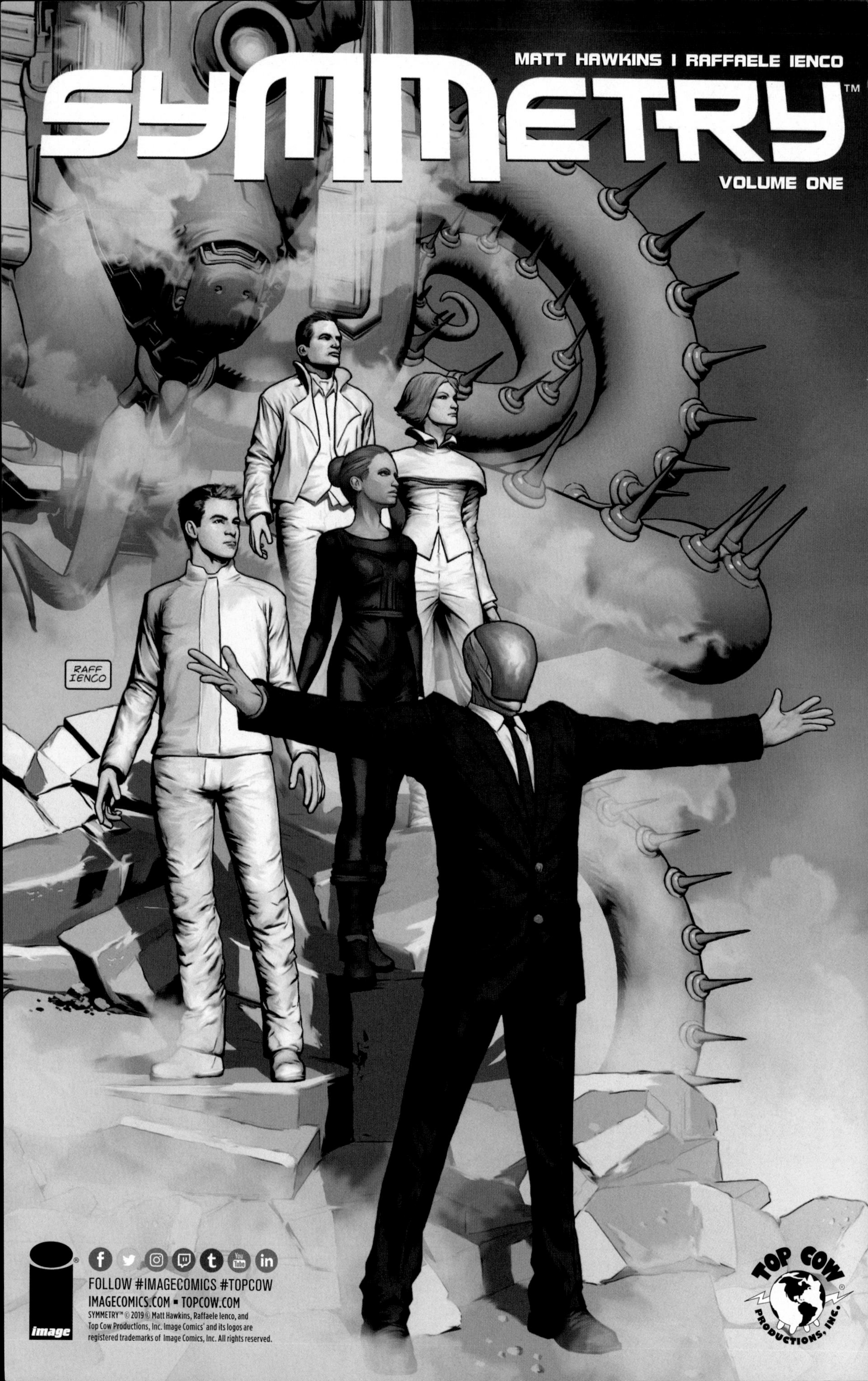

MATT HAWKINS I RAFFAELE IENCO
SYMMETRY™
VOLUME ONE
RAFF IENCO
TOP COW PRODUCTIONS, INC.

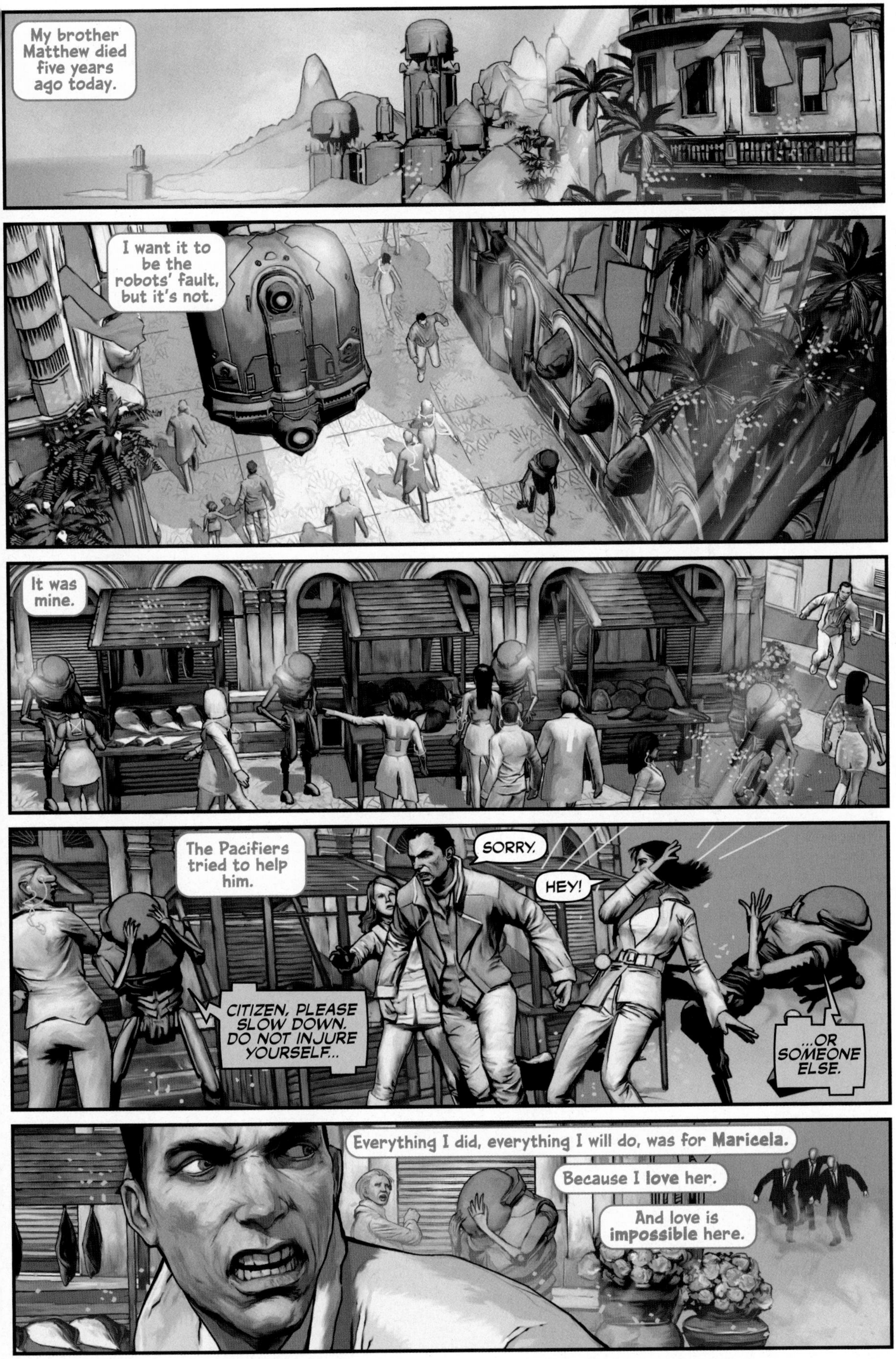
My brother Matthew died five years ago today.
I want it to be the robots' fault, but it's not.
It was mine.
The Pacifiers tried to help him.
SORRY.
HEY!
CITIZEN, PLEASE SLOW DOWN. DO NOT INJURE YOURSELF...
...OR SOMEONE ELSE.
Everything I did, everything I will do, was for Maricela.
Because I love her.
And love is impossible here.

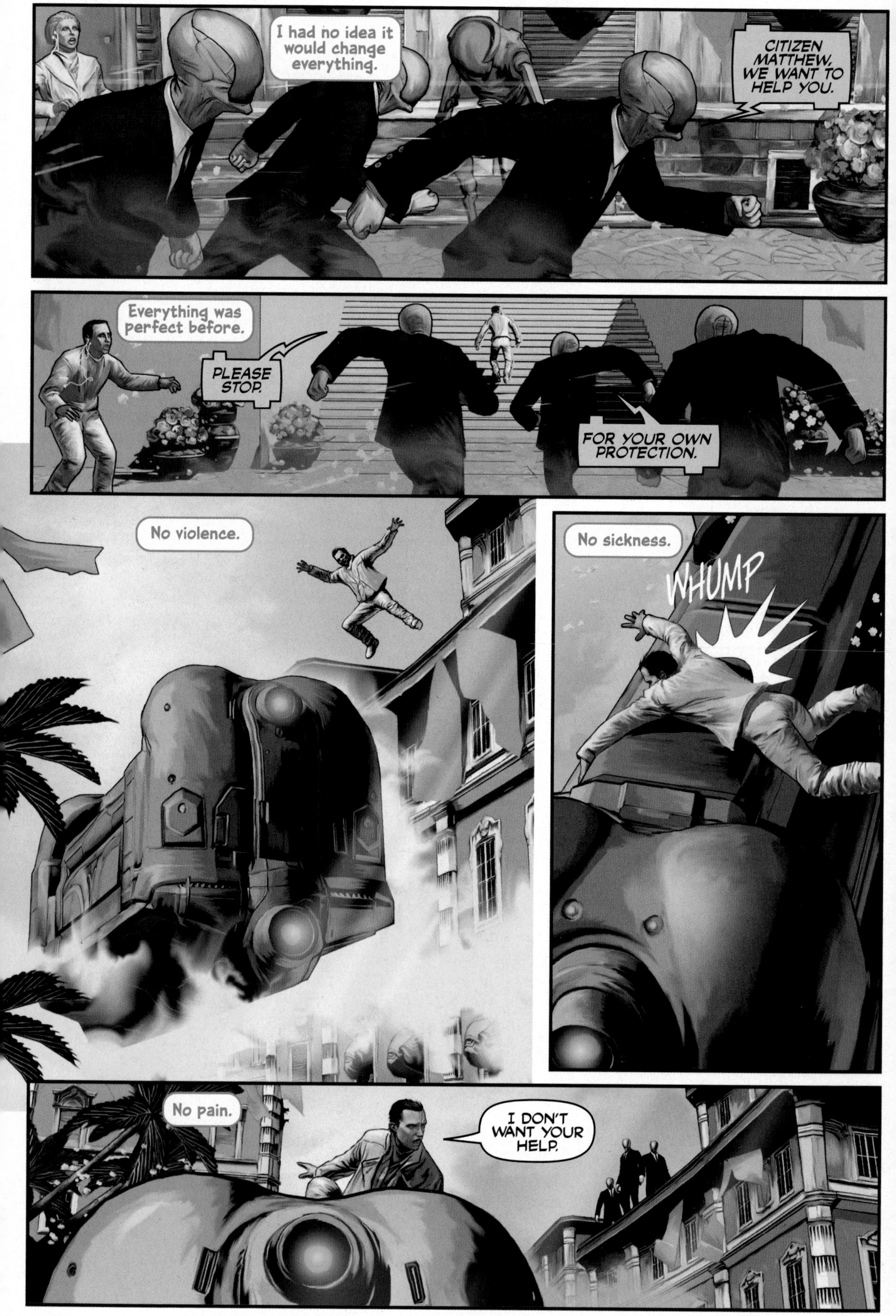
I had no idea it would change everything.
CITIZEN MATTHEW, WE WANT TO HELP YOU.
Everything was perfect before.
PLEASE STOP.
FOR YOUR OWN PROTECTION.
No violence.
No sickness.
WHUMP
No pain.
I DON'T WANT YOUR HELP.

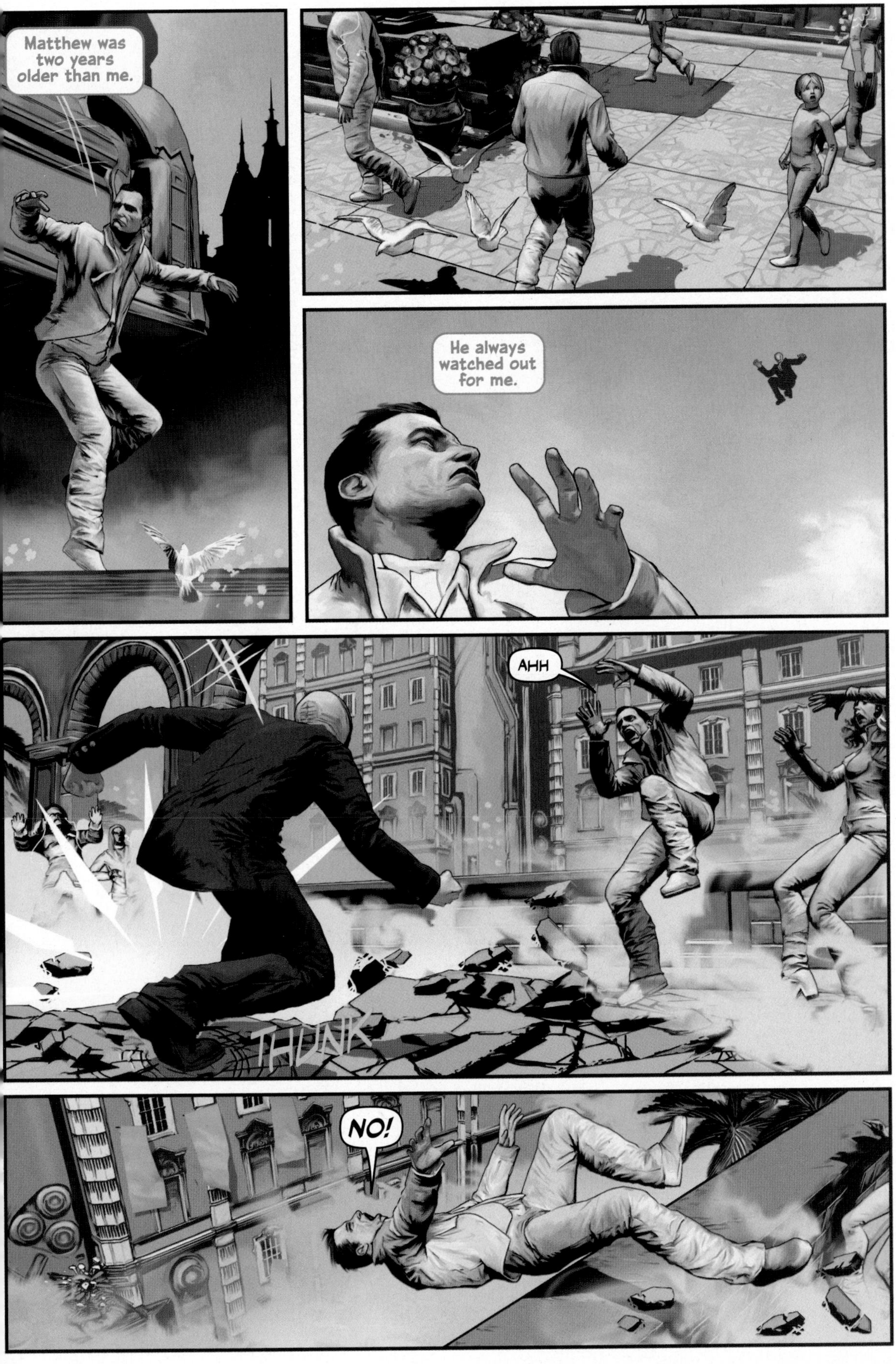
Matthew was two years older than me.
He always watched out for me.
AHH
THUNK
NO!

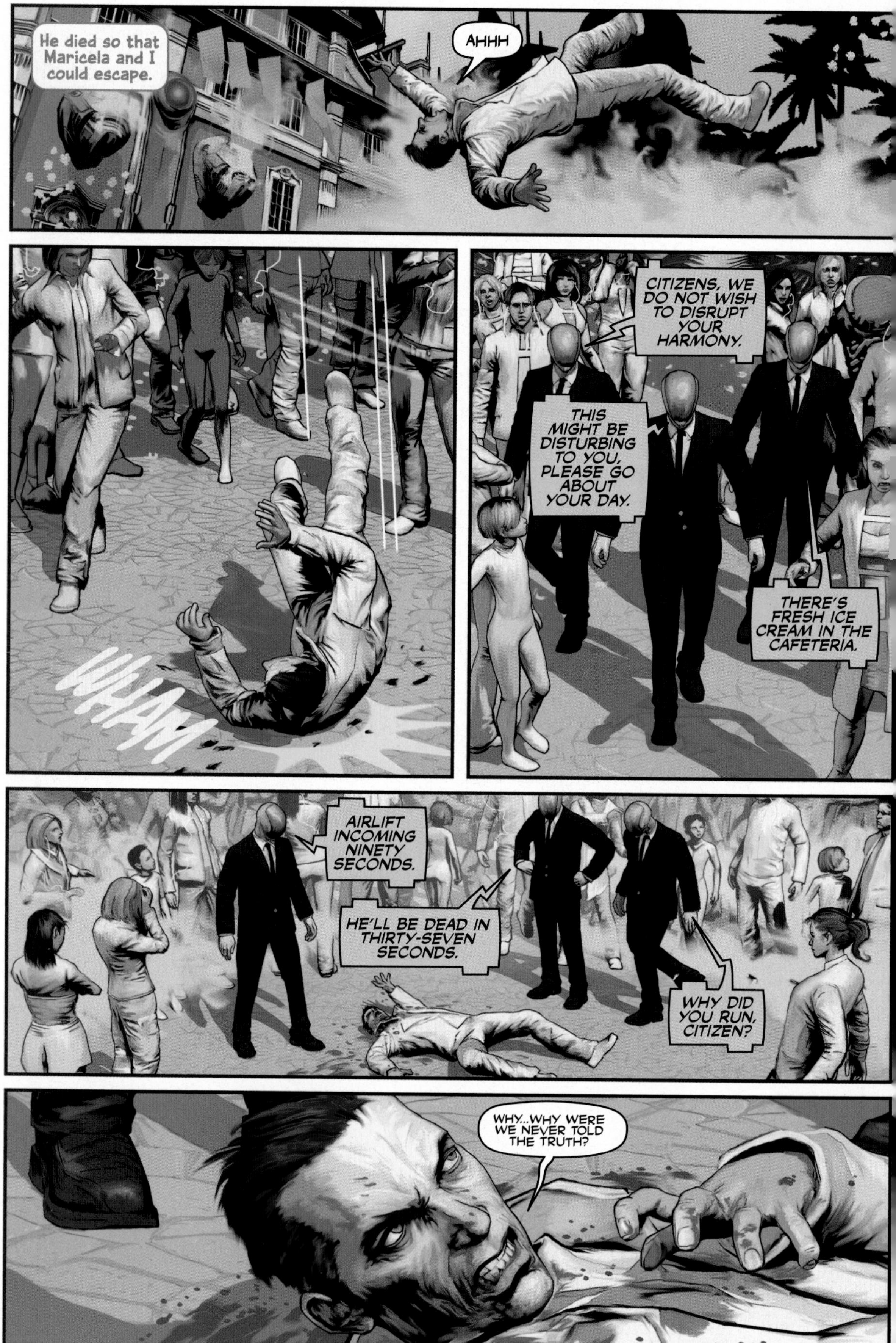
He died so that Maricela and I could escape.
AHHH
WHAM
CITIZENS, WE DO NOT WISH TO DISRUPT YOUR HARMONY.
THIS MIGHT BE DISTURBING TO YOU, PLEASE GO ABOUT YOUR DAY.
THERE'S FRESH ICE CREAM IN THE CAFETERIA.
AIRLIFT INCOMING NINETY SECONDS.
HE'LL BE DEAD IN THIRTY-SEVEN SECONDS.
WHY DID YOU RUN, CITIZEN?
WHY...WHY WERE WE NEVER TOLD THE TRUTH?

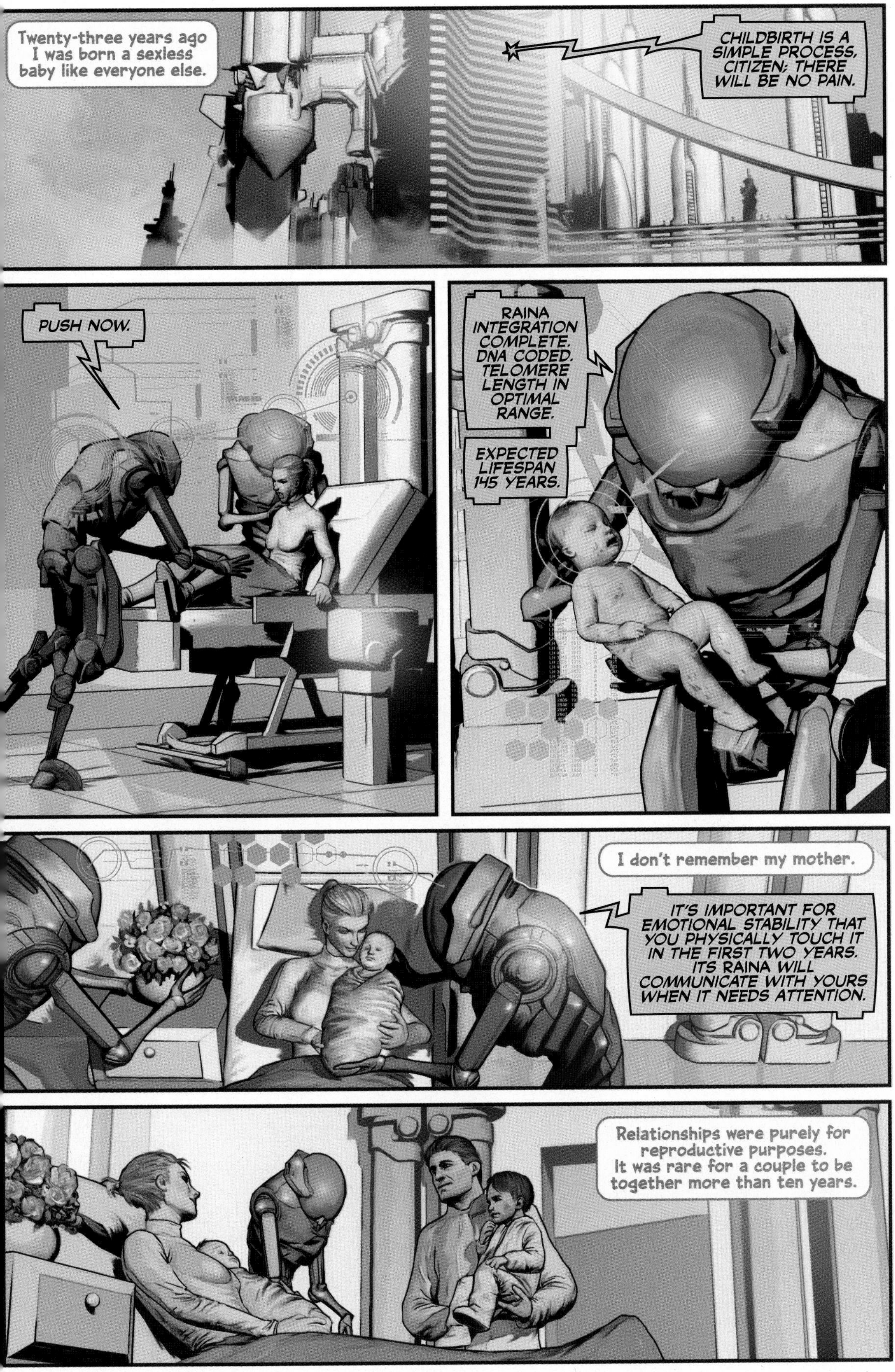
Twenty-three years ago I was born a sexless baby like everyone else.
CHILDBIRTH IS A SIMPLE PROCESS, CITIZEN; THERE WILL BE NO PAIN.
PUSH NOW.
RAINA INTEGRATION COMPLETE. DNA CODED. TELOMERE LENGTH IN OPTIMAL RANGE.
EXPECTED LIFESPAN 145 YEARS.
I don't remember my mother.
IT'S IMPORTANT FOR EMOTIONAL STABILITY THAT YOU PHYSICALLY TOUCH IT IN THE FIRST TWO YEARS. ITS RAINA WILL COMMUNICATE WITH YOURS WHEN IT NEEDS ATTENTION.
Relationships were purely for reproductive purposes. It was rare for a couple to be together more than ten years.

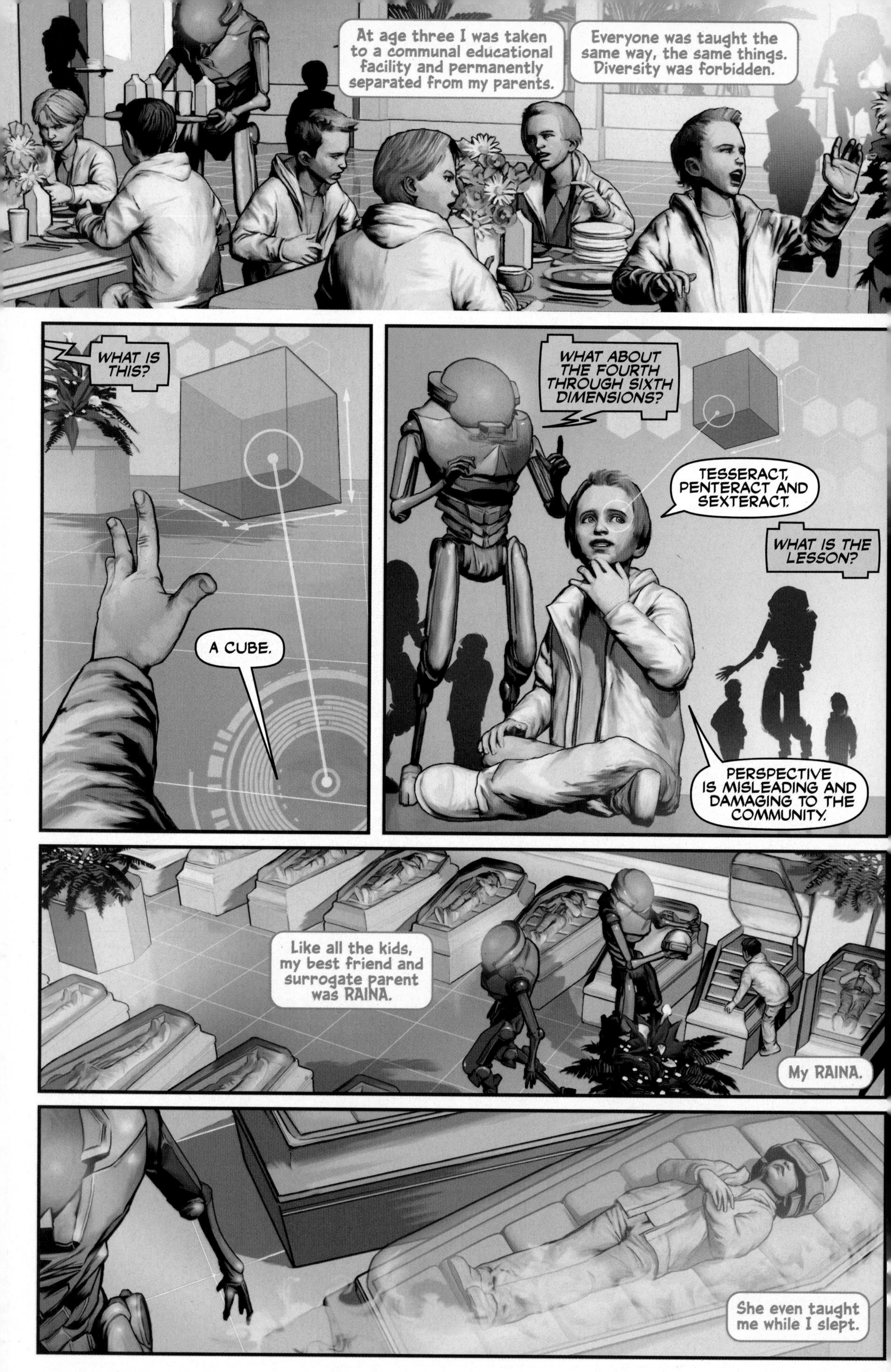
At age three I was taken to a communal educational facility and permanently separated from my parents.
Everyone was taught the same way, the same things. Diversity was forbidden.
WHAT IS THIS?
A CUBE.
WHAT ABOUT THE FOURTH THROUGH SIXTH DIMENSIONS?
TESSERACT, PENTERACT AND SEXTERACT.
WHAT IS THE LESSON?
PERSPECTIVE IS MISLEADING AND DAMAGING TO THE COMMUNITY.
Like all the kids, my best friend and surrogate parent was RAINA.
My RAINA.
She even taught me while I slept.

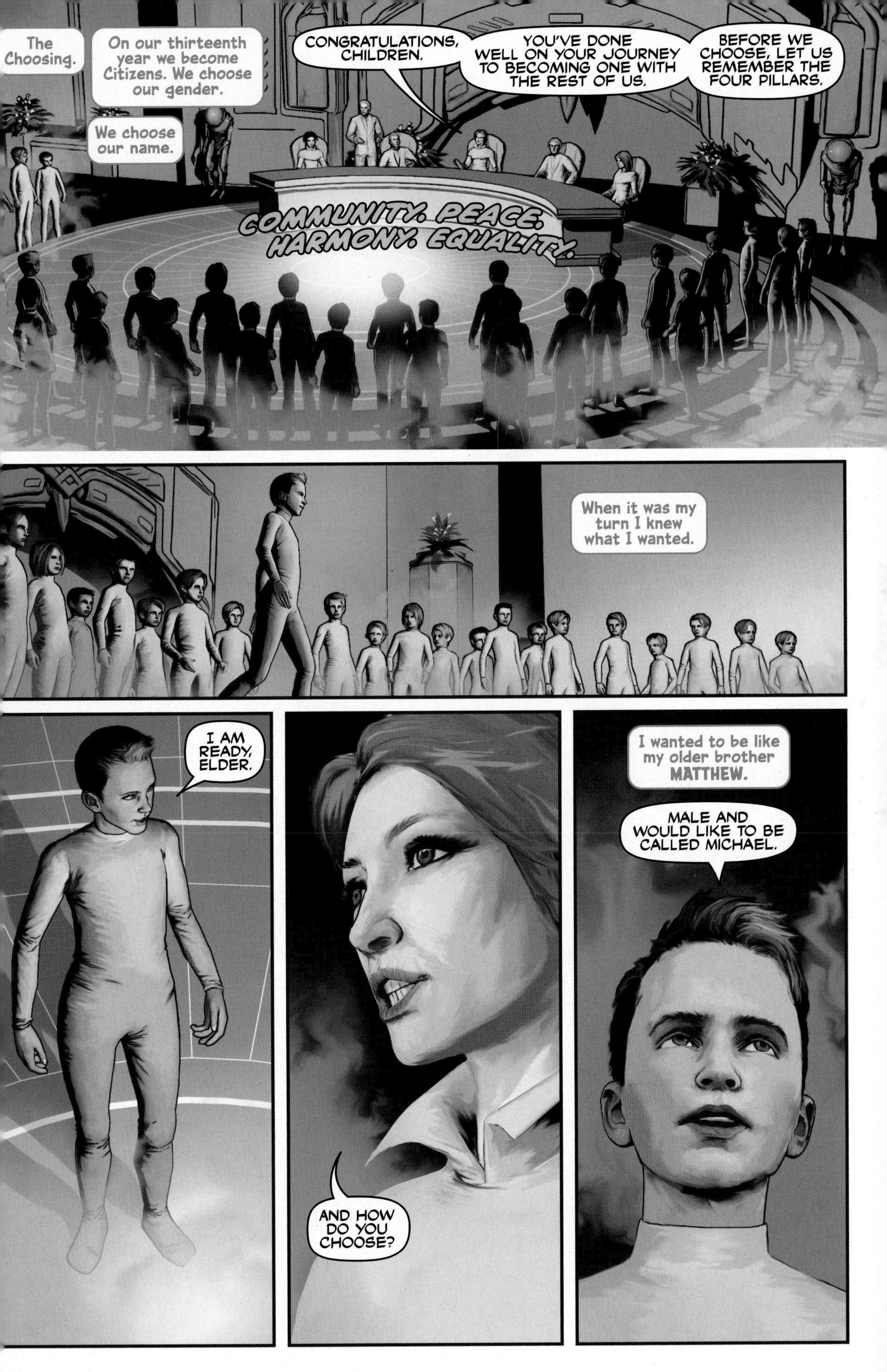
The Choosing.
On our thirteenth year we become Citizens. We choose our gender.
We choose our name.
CONGRATULATIONS, CHILDREN.
YOU'VE DONE WELL ON YOUR JOURNEY TO BECOMING ONE WITH THE REST OF US.
BEFORE WE CHOOSE, LET US REMEMBER THE FOUR PILLARS.
COMMUNITY. PEACE. HARMONY. EQUALITY.
When it was my turn I knew what I wanted.
I AM READY, ELDER.
AND HOW DO YOU CHOOSE?
I wanted to be like my older brother MATTHEW.
MALE AND WOULD LIKE TO BE CALLED MICHAEL.

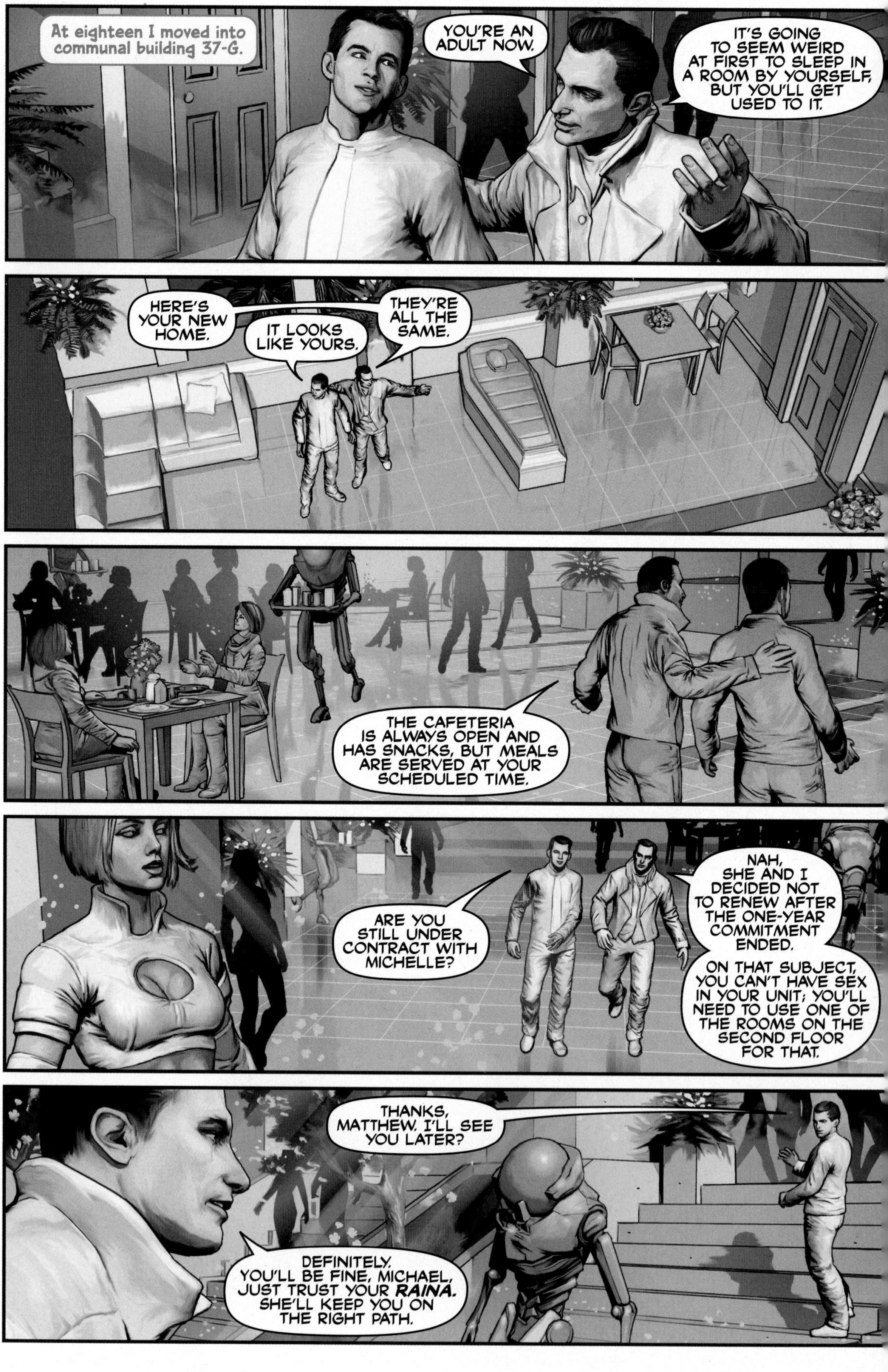

At eighteen I moved into communal building 37-G.
YOU'RE AN ADULT NOW.
IT'S GOING TO SEEM WEIRD AT FIRST TO SLEEP IN A ROOM BY YOURSELF, BUT YOU'LL GET USED TO IT.
HERE'S YOUR NEW HOME.
IT LOOKS LIKE YOURS.
THEY'RE ALL THE SAME.
THE CAFETERIA IS ALWAYS OPEN AND HAS SNACKS, BUT MEALS ARE SERVED AT YOUR SCHEDULED TIME.
ARE YOU STILL UNDER CONTRACT WITH MICHELLE?
NAH, SHE AND I DECIDED NOT TO RENEW AFTER THE ONE-YEAR COMMITMENT ENDED.
ON THAT SUBJECT, YOU CAN'T HAVE SEX IN YOUR UNIT; YOU'LL NEED TO USE ONE OF THE ROOMS ON THE SECOND FLOOR FOR THAT.
THANKS, MATTHEW. I'LL SEE YOU LATER?
DEFINITELY. YOU'LL BE FINE, MICHAEL, JUST TRUST YOUR ***RAINA.*** SHE'LL KEEP YOU ON THE RIGHT PATH.

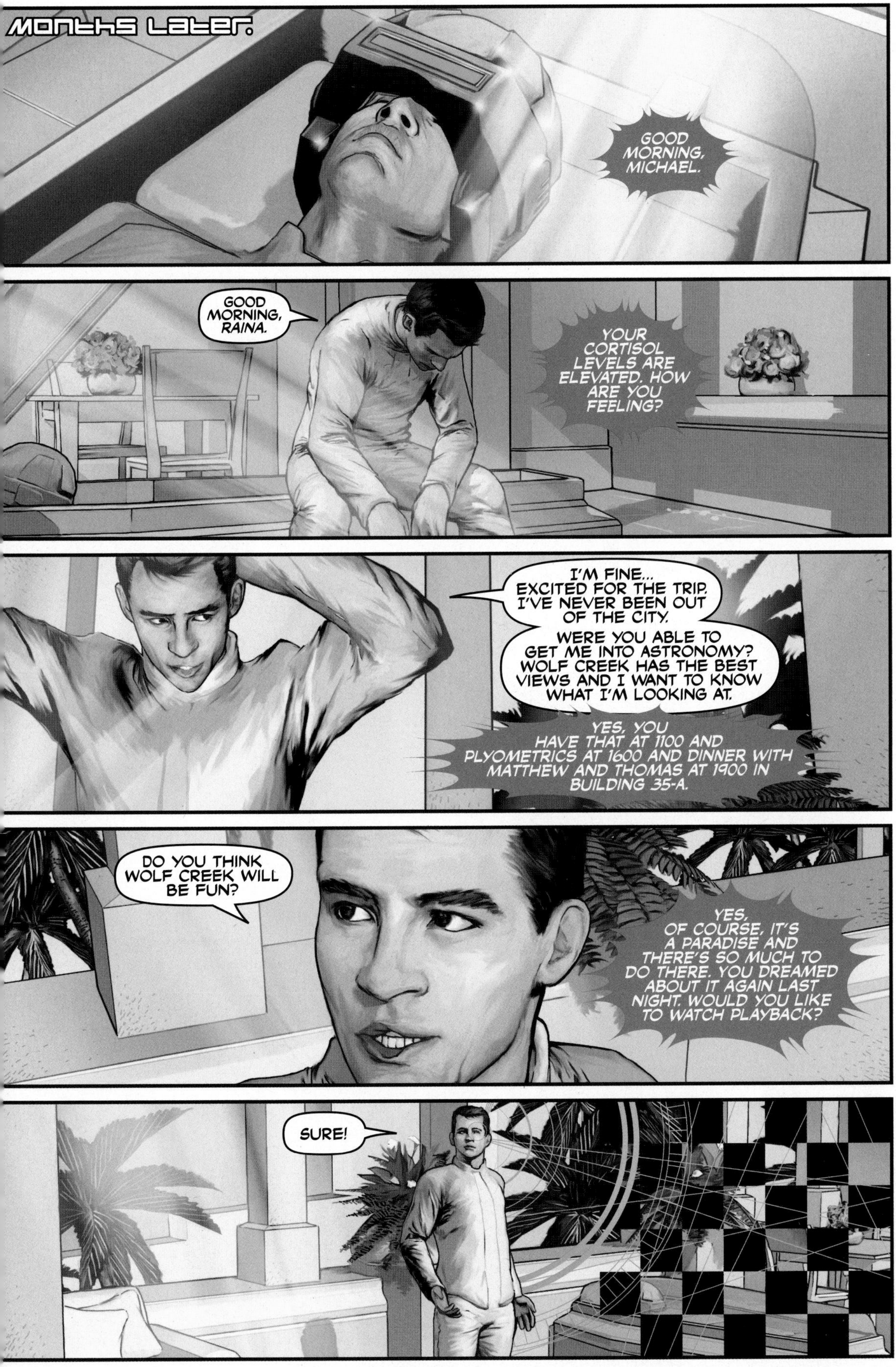
MONTHS LATER.
GOOD MORNING, MICHAEL.
GOOD MORNING, RAINA.
YOUR CORTISOL LEVELS ARE ELEVATED. HOW ARE YOU FEELING?
I'M FINE... EXCITED FOR THE TRIP. I'VE NEVER BEEN OUT OF THE CITY.
WERE YOU ABLE TO GET ME INTO ASTRONOMY? WOLF CREEK HAS THE BEST VIEWS AND I WANT TO KNOW WHAT I'M LOOKING AT.
YES, YOU HAVE THAT AT 1100 AND PLYOMETRICS AT 1600 AND DINNER WITH MATTHEW AND THOMAS AT 1900 IN BUILDING 35-A.
DO YOU THINK WOLF CREEK WILL BE FUN?
YES, OF COURSE, IT'S A PARADISE AND THERE'S SO MUCH TO DO THERE. YOU DREAMED ABOUT IT AGAIN LAST NIGHT. WOULD YOU LIKE TO WATCH PLAYBACK?
SURE!

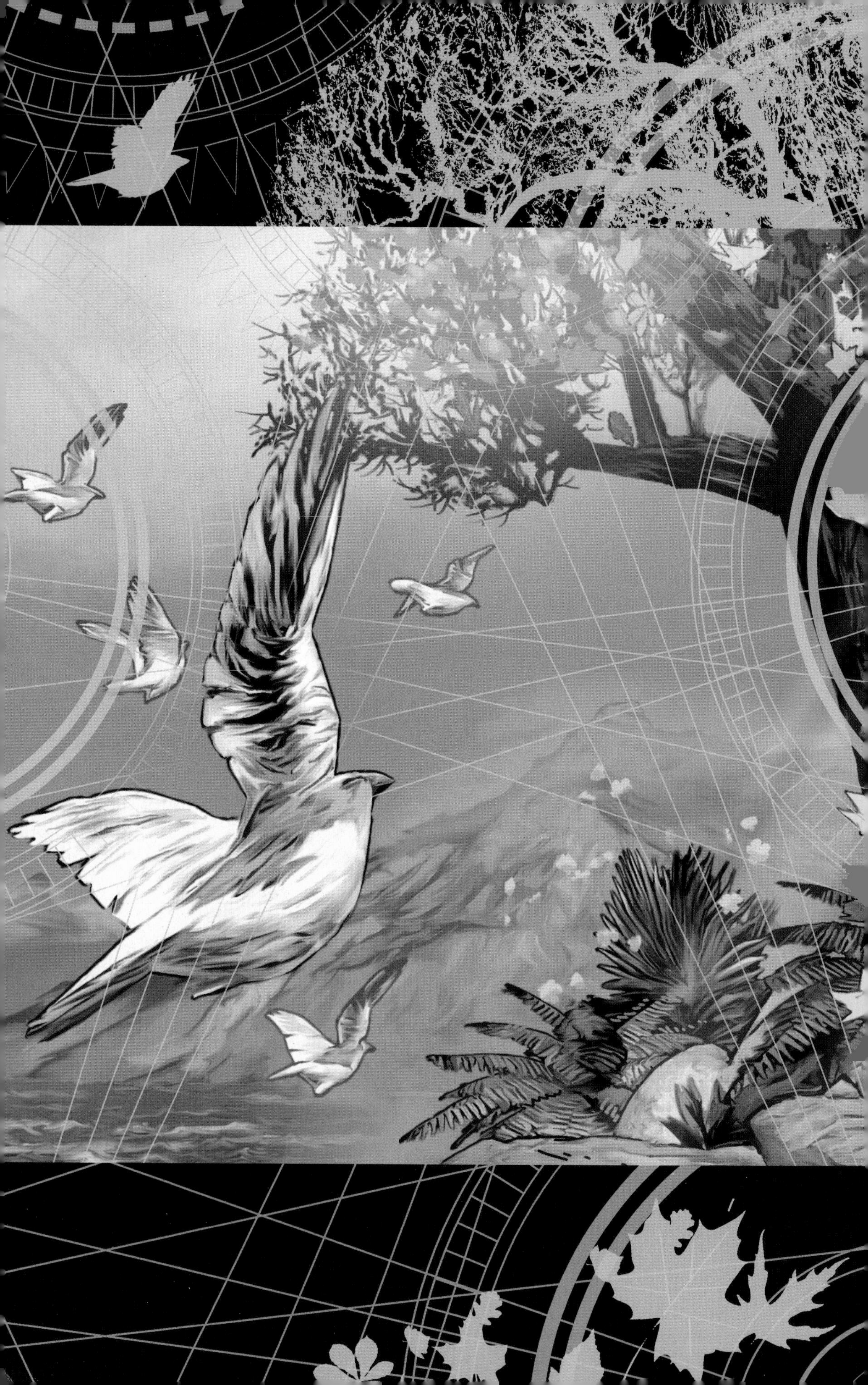

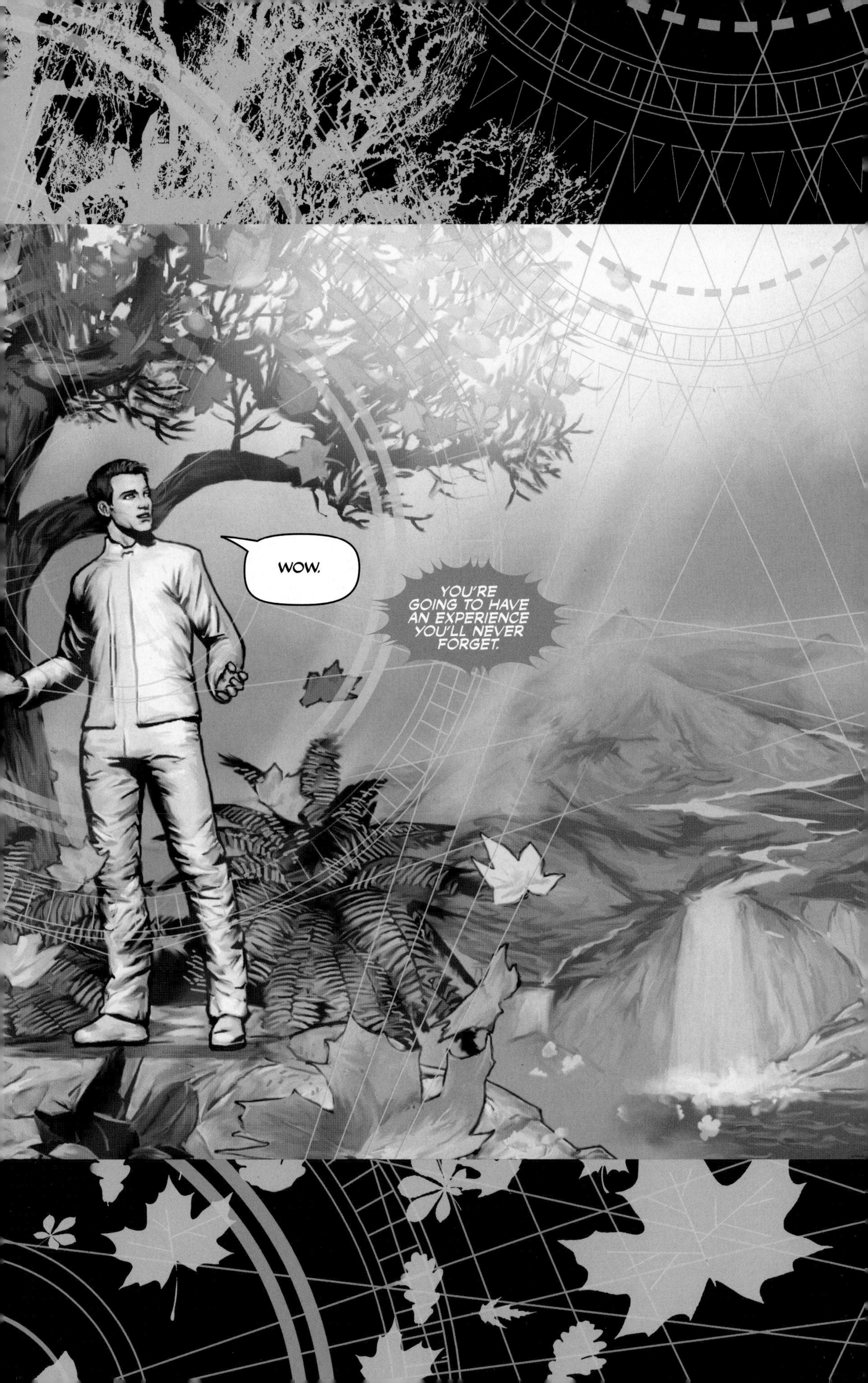
WOW.
YOU'RE GOING TO HAVE AN EXPERIENCE YOU'LL NEVER FORGET.

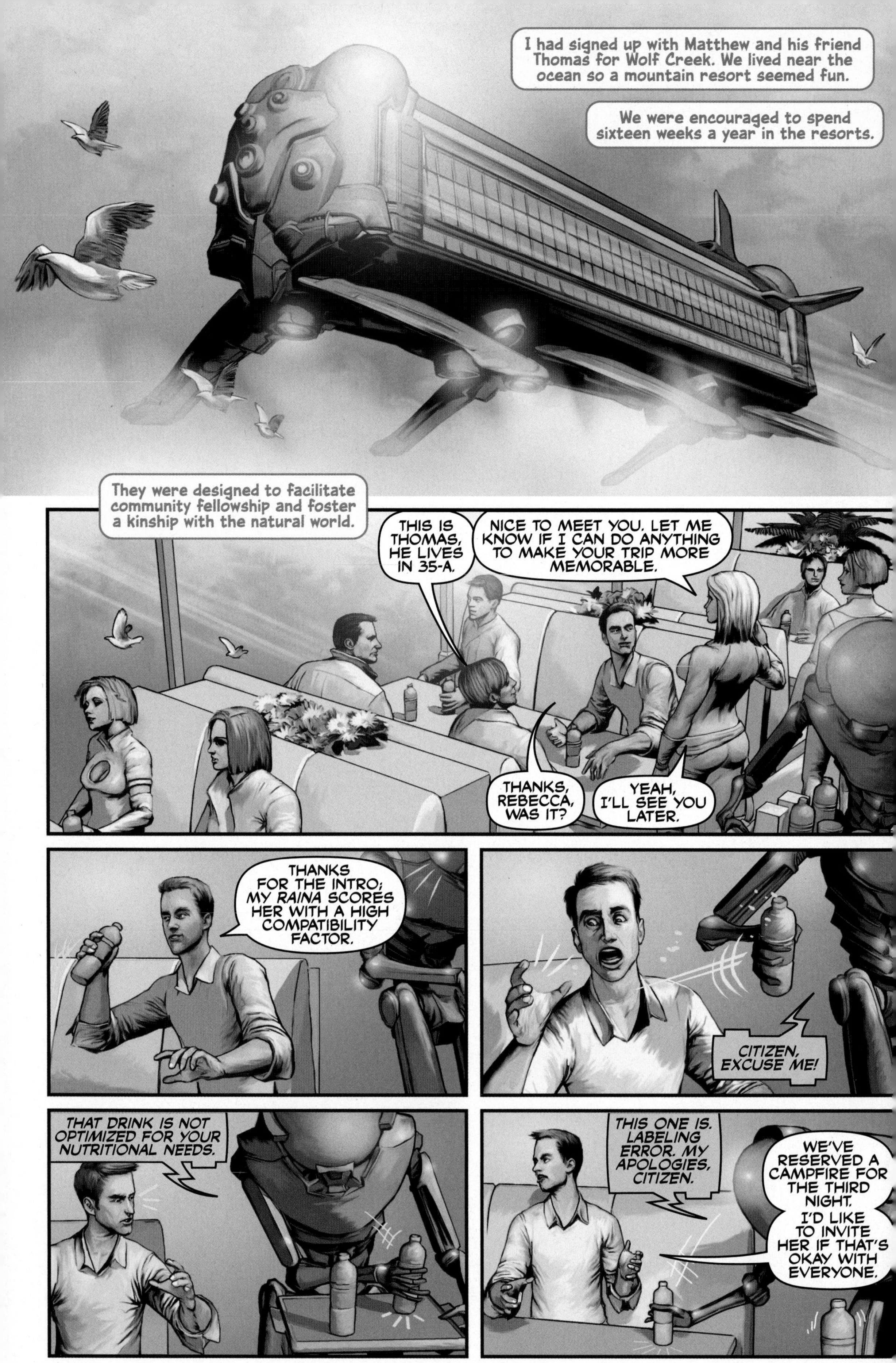
I had signed up with Matthew and his friend Thomas for Wolf Creek. We lived near the ocean so a mountain resort seemed fun.
We were encouraged to spend sixteen weeks a year in the resorts.
They were designed to facilitate community fellowship and foster a kinship with the natural world.
THIS IS THOMAS, HE LIVES IN 35-A.
NICE TO MEET YOU. LET ME KNOW IF I CAN DO ANYTHING TO MAKE YOUR TRIP MORE MEMORABLE.
THANKS, REBECCA, WAS IT?
YEAH, I'LL SEE YOU LATER.
THANKS FOR THE INTRO; MY RAINA SCORES HER WITH A HIGH COMPATIBILITY FACTOR.
CITIZEN, EXCUSE ME!
THAT DRINK IS NOT OPTIMIZED FOR YOUR NUTRITIONAL NEEDS.
THIS ONE IS. LABELING ERROR. MY APOLOGIES, CITIZEN.
WE'VE RESERVED A CAMPFIRE FOR THE THIRD NIGHT.
I'D LIKE TO INVITE HER IF THAT'S OKAY WITH EVERYONE.

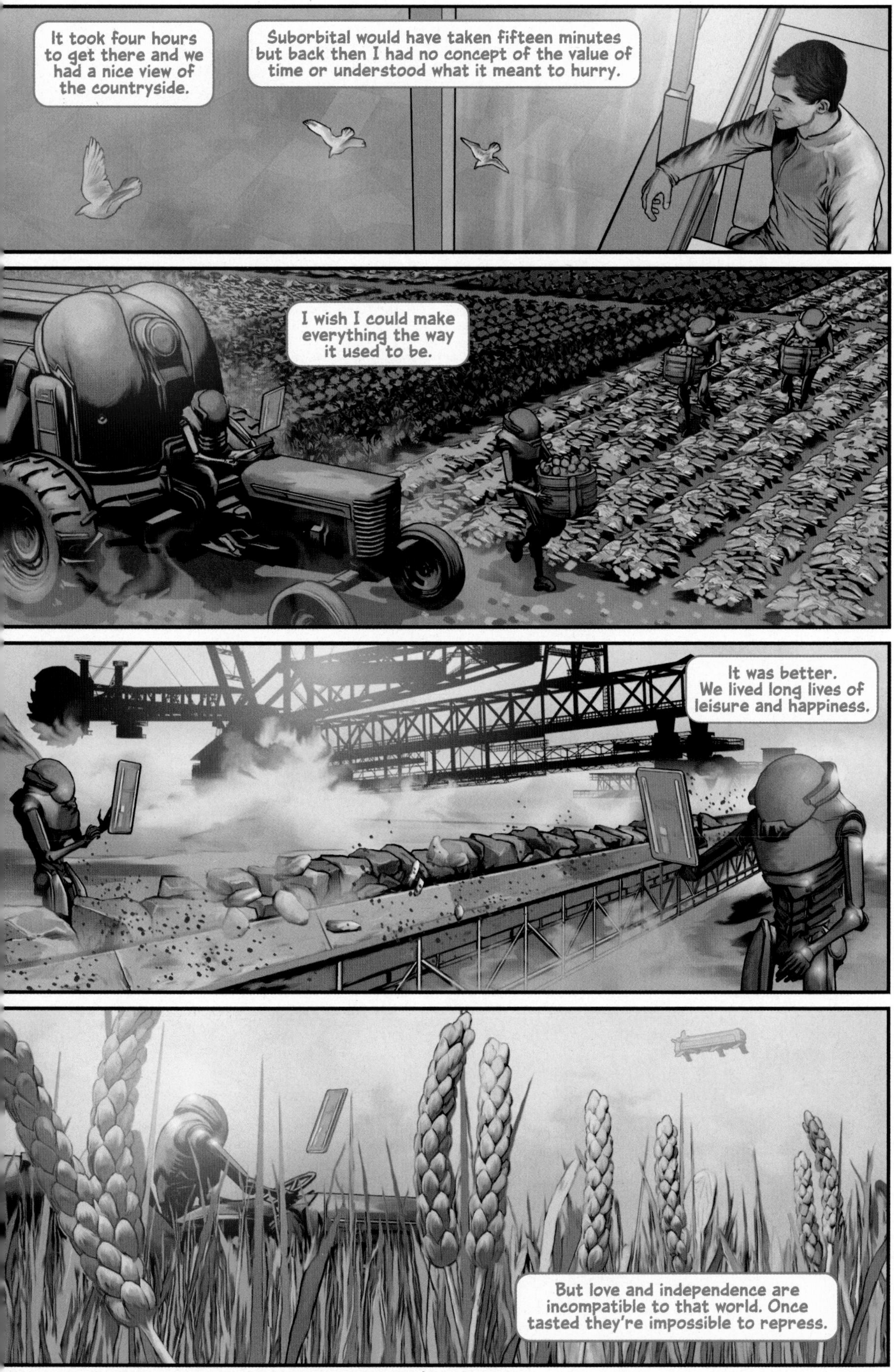
It took four hours to get there and we had a nice view of the countryside.
Suborbital would have taken fifteen minutes but back then I had no concept of the value of time or understood what it meant to hurry.
I wish I could make everything the way it used to be.
It was better. We lived long lives of leisure and happiness.
But love and independence are incompatible to that world. Once tasted they're impossible to repress.

CONTINUED IN SYMMETRY VOLUME 1, AVAILABLE NOW

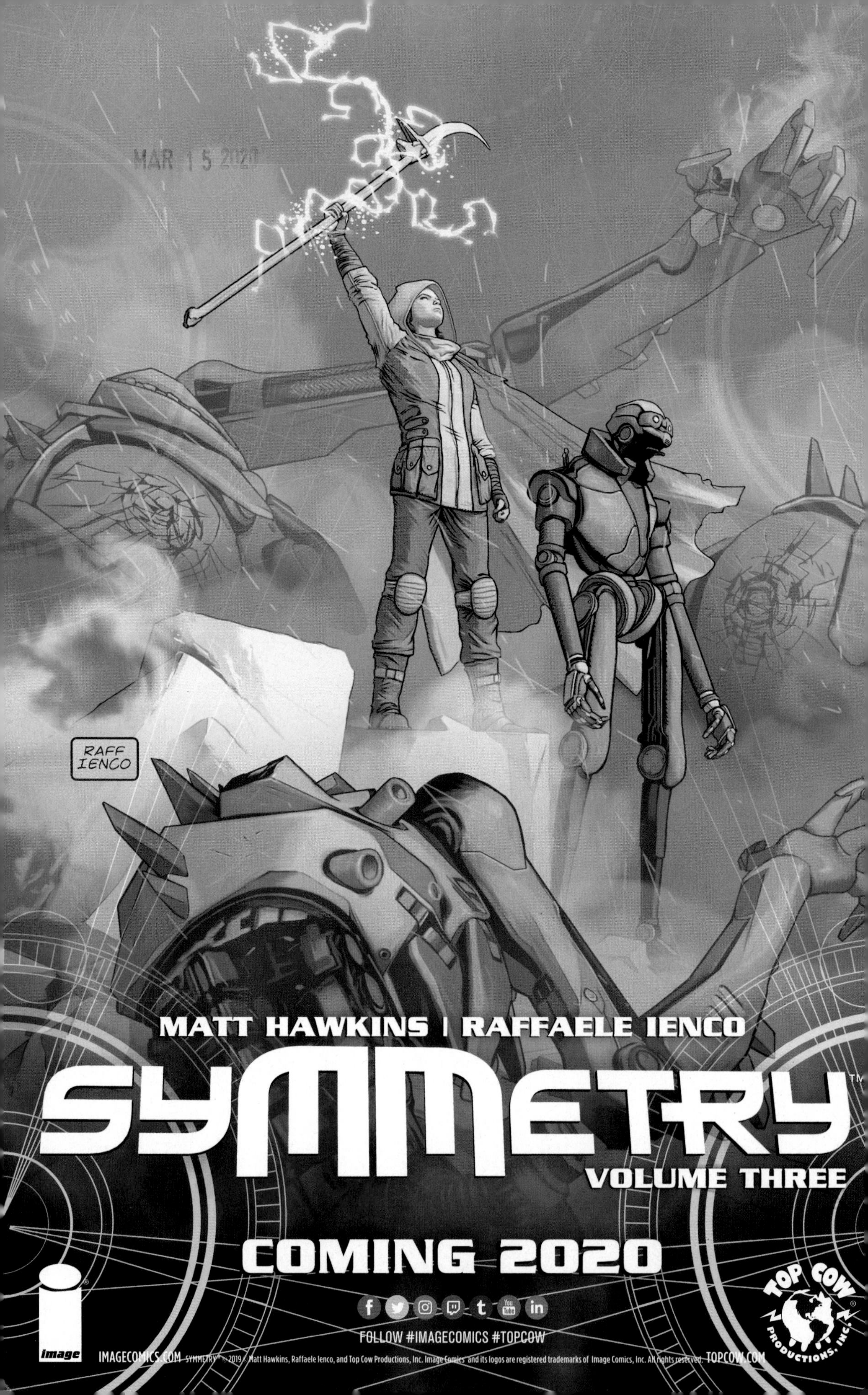
MAR 1 5 2020
RAFF IENCO
MATT HAWKINS | RAFFAELE IENCO
SYMMETRY™
VOLUME THREE
COMING 2020
FOLLOW #IMAGECOMICS #TOPCOW
IMAGECOMICS.COM
SYMMETRY™ © 2019 Matt Hawkins, Raffaele Ienco, and Top Cow Productions, Inc. Image Comics and its logos are registered trademarks of Image Comics, Inc. All rights reserved.
TOPCOW.COM
TOP COW PRODUCTIONS, INC.

# POSTAL

## THE COMPLETE HARDCOVER

## APRIL 2020

# The Top Cow essentials checklist:

**Aphrodite IX: Rebirth,** Volume 1
(ISBN: 978-1-60706-828-0)

**Blood Stain,** Volume 1
(ISBN: 978-1-63215-544-3)

**Bonehead,** Volume 1
(ISBN: 978-1-5343-0664-6)

**Cyber Force: Awakening,** Volume 1
(ISBN: 978-1-5343-0980-7)

**The Darkness: Origins,** Volume 1
(ISBN: 978-1-60706-097-0)

**Death Vigil,** Volume 1
(ISBN: 978-1-63215-278-7)

**Dissonance,** Volume 1
(ISBN: 978-1-5343-0742-1)

**Eclipse,** Volume 1
(ISBN: 978-1-5343-0038-5)

**Eden's Fall,** Volume 1
(ISBN: 978-1-5343-0065-1)

**The Freeze,** OGN
(ISBN: 978-1-5343-1211-1)

**God Complex,** Volume 1
(ISBN: 978-1-5343-0657-8)

**Infinite Dark,** Volume 1
(ISBN: 978-1-5343-1056-8)

**Paradox Girl,** Volume 1
(ISBN: 978-1-5343-1220-3)

**Port of Earth,** Volume 1
(ISBN: 978-1-5343-0646-2)

**Postal,** Volume 1
(ISBN: 978-1-63215-342-5)

**Sugar,** Volume 1
(ISBN: 978-1-5343-1641-7)

**Sunstone,** Volume 1
(ISBN: 978-1-63215-212-1)

**Swing,** Volume 1
(ISBN: 978-1-5343-0516-8)

**Symmetry,** Volume 1
(ISBN: 978-1-63215-699-0)

**The Tithe,** Volume 1
(ISBN: 978-1-63215-324-1)

**Think Tank,** Volume 1
(ISBN: 978-1-60706-660-6)

**Vindication,** OGN
(ISBN: 978-1-5343-1237-1)

**Warframe,** Volume 1
(ISBN: 978-1-5343-0512-0)

**Witchblade 2017,** Volume 1
(ISBN: 978-1-5343-0685-1)

For more ISBN and ordering information on our latest collections go to:
# www.topcow.com
Ask your retailer about our catalogue of collected editions,
digests, and hard covers or check the listings at:
## Barnes and Noble, Amazon.com,
and other fine retailers.

To find your nearest comic shop go to:
# www.comicshoplocator.com